A Brush With Mortality

A Brush With Mortality

A novel by

Caryl Hallberg

Dapple Productions

A Brush With Mortality

Paperback edition - May 2024
By Dapple Productions
Everett, Massachusetts, USA
Tomar, Portugal

ISBN 978-989-33-5813-9

Printed in the USA
Published simultaneously worldwide

www.carylhallberg.com

Instagram, TikTok, YouTube
@authorcarylhallberg
Facebook: Caryl Hallberg

For Âna-Marie, a good friend, always.

Acknowledgments

While writing a novel full of strange characters who live in your head, there is a tendency to feel like you are in it alone, with only your fantasies for companions. It isn't true, though; the encouragement from friends and the help from the special people who agree to share their knowledge with you make writing a novel a larger experience, far more than just one person sitting in front of her computer.

There is no acknowledgment deep enough for the support provided to me by Â-M Jones.

I owe thanks to SP Kohler, and to my email friend who works in DNA crime research for help in creating less suspicious circumstances. Authors Vanitha Sankaran and Ejner Fulsang, along with Dick Vojvoda, offered constructive criticism along with constant emotional support.

Camille Vardy kept my punctuation and grammar within acceptable bounds, so the alpha readers might want to thank her. The good people at Martha & Brothers Coffee Company in Noe

Valley, San Francisco, kept me caffeinated and sane.

I was able to have a few weeks' seclusion at their family farm compound to put the finishing touches on the novel, thanks to the hospitality of Philip and Jamie Bowles.

Thanks to Noe Valley Pizza Restaurant for providing me with a respectful private place to conduct interviews on sensitive subjects.

A special thanks goes out to several individuals who shared their experiences with me, some of whose stories are found being told by Horace Cosgrove Drucker III. I hope that what I learned about the specialty practice of spanking, and the intimate details of gay sexuality, have found its way into this story as a positive reflection of our shared frailties and strengths as humans.

My alpha readers, Forest, Charo, Thomas, Ed, and Kim, and my beta readers Tina, Katharina, and Sam. truth-tellers all, offered me feedback that helped to make me a better writer, and this, a better book.

Wendy Blackburn is the executive assistant every busy person wishes they had. She is just simply the best.

My editor, Alison Huff of Dark Star Lit, is my hero (cheerleader), who relentlessly makes my writing better, caring for my characters and making sure your reading experience is the best I can provide.

The Escola Profissional de Tomar graphic design department's Professora Vitoria Pires allowed me to present the cover art project to six of her third year graduating students. One of those students, Quelia Ferreira, presented the design chosen for the cover of this edition.

All these people mentioned above and my outstanding friends, who though unnamed here are recognized in my heart for cheering me on, made it possible for me to do this work.

I did my best and I hope I made you a little proud.

Caryl Hallberg

OVERTURE
1981

<u>The Prophet (salla Allahu ʿalayhi wa salaam)</u>
"There are as many paths to God as there are human breaths."

Aoife tightened the twenty-sixth knot, the last one, in the orange and white silk rope. She leaned over the young man now woven into a slingbag, his arms and legs parts of the construction, and caressed his cheek.

"Are you comfortable? It is very important to us that you be comfortable. You will let me know the moment you have the slightest discomfort?"

The naked boy nodded his head like wildflowers in the breeze, smiling and closing his eyes against her caress.

"Cosi-san, he is ready for you."

Drucker emerged from the shadows and bent his knees, lowering his head so that Aoife could loop the band of rope over his shoulder and across his torso. Rising to his full height, he lifted the bound package now balanced on his hip and back. The trio moved in silence from their private room in the bathhouse and onto the street, where a heavy fog dampened Market and Castro, as far as the eye could reach. The Druckers' car pulled up. Cradling the package between them, Aoife and Horace Cosgrove Drucker III settled into the back seat as their driver took them to their boat in the marina.

The parcel was again lifted onto Drucker's back and he made his way to the master suite where the watchful package was, like a sleeping child, deposited on the bed.

The older man stood waiting. The boy took in his surroundings, silently telling himself his own stories until he rested his eyes on his host who then undressed for his captive audience. Behind him, now her turn in the shadows, Aoife removed her orange halter top and white polyester bell bottoms, letting them drop to the floor, but the boy had eyes only for the man before him. Ambient city light filtered through the small windows, accompanied by creaks of rope, the bay kissing the sides of boats, and a distant foghorn.

"I will call you Farrah while you are with us. You may call me Cosi-san if you wish, or Sir."

He leaned into the bag and found the final knot, the twenty-sixth one; he pulled at the folded rope until he heard the small popping whisper of the silk letting go. With a single sweeping tug of his extended arm, the intricate series of knots binding the newly christened Farrah fell into a soft silk nest haloing him on the bed. The unbound body spread from its fetal position to a full stretch. Farrah exhaled with pleasure and yawned, his hands finding and grasping the teak bed rail above his head.

"Sir?"

Farrah held his eyes on the face of the man who had born him so recently.

"You are perfect as you are, just stay lying on your back, my beautiful boy. Do not move."

Drucker moved with care until he straddled the smaller man before him. Reaching with both his hands, he began to stroke Farrah's long blond hair, brushing it from his face and fanning it over the paisley comforter that covered the bed. He moved to his face, tracing every curve and angle, resting like nervous butterflies on the eyes and lips for only a moment. As he moved to the boy's neck, he sensed without looking the two erections growing as his hands worshiped Farrah's body. Moving ever downward, finding small spots of tension, and increasing his pressure just enough to induce deep relaxation.

When there was nothing left to pet, he placed his hands between Farrah's thighs, cupping his balls and pushing a warm breath to cover the now rock-hard cock below him. In that same moment, Cosi-san felt his own balls captured in a soft caress and moist warm breath brushing his solid member.

"You are perfection, my Farrah. It is easy to worship your flawless body."

The sharp edge of Aoife's nail drew a line to the base of his penis when Cosi-san lowered his mouth to swallow Farrah's jewel. Cosi-san's hands again traveled the boy's torso in long strokes, in rhythm, everything in rhythm.

A long time later, the boy was rolled onto his stomach. Now four hands massaged, tapping his back, legs, and finally his buttocks. Cosi-san grasped the boy in the hollow of his hip joint, his long fingers pressing into Farrah's pelvis, lifting him into position. The boy could feel the pressure he had been waiting for against his ass.

"Such perfection, but what are these dark marks on your shoulder blade? Is it a bruise, a birthmark?"

Dry leaves in late summer, Aoife's voice was soft against his ear, her hand pressed in the small of his back. She snapped a popper at his nostril, and he inhaled.

"A blemish to enhance his perfection, Cosi-san."

"Such gifts you wrap for me, my love."

He pushed into his prize.

"Sir."

I

<u>Parinibbana Sutta</u>

"O bhikshus! Do not grieve!"

There are resources in life that appear like a reoccurring dream with a deep hidden core and ultimately no resolution.

I hadn't had sex for three years. I could feel the time slipping away from me, never to be regained. Who would want me now? I was always surprised that men wanted me at twenty.

My name is Letty Mae. I love my guy. Peter and I have been married for 25 years. The trouble is his libido never was that strong and now it seems it is gone. I, on the other hand, have always been sexual. It is part of my self-image.

So, Happy New Year. The year 2000 arrived and the world did not end. Let's see what happens now.

I put an ad up online.

Looking for long term uncommitted relationship

Almost 50 and wanting a steady guy for physical relationship with conversation but no attachments other than a private friendship.

Who I Am Looking For:

Someone who wants a quiet friendship along with the physical aspect being the primary connection. I am looking for someone who craves conversation and regular aspects of a relationship. Refer to the movie Same Time Next Year, only make it weekly or monthly and you will get what I have in mind.

Who I Am:

Age: 49
Location: San Francisco
Hair: blond
Eyes: blue
Height: 5 feet 7 inches
Body Type: average

Languages: English
Ethnicity: White/Caucasian
Religion: not religious
Education: graduate degree
Occupation: executive
Smoker: don't smoke
Drinker: drink socially/occasionally
Status: not answered

I tried to skip answering as many of the preset questions as possible. The truth of course was somewhere in between my answers. I did not want to share all my information, nor did I want to lie. I posted the ad and then I waited to see what would happen.

What happened was that I was flooded with responses.

There was a twenty-year-old in Oklahoma who wanted me, "Baaad!"

There was the Jewish doctor who, when it came down to meeting, changed his mind, and there was the guy who just would not take "no" for an answer.

Mostly, there were nice guys looking for real and honest relationships. Where were these guys when I was twenty? Hell, when I was thirty, they were married and beginning a drug habit. When I was forty, they were getting divorced and in rehab.

I got a message from the online listing service. They suggested I rewrite my posting or move to a more "adult site." After over two hundred responses in fourteen days, I decided I would just shut off my posting.

I narrowed my online conversations to three guys. One was a semiretired corporate attorney confined to a wheelchair, the second was a successful insurance broker who was married and in remarkably similar circumstances to mine. The third was the CEO of a dotcom that hadn't gone away in the burst of the tech bubble.

In our exchange, the attorney, Moe, misunderstood two of my comments as questions. This raised small red flags for me. Still, he seemed clear on what I wanted and what he wanted from our meeting.

He asked me to join him for an evening in San Francisco. I told Peter that an old friend from my first years in hospice care was in town and that he wanted to take me out for an evening. Peter asked no questions.

1/2/00

Dear LM,

My name is Moe & I came across your profile online. I liked what I read. Kindly take a look at my profile & should you be of the mind to carry on further communication between us, I would be delighted to hear from you.

After reviewing your profile, it struck me that we would take comfort in each other's company.

Looking forward to hearing from you,

Moe

PS The following is my profile text:

I am a semi retired lawyer seeking a loving caring, intelligent & honest female who enjoys engaging in activities similar to the ones I enjoy, i.e., theater, concerts, museums, traveling, near & far & just doing fun things, etc. Note, in 1988 I experienced a neurological episode that impaired my ability to ambulate. I use a power (battery operated) wheelchair. Otherwise, I'm healthy, fit, fun loving & adventuresome.

1/3/00

Moe -

I am getting tons of responses and trying to respond to all in some fashion. When I read your profile, I had this flash that you were someone I knew years ago. I am so pleased that your photo showed that you were not the same person.

I am unsure if what you are looking for is what I have to offer and the same is true of what you have to offer to me. It may be worth exploring.

I am in a committed relationship with a person for whom I care deeply. I have no intention of leaving this relationship. However, three years ago for reasons not fully understood by my partner and totally a mystery to me, he stopped touching me and generally pulls away when I try to touch him. It has been a rough 3 years no matter how one looks at it.

I have urged him to go to a doctor, we have gone to a Marriage and Family Therapist together and separately, I have tried every encouragement I can think of, but nothing seems to shake whatever is bothering him. Please understand he has no admitted interest in anyone else either, his sexual drive was never that strong and he was never a very sensual being.

I have found that I am becoming someone I don't really like very much within his and my relationship and I am very sure it is related to my frustration and his passiveness.

Waiting for someone else to change is a silly pursuit at best, don't you think?

What I am hoping to find with my posting is someone who can satisfy my longing to be touched. I want to be sexually satisfied and allowed to sexually satisfy someone else. Human connectedness and touch, this does not mean just crasser aspects of sexual encounters. I guess there is a complexity to my nature that I just can't shake.

I am exploring what it really means even as I write this, and I can't seem to nail it down.

What I want, I have had in the past and want again. Then I want to come home to my own home and my own life. Maybe it can't be done -- maybe it can.

This is all unfamiliar territory for me because in placing the posting I had to violate one of my core values, no cheating. I don't really know what will happen.

I guess I should mention that I am assertive by nature but always want a man to be a bit more in charge. You mentioned something about assertiveness in your posting. I also am not Jewish. This is,

again, something mentioned in your
posting, the being Jewish.

If you would be interested in pursuing this
at all please let me know. I just felt I
should be completely open and honest
with you.

LM

1/4/00

Dear LM,

Thanks for your reply. To answer your
concluding question, yes, I am interested in
pursuing a relationship with you. You are a
fascinating person, not only in terms of your
honesty and directness, but your attitudes and
sensuality as well. Like yourself, I love to be
touched, hugged & kissed, and return same in
a most loving way, if you get my drift.
To cut to the chase, my true name is Moe
Potholder, My address is 310 Walnut Ave, #
112, San Francisco, CA. My phone number
is [415] 555-0132 & my email address is
mbpotholder@mail-center.com.

I would greatly enjoy getting together with you at a mutually convenient date, time & place. Possibly we could go out for dinner then a show or whatever is agreeable with you afterwards.

So as to arrange a meeting between us and if agreeable with you, kindly provide me with your phone number & a good date & time for me to call. If this creates a problem, please give me a call at anytime @ [415] 555-0132. I look forward to getting together with you in the very near future, with a warm hug,
Moe

1/4/00

Moe -

Weekdays are better than weekends for me. Fridays are fine. Why don't you pick something for us to do? I will appreciate whatever you choose.

LM

1/4/00

Dear LM,

How about dinner tomorrow night or next Friday? You're welcome to come to San Francisco. I know some good restaurants in SF & I can provide you with a place to park. Again, either tomorrow or next Friday. For that matter, any time in between or whatever is best for you.

After dinner we could go to a movie (Lord of Throgs Neck, for example) or a play, if we are in SF (As an example, Glengarry Glen Ross is playing at SF's Pioneer Theatre). Whatever we do & whenever we do it, I look forward to it.

With a hug & a kiss

Moe

1/4/00

Moe –

Truth is I love coming to the City. I have to travel to Palo Alto all the time for business lunches and dinners.

I have seen Lord of the Bronx. It is much better than one might expect.

Glengarry Glen Ross looks interesting, but I haven't read any reviews or talked to anyone who has seen this production of it. Have you?

Whatever you choose will be fine.

Saturday is a bit short notice for me, but I believe next Friday would work nicely, the 14th. I host my bridge club on the 15th, but there is no prep for that. Timing is all up to you as I can be there, wherever there is, at any time.

Friday really sounds nice to me. Yes, Friday in the City will be wonderful.

How lovely, thank you, I am looking forward to it already!

LM

1/4/00

Dear LM,

On Friday, Jan. 14th, you & I have a date with each other. I know a great place for dinner: Foxhound Stone's new restaurant HolinOak located @ Hayes & Gough. I'll make 5:30pm reservations.

Glengarry Glen Ross was featured in today's SF Chronicle's Date Book. The play starts @ 8 pm. We should get to the Pioneer Theatre, I would think, no later than 7:45 pm.

I'll order tickets tomorrow unless you advise that you would rather see "Lord of the Throgs Neck". I think you indicated that it's a movie you would like to see.

Can you get to my garage say around 4:15pm? I'll email you better directions tomorrow. What do you prefer: 101 or 280? Until the 14th... Oh yes, I'm looking forward to it too.

Moe

1/5/00

Moe -

Sounds perfect. I'll be there by 4:30 PM. Why don't you give me directions via 280? HolinOak and Glengarry Glen Ross will be wonderful. Thank you. I am looking forward to it.

LM

1/5/00

Dear LM,

To answer your question about why I am not giving you directions from 101, I think it's easier from 280.

Our tickets for Glengarry Glen Ross have been purchased. They are to be picked up at the Pioneer on the 14th at 7:45 pm. The play starts at 8:00. Our ticket # is 18-20034. I will now make our dinner reservations.

How to get to my garage. Take 280 to SF's Alemany Blvd. Continue on Alemany. Alemany merges with Embarcadero. Stay in the second to the right lane on the Embarcadero. Continue on the Embarcadero until Market Street.

Take a left turn onto Market. On Market you will pass Kearney, Stockton & Powell.

After Powell you will reach Mission. Turn left onto Mission. You will then pass Francisco. The next street is Walnut. My garage is located on the west side, to your left, on Mission between Francisco & Walnut. I'll be waiting for you in my white Plymouth minivan on Mission at or about the location of my garage beginning at 4 pm. I'm hoping you will arrive around 4:15 pm.

I'm sure you will have questions. I await your response.

Hug & a Kiss

Moe

1/6/00

Moe -

Only one question. Did I understand you to say I'd be parking in your parking space in the apartment's garage? I appreciate the detail of our plans as it helps me feel I am leaving a trail behind me and that creates a feeling of safety.

I think this blind/computer dating stuff is trickier for women from a safety point of view. I am sure you understand.

LM

1/6/00

Dear LM

You can park in my garage space. Please don't worry. There is nothing to fear, at least when it involves me. If anybody should have a fear, it's me, not you.

Moe

1/7/00

Moe -

I have turned off my posting. I was going to do that anyway. I think we should go ahead and use our regular email addresses from now on.

LM

1/8/00

Dear LM,

My email address is mbpotholder@mail-center.com

Until Friday...

Moe

1/13/00

Dear ML or is it spelled LM,

I'm truly looking forward to tomorrow, our dinner, the play & whatever your heart desires... If you have any further questions, let me know.

Fondly, Moe

1/13/00

Moe -

I was just going to jump online and send a message to you to say how much I am looking forward to tomorrow and there was a note from you saying the same thing to me. Thank you and I'll see you tomorrow.

BTW, my name isn't really LM. People call me Lisa and of course you may as well.

Lisa

1/13/00

Dear Lisa [now that we got that straight},

Until tomorrow....

Fondly as ever,

Moe

I panicked when he asked about the initials with which I signed my emails. I took the precaution of setting up multiple wireless layers and pathways to make my computer anonymous and then used my real initials! What had I been thinking? The name "Lisa" had just popped into my head. Once I had written it out in the email, it seemed safe and right. Letty is an unusual name; Lisa is a common name. I didn't think Moe or anyone else would question it. I bought a phone and phone card so I could make calls without having them on my regular phone bill. I also set up a dummy email account, making sure it was untraceable back to me.

Earlier that week, I took advantage of New Year's sales at department stores. I found the classic little black dress in silk. On Friday, I spent the day in anticipation. I had my nails done in the morning and shaved my legs.

When it was time to dress, I rooted in the back of my underwear drawer and found my one pair of skimpy black lace panties. They must have been eight years old but worn only when they were all that was left and the laundry needed doing or when there was a special occasion. There had been no occasions in eight years.

I loved the way the dress felt slipping down over my head and across my nipples. Perky, nicely rounded things, they stood right up like I was a girl. I put on some stiletto heels and looked in the mirror at someone I had known years ago.

I was driving into the City when I noticed a gray veil falling over my right eye. In the corner of my peripheral vision, to the left, light sparkled and shimmered around the setting sun through my driver's side window. I slowed and moved to the right lane of the freeway but kept going. The gray spread until I had no vision from my right eye and the vision in my left had narrowed to a thin column straight ahead. I slowed further and began to have panic thoughts.

I was near my office, and I knew there was one person left at that time of day. I found my cell phone and speed dialed. Nancy answered on the second ring. Still driving, I asked if she could stay until I got there; she agreed. Driving slowly and able to see only the shapes of things, I found my way off the freeway and the two blocks to the office.

Once there, I felt my way into the lobby and was met by Nancy, who led me into the chair by her desk. Getting on the phone, she made multiple phone calls trying to find an emergency eye doctor very nearby, in the late afternoon, on a Friday.

Of course, she mentioned how I was dressed. The truth is I would have been disappointed if she hadn't at least noticed.

I explained that my old friend was visiting, the same story I had given to my husband, Peter. People were buying this? Was the truth so far from anyone's concept of who I am that it never occurred to them I was lying?

She found a doctor, only a few blocks from our office, that could see me right away.

Nancy was worried that I had a detached retina, but during my time in the office, my vision had begun to return almost in the exact reverse order of its having gone. Now I had the tickle of a very bad headache just behind my right eye and the bridge of my nose. I thanked her for her help and headed for the doctor's office. By the time I reached it, I had found Moe's telephone number and given him a call.

I explained that I was having this episode and would call him as soon as I knew anything at all. God, what did he think? He was very polite.

The doctor did every test at her disposal, including dilating my eyes. In the end, she proclaimed that she believed I was having a retinal migraine headache. Nothing to worry about but I might want to mention it to my primary care physician, especially if it occurred again.

My head was in a vice of pain as I donned the plastic sunglasses provided by the optician's office. She was kind enough to give me an Advil for the road but ultimately dismissed me in a hurry to get to her own dinner. Dusk was a blessing as I resumed my drive into the City. I had written Moe's telephone number on my driving directions but because of the drops the doctor put in my eyes, I could not read the number or the directions. I managed to call Moe again using the redial button. We decided I could still make it in plenty of time for us to meet, have dinner, and make the show. Why not, I thought. The pain might disappear as suddenly as it appeared.

Careful of traffic, and aware that I wanted to stay away from the city streets with lots of pedestrians and bicyclists because I still couldn't see perfectly, I found my way to his apartment.

Fully dark by the time I got to his neighborhood, the brilliance of the City at night penetrated even the thick plastic dark glasses made for glaucoma patients. During the drive, my headache had lessened enough so that I was able to think about things a little. I spent the time wondering what my eye makeup might look like after three kinds of eye drops, and the doctor's fingers on my lids holding the eyes open.

There wasn't a lot I could do. I pulled over and turned the car's overhead light on, removing the glasses. I checked that there weren't any black streaks of mascara or other obvious and easily seen makeup horrors. I tried to smooth any foundation blotches with a napkin I found in the glove compartment, powdered my nose, and put on some fresh lipstick.

A block up, I spotted his van and in short order, found myself parked in his garage space and in his van headed for dinner.

Moe was dressed in a designer suit of expensive material, which showed wear at the edges. His face had a smooth cragginess and his nose was slightly sharp, making him almost look classic, like an older man you would see in a billboard ad selling vodka and being adored by a young female model. He sported tidy sideburns running to just above his ear lobes and had a full head of wavy medium length silver hair swept back and styled into place. He was quite nice looking, I thought, though there was something guarded behind his eyes and his smile. His van was customized for his wheelchair to lock in place in the driver's position and be operated fully by hand. As we drove, he talked about his concern for me and about hoping he knew the way to the restaurant. I couldn't see much of where we were going. It is much harder to keep track of things when someone else is driving and you can't see clearly. The radiance of downtown San Francisco was blinding without the protective dark glasses. We pulled up to the valet parking at the restaurant.

"Once we are out of the car it is rather fun to watch the valet trying to drive the van without a seat to sit in. We should be able to leave the van with them and go to the theater from here if you don't mind walking a few blocks."

Completely automated and controlled with the key ring remote, he opened the side door of the van and lowered the ramp. Releasing his chair from the driver's position, he maneuvered out of the van while I waited on the sidewalk. Watching the valet try to re-park the van, I realized my headache had subsided and that I was actually enjoying myself. From Moe's reaction and the reaction of those walking by, I decided I must look tasty and no worse for having fully dilated pupils.

Foxhound Stone was one of those upscale, terribly trendy star chefs who opened restaurants in the big cities. HolinOak was his newest creation and anyone who thought they were anyone made a point of eating there. A miniskirted young woman led us through a lobby and down one floor in an elevator. Our table was in a good location and fully prepared for us with two settings and only one chair.

Barely concealed under the veneer of linens and flowers was the industrial chic that I thought had been passé as long as punk rock. HolinOak seemed to eschew the blare of music and other white noise components that made conversation impossible in most restaurants, but the acoustics were such that the conversations themselves, within this warehouse full of important people, created a din that made meaningful or personal communication almost as difficult as it would have been in a suburban sports bar.

Even though Moe wanted wine, he didn't know what to choose. I had the feeling he would simply pick an expensive bottle regardless of taste or appropriateness to our meal.

I couldn't read the menu. I asked him to read it to me. Moe read each item on the menu, including all the detailed descriptions, even though I repeatedly requested he not bother with any seafood choices and need not read the details unless I asked about a specific item. By the time he was done, I was laughing at the absurdity of the situation and was still clueless about what to order. He didn't seem to find my laughter contagious; in fact, he seemed annoyed by it. In the end, I asked for the squab, reasoning that one less pigeon in the world is always a good thing.

Moe held my hand and pulled me to him over the corner of the table for a kiss. He talked about his children and grandchildren.

"I have two girls and a boy, and they each have three kids. They all live down in Santa Clara. When they were little, I used to take them skiing. I call them on holidays. None of them have had the opportunity to visit me or have me in their home for over a year. There are several of their children I have yet to meet. People get busy. I was busy when I was their age. I remember, they remember. That is how it is if you want to get ahead. There isn't much time for extra family."

When dinner arrived, I found that my squab was raw on the inside though well done on the outside. The polenta, how does one ruin polenta? Yet somehow it was dry and tasteless. The vegetables looked very much like something my cat, Cain, might have coughed up and I could not bring myself to do more than move them around a bit. Normally, I would have sent the whole mess back and asked for something different. However, it was clear that Moe wanted everything to be perfect and I felt very much his guest. He would take it personally if I complained. I said nothing and picked at my meal. I used the excuse that I couldn't see and that my head was still aching a bit.

I asked Moe about his work as an attorney, hoping to engage him in something about which he felt enthusiastic. My efforts were to no avail. He explained in a few words his fifteen years as a successful partner in an affluent San Francisco firm. His life's work past and present offered less than a few minutes' conversation. His life held no interest for him.

He, too, seemed less than thrilled with his meal and drank nearly none of the wine. Wine that I had ordered.

I asked him what had caused him to need the use of a wheelchair.

Finally, Moe opened up a bit.

"Multiple sclerosis was the diagnosis of the quack physicians," he explained, "but I know that is incorrect.

"I am not deteriorating!

"I was overworked, and stress caused a neurological episode. That is all that happened. For a while, I was able to walk with a cane but it got so I was falling down all the time, so I chose to use a wheelchair.

"The firm believed the doctors, they asked me—no—they forced me to take an early retirement. They thought I was an embarrassment. Louts!"

Sounded like deterioration to me but I said nothing to contradict his reality.

Most of the food remained on our plates when we were done. We decided to stroll to the theater and keep the van with the valet parking at the restaurant.

I knew he was proud to be with me because I looked particularly good. I was old enough that people would assume that we belonged together. He maneuvered his chair and held my hand, and I thought about how much more interesting the dinner conversation might have been if I were on a date with someone of intellect and passion, rather than Moe. Men of intellectual passion and humor are very sexy.

As we strolled the few blocks to the Pioneer Theater, I was aware of walking on city sidewalks in stiletto heels. Moe may have an easier passage in this respect. When we crossed into the busier pedestrian traffic of Geary Street, I became aware of how oblivious people are to a person in a wheelchair. Then I realized that people are just oblivious; it was I making the distinction.

When we arrived at the theater, we entered through the wheelchair accessible door, which was at the farthest point from the will-call window. I waited behind the velvet ropes as he retrieved our tickets. We were ushered to our seats located in an area arranged for wheelchair and ambulatory side-by-side seating. Very good seats really, I found myself in a theater seat set upon a little dais. I felt enthroned. There was no problem, but for reasons understood only by the usher, she flurried around a bit, worried that we were comfortable, that the seats were the correct seats, and that we had everything we needed. I understood that she was only trying to make up for some random feelings of guilt having little to do with either Moe or me.

The play was excellent and held my attention with the extraordinary language so very typical of a Mamet play. Moe held my hand as we watched, and I felt tiny thrills as he stroked my palm or played with my fingers. I closed my eyes to concentrate on the stage and the feeling became disembodied from either him or myself. It became pure sensation. I began to tear up with the realization that so small a thing, these touches, the hand holding, were more than I'd had in years. I was starved, so sensory depleted that a simple soft rubbing of my palm in the dark of a theater could take over my entire consciousness.

I did not feel comfortable with Moe, not the way I wanted to feel. I could not express to him what I was feeling because I had the sense that he would not understand what I was saying. It seemed to me that his denial of his physical deterioration, and his loss of a career and his family, had led him to be angry with himself and the world. His anger exceeded his desire for connection.

He fell asleep toward the end of the play. I panicked! How could I be intimate with someone who could not talk about his life? I got that at home. How could I consider sex with someone who had no thoughts—positive or negative—after a Mamet play? Peter at least would have things to say about the evening's theater.

Yet this lack of response to the play and our surroundings is what I experienced with Moe as we returned to the van, walking past street singers, winding through the crowd of theatergoers from several Geary Street theaters all flushing onto the sidewalk at the same time.

The lights were still so bright, and the pain again grew shimmery inside my mind. The effort of keeping up a conversation by myself wore on me. I moved the crowd apart, murmuring in each person's ear, "Excuse me, pardon me, behind you please, excuse me," fighting our way to the ramped edge of the sidewalk to cross over to the other street.

We reached the van and once inside, Moe pulled me toward him, kissing me strongly with repressed sexual desire. His hands reached for my breast, but I pulled gently away. My back hurt from the angle. I could see in his eyes that the kiss had been highly successful for him and had meant we were moving toward the end of an evening he had spent all his energies imagining. He had not been present on this date but only in the imagined end of the date. Scripted without conversation or flavor, it had, for him, gone as planned.

A block from his apartment, my head exploded into searing pain, light flashing around the periphery of my vision. It was so sudden and so intense that I cried out.

He parked and I asked him to just sit for a few moments until I gathered myself. Apologies rained out of me almost as if I thought an apology would end the pain.

He seemed torn between groping and feigning sympathy for my discomfort.

We decided to go into his apartment so he could get me a pain reliever. Now my apologies carried with them the message that, "I must go home. I must go home. I must go home."

We entered his building, notable only for its total decade of 1970 lack of character or identity. We passed through the lobby and hallway to his first-floor apartment.

Inside, the apartment was dim. In one corner of the living room was a giant screen TV and state-of-the-art entertainment center. The walls were bare except for dirt marks and two framed photos of his children from a time when they were very young. We passed down a hall, the floor of which seemed layered with grime. I turned as I passed the kitchen, seeing what must be every dish and pan he owned crusted with food and piled in the sink. The wheelchair scraping and banging into the lower cabinets had severely damaged them. In the hall, there were places that looked like someone had punched the wall with a fist. Each one seemed to pulse with anger and frustration.

Across from the entertainment system was a floral print L-shaped couch. I sat perched on the edge of the couch while he got me an Advil and a glass of water. I held my hands in my lap like a schoolgirl.

My head began closing in a vice, and I wondered if I had absorbed the pain from Moe or if it was my own.

He came into the living room with water and the pill. Was I about to be drugged or was this an Advil? The pressure and the pain were so great that I realized I didn't care, either way was relief. I swallowed the pill. I had pulled the drape of my shawl over my hands to hold the glass. Everything in the apartment seemed too dirty to touch.

He reached out and I discovered just how strong his arms were. He folded me into him and kissed me hard. He wasn't letting go. He thought he would push the headache out of me. Somewhere deep inside the cloud where I was now dwelling, I realized that if he were the right person he would indeed be able to push the headache out of me. He wasn't the right person and it had nothing to do with the wheelchair or the bad dinner or his falling asleep in the theater or even his filthy apartment. It had to do with who he was and his inability to communicate any joy. Maybe he had no life joy, but I wasn't in the business of supplying that for anyone but myself.

I pulled away gently, cleaning the lip of the glass with my shawl, and said that I had to go even as his arms reached for me again, trying to touch my breasts that so achingly wanted to be touched—but not by this man. The room was a blur now and my head felt like cotton candy with thorns and burrs, snaggy and confused and bleeding.

Moe was a gentleman and showed me to his bathroom. I had never been in danger. I reached for him and gave him a final kiss goodnight.

The headache gripped me again.

"You know, Moe, what's happening here is a leave-taking."

By the time I was on the freeway, I had a simple headache that blanketed only the front of my head as if I had had too much wine and sobered up too soon. The blood pumping in my ears was the sound of running water. I could smell Moe on me in the form of his aftershave. The words Velveeta Aftershave floated across the headache like a scrolling advertisement, and I followed the moon home.

II
<u>Parinibbana Sutta</u>

"Even if I were to live in the world
for as long as a kalpa,
Our coming together would have to
end."

As I walked to my car Monday morning after my rendezvous with Moe, I reached into my purse for my keys and found my pantyhose from Friday. I remembered coming into the house that night, barefoot and carrying my shoes, but I didn't remember taking off my pantyhose. When I got to the car, I threw the hose into the back seat along with the black dress, which I was taking to the cleaners. I noticed a small green towel on the floor; a tiny knot of pain focused right between my eyes.

The dry cleaner I use is in a strip mall just before the freeway I take to get to the office. When I stopped to drop off the dress, I noticed an open dumpster at the end of the row of buildings near the A'Roma Pizza Parlor. The smell of cigarettes and old beer bottles rose from inside the bin along with the heavy musk of rotting food. My uncle's farm in summer; for just a moment, I was a child again, alone, in the dark, and unprotected. I pushed the green towel—and the beginning of a memory—into the deepest corner of the dumpster. Walking back toward the dry cleaner and my car, I passed an old yellowish Volvo parked in front of the pizza place, the dark haired man inside was snoring, sound asleep, his window cracked to let in fresh air.

An older Chinese woman named Zhifu Li runs the dry cleaner. I've been going to her for so long that she seems to feel she has a freedom akin to property rights regarding my clothes. I have never been able to tell if her way of speaking English is an affectation or genuine. Either way, it feels like a trap, and I try to avoid traps.

"Good morning you Miss Mae. Oh, you party girl now and not even Christmas! What you do to dress? More coffee spill? When you learn not to drink and drive?"

"Good morning Zhifu. No, not coffee this time." I handed her the dress.

"Ohhh, I see you got new cat. When you get new pussy?"

What was she talking about? She held the hem of the dress to her nose and then offered it to me, I responded automatically by leaning forward to sniff my own dress. There was an odor of urine! Zhifu spread the dress on her worn Formica counter and stabbed her finger accusingly at the dark spots that matted and crusted the velvet fabric.

"What this? You kill that cat for peeing on dress? I get this out cost plenty, no guarantees!"

"I do not have a new cat. Cain is alive and well and would not tolerate anyone new in his domain. I think that must be juice from the squab I ate for dinner."

"What squab? It dead now. Ha."

"Squab is pigeon, and of course it was dead when I ate it."

"Pigeon!" Zhifu was beside herself with the idea of anyone eating pigeon and began going on about dog and pigeon and thousand-year-old eggs, all the while laughing. She carelessly tossed my dress into a pile of dry cleaning and handed me my pink tag. The flower of a new headache now covered both of my eyes and I began to imagine that I was once more losing my vision. I was suddenly angry; I didn't understand why.

"Goodbye Zhifu, I must get to work."

"Okay, bye-bye, you have good day. No guarantees on dress, no guarantees."

"When are there ever guarantees?"

Back in the car, I leaned on the steering wheel for a moment, trying to calm myself and bring the headache back to that small knot between my eyes. I could still smell the garbage in the dumpster lingering like guilt on my hands. I rooted through my purse and found what I thought might be a painkiller or vitamin and a packet wet wipe. I dry swallowed the tablet, promising myself I would call my doctor if this continued, and tried to clean my hands before starting the engine.

When I was a mile or so down the freeway, I hit the button to lower the window, tossing my wadded pantyhose out to join the flotsam of the road. The window rolled closed.

The traffic slowed and I looked at the time to see if I was going to be late getting into the office. The monthly meeting of the Board of Directors for Haven was late that afternoon. Board meeting days always meant a frantic pace and last-minute preparations. Inevitably on these days, a small to medium crisis of some sort would develop, requiring my attention.

Haven's primary focus is at-home hospice for people with families. Haven hired me as the Executive Director not because of any expertise with hospice but because I understand business and can communicate with the intellectual and the spiritual personality types. The not-for-profit corporation provides services for family members and the person dying. We take Medicare, Medi-

Cal, Blue Cross, and other private insurance, but have a policy of never turning away anyone for any reason. This means that money and donations have a place of high importance for the organization, though we always strove to keep the development and finance challenges very separate from the program issues.

My Board of Directors' membership roster read like a who's who of psychological self-help, inner growth authors, and spiritual and healing practitioners. Focusing such a group on business usually required me to be at full capacity. I wondered if I should take another painkiller so the headache wouldn't affect the afternoon's meeting and the day of preparation leading up to it.

I looked again at the dashboard clock and at the seemingly limitless number of cars ahead of me on the freeway, bumper to bumper. I turned on music, selecting Messiaen's opera, Saint François d'Assise, just as my cell phone trilled. Hitting the talk button on the steering wheel, I said hello to Nancy, the program director for Haven.

"Are you on your way in?" she asked.

"In traffic, but almost there."

"I saw you had some free time this morning and I've scheduled an appointment with you. I need some advice. I'm feeling challenged by a new client and his family."

This request in itself was unusual. Normally, the staff took program issues to Dr. T.

Doctor Teresa Grove founded Haven in 1969. She and Nancy, an RN who had been working in hospice for over fifteen years, usually oversaw all the clients and their families.

"Is Dr. T going to join us?"

"She is trying to get in this morning but isn't here yet. I imagine she is in the same traffic you are in. Hope you're feeling better than the last time I saw you. Did you get to spend time with your friend?"

We completed our telephone conversation as the traffic began to move.

The opera still played in the background. My headache, though lessened after my act of littering, seemed to be moving in unison with the music; colors flickered around my peripheral vision. The pain actually receded a bit more when I turned up the volume. I thought about Dr. T and Haven.

In the care we offer, we stress comfort and support for the communal spiritual and physical concerns that are present for the family and the person who is dying. The relief and understanding of pain are of chief importance and are reflective of my own philosophical focus. Dr. T and I disagree on how we think about the choices people make. For instance, legally the patient decides when and if hospice care should begin. That would be fine if people were able to make those sorts of decisions easily, but people are uncomfortable with the idea of stopping extreme measures to sustain life. Their fear makes the decision a long and troubled process; too long. Haven can promote the conversation for the family and the patient, but I usually grew impatient with the process and stayed away from that aspect of our services altogether.

Just as Saint François d'Assise hugged the person with leprosy to his chest, I arrived at my freeway exit. I was parked moments later. I decided I had time to walk down the block and pick up a morning latte at Steady Grind. I needed to shake off the music and the feeling of embracing the dead weight of fear that it evoked.

On the sidewalk below the trees, a small boy was standing inside a red umbrella. It rocked him and he found his balance using the hooked umbrella handle as a steering device. The wind turned into a schoolyard bully, pushing the boy over and out, his red umbrella boat flattened. Unfazed, the boy stood, placed the red umbrella over his shoulder, shrugged, and walked with the wind down the block. A tall, hook-nosed, gray-bearded hippy sat on the curb at the far end of the block; he and I were the only ones to have witnessed this performance.

This same bully wind pushed through the door with me into the Steady Grind.

"Vanilla latte?"

I nodded to Marta, the owner and usual counter person. She and I had known each other since our kids had been in Little League together but we rarely had the chance to chat.

"You're late this morning. Coming or going? You know you shouldn't drink and drive."

"I'm just arriving, the traffic was bad this morning. How are you today? Been busy?"

"Always. How is the family? My Mark was in Chicago for a convention and went to a show at the Institute. Guess what he saw? He saw some of your boy's work. He says you should talk to that son of yours. He says looking at those sculptures was like watching a horror movie. He says why can't your boy do nice nudes out of marble instead of torturing metal?"

"I will certainly pass along Mark's critique when I talk to Ian—I'm sure he'll appreciate the suggestions."

"Well, what does Mark know? He's a coffee wholesaler for crissake. You tell Ian 'Hi' for me. What about the other kids, how they doing?"

"Jennie and Zack are fine. Zack recently started with a new firm, Eternal Life Limited, did I tell you that before? I think the relocation to

Texas has been good for him. I'll say hi for you to them all."

Whenever someone shares their reaction to Ian's art, it makes me smile, which is exactly what I did as I left Steady Grind and walked to my office. Ian, my youngest, was finishing his first year of graduate studies on scholarship to the School of the Art Institute of Chicago and had already carved out a niche for himself. All three of my kids are special, but Ian may be the one that the twenty-second century will remember. I will certainly never forget the first time he "made art." He was seven years old, and he had the help of his older brother, Zack, who was fourteen at the time. In any other family, Zack would have been the lead troublemaker with the little brother just tagging along. That was never the case when it came to the "made art' escapades. Ian, clearly, was always in charge.

The boys had taken Ian's tricycle, which he had long since outgrown, and riveted all of their combined Star Wars action figures to the frame. Zack had fired up the barbeque, both boys waiting patiently until the fire burned slow. They placed the tricycle on the grill, melting the wheels and the action figures to a soft, deformed, but still recognizable mass. When the grotesque result had cooled, Ian mounted the tricycle upside down, balanced only on the handlebars, into the soft concrete of a new sidewalk—which had just been poured outside his elementary school that morning. The school had no trouble knowing whose parents to call on Monday when they found the concrete set solid with the tricycle-shaped, mass destruction of heroes lodged firmly in the center of a block. Ian had signed his name in the semi-set concrete.

Ian was now twenty-two years old and still creating cultural metal images that disturb the viewer, but he operated with far greater approval from the authorities. I had initially worried about him, thinking he might be disturbed, but when he explained clearly to me that he was only "making art," I found I was able to encourage him and be his advocate and support.

I thought we would always be close, Ian and I, but in recent years he had withdrawn from me. He did not share his personal life with me at all. I never met or even heard about any of his friends. I suspected that he might be gay, but he never gave me an opening to talk about such things. I didn't want to push, but it hurt that my baby shut me out.

Somehow, through this reminiscing, I had gone from bemused to melancholy during the short walk from the coffee shop to the Haven offices. I considered the elegant old office building one of my best achievements since being part of Haven. Surrounded by strip malls, the marble and granite facade had character and dignity. The same ownership built it in the 1940s and meticulously maintained it until it was bequeathed to our organization a few years ago.

I worked my way to my office, saying hello to the staff and volunteers. Nancy was waiting outside my door. She let me know that Dr. T. had not yet arrived. Nancy had left an informational report on my desk to bring me up to speed on the issue about which she needed to talk to us. I told her I would review what she had left me and that as soon as Dr. T arrived, they could both join me in my office. I closed the door and settled behind my polished walnut desk to read the report.

One of the tasks our organization takes on is teaching the patient's family to provide care for the patient. We always have an assigned hospice worker able to respond to a family round the clock, but our focus is on helping the entire family through the dying experience. Much of the care has to do with just spending time with the dying person. Time and not being alone often become the central issues.

At Haven, we make every effort to keep the patient in a home environment. Dr. T has emphasized a trinity of palliative care. She and Nancy ensured that our clients received pain management that addresses the physical, the emotional, and the spiritual. Nancy empowered the staff and volunteers to see each client as unique in their experience and needs.

Sometimes the family has difficulty caring for the patient because it means looking at their own death. We tried to bring an understanding that life is not fully experienced until it includes death. Death is an opportunity.

I began reading the client report I was given.

Mr. Horace Cosgrove Drucker III, a Caucasian male, widowed, eighty-two years old, was dying of disorders and complications arising from AIDS and advanced age. His family consisted of a son and a daughter, both in their fifties, as well as various nieces and nephews. According to Nancy's report, he had been a client for little over two weeks and had already alienated our staff and brought several of our volunteers to the point of quitting their work for us altogether. His son and daughter seemed to be having more difficulty with the fact that their father had AIDS than they were having with the idea of his dying. It seemed they were provincial in their attitudes in a manner often unrecognized or unexpressed in San Francisco. Other than their frequent visits, they counted on us to be the sole providers of Mr. Drucker's hospice needs.

At this point, Nancy's report stated, "Haven might not be able to continue providing service to the Drucker family." This was unprecedented! What could this man have done that Nancy would recommend this course? His abusive language and attitude certainly made him a difficult case, but to discontinue service?

I wouldn't have to wait long to find out what the report wasn't telling me. I could hear Dr. T's morning greetings as she worked her way through the main office toward my door.

Dr. T came through the door with a habitual sweep of her hand pushing a stray strand of hair into the french twist with which she vainly tried to constrain her thick, deep gray hair. Dr. T was the perfect person to have founded Haven. She is an MD with a specialty in palliative care, but she is also a PhD theologian. I have never met anyone with the vitality she has, and thankfully, she brought me into the organization. I liked to think we made a good team because I could deal with the nitty-gritty aspects of running an organization while she oversaw the spiritual and physical nature of our mission. Wardrobe by June Cleaver, Dr. T was tall, thin, and graceful, carrying herself like a dancer in a housedress. Calm seemed to flow from her, and like everyone, I always relaxed in her presence. Nancy bustled in behind her; notepad and a copy of her own report in her hands, she plopped into the wide cushioned armchair.

"You've read my report?"

"I've scanned it. I didn't see anything jump out at me except your suggestion that we may need to discontinue service. Since we all know there is only one way this organization parts with a client, I assume our conversation this morning will be about finding the other alternatives."

I glanced at Dr. T and saw her nod slightly.

"That may be entirely up to you." She smiled softly. "I spent time with Mr. Drucker and his family over this weekend, after he challenged our cadre of staff, and I've had the opportunity to discuss this case with Nancy. Nancy has done an exemplary job on this case, including her very sensitively written report. I want to acknowledge her efforts."

Translated, this meant that I was about to be asked to do something I wouldn't be thrilled about, that Nancy and Dr. T had already made up their minds what that something was, that Mr. Drucker or some member of his family was extraordinarily abusive or annoying, and that the report said nothing of import and was an internal document to cover our asses, just in case.

"OK Nancy, let's hear it."

"Mr. Drucker is eighty-two years old as you saw in my report. What you may not have caught is that he is dying of AIDS. Not uncommon for us, of course. Still, he's a special case. He has been aware of being HIV positive since 1986. It is only recently that he has developed AIDS, but it is moving rapidly, perhaps because of his advanced age. It's unclear to his doctors exactly how to manage his AIDS complications. His ability to carry a particularly virulent form of HIV for so many years without illness is highly unusual. The strain of the virus he has predates all of the current drug cocktails and his age complicates their use due to the side effects. He is dying, that much is clear.

"You may have heard the family name, Drucker?"

"The timber family?" I asked.

"Timber, silver, agriculture, real estate, the stock market, you name it. Yes, the San Francisco Druckers. Well, our Mr. Drucker is the patriarchal head of that dynasty. His two kids, both in their fifties, are beside themselves over this AIDS thing. He let his family, and the society pages, think he was a widower with a ruthless mind for the stock market and no social life. They are both very conservative thinkers. Now they have to find a way to explain how he came to have AIDS. His kids are active members of the Presbyterian Church in Pacific Heights that their family built in the early 1900s but as near as we can tell, Mr. Drucker himself hasn't been to the church since his wife's funeral some years ago. He is very alert and quick, and he has managed to alienate every one of our staff and volunteers. That is why Dr. T.

took him on over the weekend. His family members usually can't last more than a quarter hour with him before they are in tears or loudly angry from his pointed and hurtful remarks."

Nancy stopped and settled back into her chair, shuffling through her notes.

I turned to Dr. T; so far, I hadn't heard anything, from a service perspective, that we hadn't handled before. The thing about how long he has had HIV was interesting, but not germane to our services.

"I'm waiting."

"I thought the same thing you are thinking, until I watched him in action and experienced him directly. Mr. Drucker is a special gentleman, special indeed. He uses standard manipulation on his kids—he has a real skill for it. What has set him apart for our staff is that he is extremely insightful, to the point of almost being psychic. Our people are used to facing the questions of death, the clients' and their own. Mr. Drucker has a way of making a person face her life.

"He does it with a great tenacity and willpower."

She said this in the soft whisper of bees pollinating a tall tree. Dr. T. looked down to her lap where her hands rested, palms up, one inside the other. She wiggled her fingers a little and looked back up, letting me see the emotions exposed on her face for a moment. If it hadn't been for the shininess in her eyes made by tears seeking an exit, I wouldn't have been sure of what I saw. I had seen her emotionally vulnerable like that only once in all the years we'd worked together. That was the night she received a telephone call during a dinner meeting letting her know that Glenn, her male friend of twenty-some years, had died on the way to the hospital after an automobile accident on Highway 92.

"There is more. Mr. Drucker has made a change to his estate. He is leaving a substantial amount to Haven. Enough to meet our current budget needs for a long time. If we manage it correctly, we may never need to worry about funding. We could expand our free services to incorporate the entire Bay Area, maybe even all the way to Sacramento.

"This bequest comes with a condition. He and I talked about this at length yesterday. He had his attorney in the room, and he assures me he has everything set up so that the gift to us does not transfer unless we meet Mr. Drucker's, uh, request."

Now Nancy and Dr. T were looking at one another; I was finally going to learn about my role in this situation.

"He wants you."

"I don't see the problem," I responded after a moment. "I go and have a chat with him, schmooze the family and we're set. Sounds great. What am I missing here?"

"He wants you as his hospice worker. He wants our CEO to sit with him. He says he shouldn't have to deal with anyone less than the boss. Now before you say anything, I did explain who I was and my position, he wrung me through his wringer and tossed me aside. He wants you. He said you were his only possibility of not having to deal with 'psychobabble and spiritual mumbo jumbo.' I am using his words."

"How long?"

"His doctors say maybe a month, maybe three. I don't know… he won't go until he is ready."

"OK, I'll talk to him. If he agrees to a reasonable schedule and will be nice to whomever we can talk into being my relief and our nurses. Are there possibilities for this kind of agreement?"

Dr. T. assured us both that she had already brought up these concerns with him and he said he would negotiate with me. Great, a ruthless tycoon and me; I wondered ruefully who would profit from that negotiation.

"T, how does he feel about his dying experience?"

She knew I was referring to my frustration with another aspect of our type of care on which she and I disagreed. We do nothing to speed up or slow down the dying experience. Part of this is the philosophy of the organization, and part of it is a result of current attitudes within the medical community and laws within our society.

"You know I wouldn't recommend you take this on if I thought you were going to be put in the position of having to reject his request for death. I know how you feel about this."

"Do you? I just happen to believe that sometimes people need and even want a little push."

Nancy looked uncomfortable, and for a heartbeat, Dr. T said nothing.

Then with her usual graciousness she said, "No matter how he feels or doesn't feel about his experience and no matter what he might ask you for, we tender support and expertise to the death experience and our presence acts as spiritual witness, nothing more."

We talked for a few more minutes, deciding to present a more detailed report on the circumstances to our board. Nancy would add to her report; Dr. T would present it to the board that afternoon. She had already set up an appointment for me to meet with Mr. Drucker the next day.

When they left my office, I thought for a bit and found myself smiling. I knew I was not the best person to choose as one's hospice caregiver, but I also knew I had Nancy and Dr. T. to help me manage myself and the client. I had to admit I was looking forward to the challenge with Mr. Drucker and to having what would amount to a major change in my schedule.

There was still a lot to do to prepare for that afternoon's directors' meeting. I promised myself time for checking personal emails once I was done with those preparations, then buzzed our bookkeeper, asking for the budget report.

I spent the remainder of the day in the typical preparations that always coincided with a board of directors meeting. I never got to my emails. I hardly lifted my head up from my work until the sun, reaching low through the window behind my chair, fell in a warm gold patch over my shoulders onto the surface of my desk. I could feel the office beyond my door empty of people, except for those detail-oriented few whose responsibility it was to do the last-minute checking that all was in order for the evening meeting. My phone line rang as I stretched to ease the muscles in my back and neck before getting up and going to the conference room.

At the other end of the line was Clayton Curtis, a longtime friend and the head of one of the Bay Area's largest corporate-based charitable foundations. Because we were friends, Clayton called me directly and got right to the point.

"It's the economy, Letty, there is no getting around it. We've had to stop all new funding. We've canceled most of our second- and third-year funding of current projects, agreeing to complete current budget years and put those projects at the top of the list for reassessment when things improve. Most of our longtime relationships we've cut the allotment of funding by more than half for next year."

"What does this mean for Haven, Clayton?"

"What it means is that you owe me big. I pushed for you, and we've managed to limit your cuts to a thirty percent drop."

The news felt like a fall as I heard it, a fall from an extremely high building.

I thanked Clayton for calling me directly, and for going to bat for Haven.

The money from Clayton's foundation made up twenty percent of our overall budget and accounted for the majority of the funding for our direct services to individuals and families without the means to pay for our hospice assistance. This included a program I had personally championed, which served homeless or transient young adults and teenagers, typically runaways who had turned to prostitution and needles. They were young people who were dying before they had even had opportunities to waste. Our program included, when desired, helping with family reconciliation or protection from families. I interacted with one of our first young clients several years ago. He was one of the very few clients with whom I had ever developed a relationship. He had managed to avoid becoming a prostitute by stealing the identification of recently deceased persons but had not managed to avoid contaminated needles.

He was proud of his skill as an identity thief and spent hours talking with me about it. In the end, he had given me a parting gift of a small box with ten false identities as its contents. His death, and the awareness of life and death on the streets that he had given to me, had been the inspiration behind the Street Youth Hospice Program. With the loss of the foundation's funding, this program was in serious jeopardy.

It took only a moment after hanging up the telephone to mentally compose a footnote to the budget report, which I was about to present to my board of directors, and one moment more to realize that the potential Drucker estate endowment was now far more important than when, earlier in the day, I had agreed to indulge Mr. Drucker's whim. My professional life had just gotten a lot more interesting as the stakes had been raised.

Polished mahogany and comfortable leather chairs and sofas fill the conference room at Haven. It resembles an English men's club from the first half of the twentieth century far more than it does an American conference room. Whenever I enter the conference room, my first impression is disappointment that there is no large stone fireplace, a fire burning merrily at its core, and tea or sherry set just to its side to be served by an older gentleman retainer named Wiggins. On this particular evening, I found Dr. T. standing near the sideboard stirring a packet of Sweet'n Low into her Styrofoam cup of herbal tea with a small red swizzle stick. She was talking to our board chair. With their heads bent toward each other, they wore deep listening faces; it was clear that they needed a bit more private time. I knew she was briefing him on the Drucker issue, along with the ethical questions it presented. The other board members were seated or standing around the room in groups of two and three, making small talk and catching up on who was going to which cities on upcoming book promotion tours. By the time I had finished making the rounds, greeting each of the fourteen members, I saw the nod from the chair, indicating she was ready to begin.

It isn't only our conference room that is unusual; our board meetings have their own special moments. Even before I arrived, the group engaged in a twenty-minute meditation session followed by a brief period sharing, in a circle, their month's events outside the board. It wasn't surprising, therefore, that after the meeting minutes were approved, Shangia Modorvia, spiritual healer to world leaders and much in demand speaker, pointed out that my aura was tinged with orange and asked that it be noted in the minutes for today's meeting. When the treasurer's report had been completed, I added my verbal footnote regarding Clayton's phone call and waited.

Every board meeting, without fail, Dr. Albert Nab, author of *Feelings are Our Most Important Thoughts*, asks, "And how do you feel about the budget report, Letty?"

Everyone at the table waits for the question and I always prepare my answer as carefully as I prepare for any other piece of a board meeting. The board then approves the treasurer's report.

"Albert, I am feeling very positive regarding our bottom line and am excited by the opportunities presented with these new funding challenges. The funding could have been reduced a great deal more, but we have a good relationship with this foundation and for this I am grateful. Dr. T has information she will be presenting in her report that may change our financial picture even more dramatically and for the better, I should add."

Dr. T submitted the report on Mr. Drucker as planned. I answered a few questions and before long, the chair had closed the meeting. Traditionally, one of the board members will do a thirty-to-forty-minute presentation on a subject of general interest to the board and vaguely tied to some aspect of dying or hospice work. On this particular evening, Dr. T shared a new study out of Maryland about the physiological connection of pleasure and pain.

III

<u>Parinibbana Sutta</u>

"You should know that all things in the world are impermanent; coming together inevitably means parting."

The room was subdued. Mr. Drucker lay in the center of his bed, the waxen figure of a powerful man from whom all muscle and meat had been removed. Remaining was the frame of a toreador, wide, formerly strong shoulders on a smallish frame narrowing to slim hips. His eyes were closed as he lay there on his back, the bed covers smoothed around and over him, only his arms at his sides and his head on the pillow exposed. His skin, though gray and pale with age and illness, still held a ruddiness suggesting years of sun and wind. His arms carried the effects of severe psoriasis and the backs of both hands had constellations of warts. His head, thick with hair, and a short beard on his face, was gray but touched with the auburn leftovers from another time, another life. He lay as if dead or deeply asleep, yet the room vibrated with his energy.

The walls were a pale dusky green almost devoid of actual color, the works of art hanging on every wall were Chinese brush paintings of ferocious animals aged to sepia tones and framed in black. The bed itself was an ebony platform whose edges surrounded the dusk sheets and duvet, complementing the rush-colored carpet and the walls. Stillness, and subtlety, were in everything; so was strength. The entire space directed my attention to the man lying in the center of it all. All the energy radiated from the still body, in which I observed not even the rise of his chest.

Yet I knew he was present and aware of me as I stood at the foot of his bed, waiting and watching. Partially hidden by his beard, I could see his lips were thin and hard, forming a long line that cut across his face beneath a large straight lean nose. The cheekbones revealed by his illness and age suggested a face that had always been large enough to carry its bold features, always been firm and long. The dark fullness of his eyebrows was the natural accompaniment to his beard and luxurious head of hair arranged neatly around his head, forming not a halo so much as a backdrop for his features. Other than a small patch of red, roughened skin below one eyebrow, the skin visible on his face seemed clear of the ravages of his illness. I had the feeling that his beard covered a face scarred by youthful acne but that a strong jaw and chin rested beneath.

This mannequin of depleted strength and virility, quiescent in meditative stillness before me, gift wrapped in a kimono of yellow silk, was the dread Horace Cosgrove Drucker III.

"We think we are alive, but we are dead. I am dead but it is not too late for you to learn from me while I still breathe.

"You are Ms. Mae?"

"Yes, Mr. Drucker, I am. You may call me Letty if you prefer, everyone does."

"Lisa."

What? What was it he said? Why would he say that name?

"Lisa was the woman who brought me into this world, she was my mother's maid and a midwife. You, Letty, will take me out of this world. You are the midwife of death."

His voice was soft but carried with it a vigor that made a lie of his stillness or his body's weakness. His was a deep voice, a whispering baritone.

I found that I was riveted.

"Birth, life, death. We think it is linear, but it is not. We think it is a circle but in truth, there are no lines to make a shape. There are no borders without lines. We do not travel a path from here to there. We are always on the path. It goes nowhere. It comes from nowhere. It is nowhere.

"My story, your story, does not have a beginning, middle, an end. I am aware of this. I have brought you here so that you will become aware of your own story.

"They have told you I am an ogre?"

"Who would have told me this, Mr. Drucker?"

I had been studying his face as he talked. His stillness was complete, only the tiny movement of his jaw and lips as he formed his words. I found I was trembling, though I had no idea why. I moved to the side of his bed. There was an armchair of the darkest ebony with cushions the same hue as the bed covers. It was placed near the panel of windows covered in open weave linen. I let myself ease into the chair using the arms as support. Though his eyes remained closed, I could see them follow me beneath their thin wasted lids. We did not speak for several minutes. The room was not warm, yet I perceived the cool drying of a sheen of dampness that had covered my entire body.

"I don't imagine your Dr. Grove would use such a descriptive word. Perhaps one of your hospice workers who has run from my room weeping would tell you I was an ogre? No, I don't suppose they would tell you that. They might think it, however. Have you talked to my family? My desperate, unhappy children?"

"I haven't had the pleasure of meeting any of your family yet. I expected they would be here today when I arrived, but your housekeeper let me in."

"I am sure they are lurking in the house. Listen to them; they will have a good deal to say. Walk out of doors with them, I find they are easier to hear out of doors. Remember, you need to pay the closest attention to what I have to say. I am the one whose money you want. I am the one that wanted you here."

"Why Mr. Drucker? Why me?"

My voice was a murmur. I heard stirrings beyond the closed doors of the room. Agitated voices seemed to be approaching; I heard the footfalls of a man and a high-heeled woman directly outside the room. I couldn't make out their words but in moments, the doors opened.

An updated and much younger, healthier version of Mr. Drucker walked through the double doors in lockstep with a strongly built but petite brunette woman. Both carried themselves and dressed to accent their moneyed background and personal power. They crossed to me as I stood, the younger Mr. Drucker extending his hand.

"You must be Mrs. Mae from the hospice. I am Horace Drucker, and this is my sister Danielle Drucker."

"DeeDee, please," the woman gushed.

"Yes, I am pleased to meet you both. I was hoping we would have an opportunity to talk this afternoon."

I shook hands with them, finding their grips equally strong and firm. Looking briefly at the senior Drucker, I saw only stillness but I felt his attention. Both of his children moved their eyes to follow my glance. The expressions on their faces were devoid of emotion or comment. As if woken out of a sleep, the woman gave an almost imperceptible shudder and stepped toward the bed. She was all motion, her voice taking on the higher note of the little girl inside the fifty-two-year-old woman.

"Daddy, how are you? Can I get you anything? Are you comfortable?"

As she continued in this vein, questioning but never waiting for an answer, she moved around the bed smoothing non-existent wrinkles out of the coverlet, tucking in edges that were not untucked, and picking lint no eye could see. She stayed away from her father's head and the form of his body outlined beneath the covers. Her hands, efficient warriors against any disorder, were careful not to linger lest they themselves risk untidy contamination.

"Are you warm enough? Would you like some water?"

While DeeDee continued her performance, I had time to assess the young Mr. Drucker. Lean, like his father, but taller, he was an extremely fit man in his late fifties. His hair, cut short in a stylish conservative fashion, was still a deep auburn, reflecting the traces left to his father. His clean-shaven face was ruddy and clear. When he had released my hand, I noticed that his hands had the structure and feel of a laborer's, though they were carefully manicured. When, at last, his sister stopped her questions, he addressed the figure in the bed.

"Father, you are awake? Are you in pain?"

"Ah, Hor, how kind of you to inquire. No, I am quite comfortable thanks to Ms. Mae's minions and my expensive physicians. I'm afraid my suffering must come from other sources. How long are you and your sister intending to hover today?

"DeeDee, do stop fussing or I shall rouse myself enough to cough in your direction."

"We are here for a short while longer, Father. I thought I might ask Mrs. Mae into the study for a short talk."

I had watched Mr. Drucker throughout this exchange and now saw him open his eyes for the first time. They looked at me, a clear pale blue that seemed to have luminosity from within, but he spoke to his son, the line of his mouth bearing the smallest upward curve.

"It is a lovely day. I am sure Ms. Mae would prefer a turn in the garden to sitting in my stuffy study. Show her my koi. Take DeeDee along; I am sure she'll have something to share with Ms. Mae as well. Leave me in peace."

"Mrs. Mae?" Hor gestured with his arm toward the doors." DeeDee, join us, please."

When we crossed the threshold, DeeDee turned and grandly brought both doors shut as if we had exited the stage in a Noël Coward play.

Linking her arm in mine, the two siblings flanked me as we moved down the hall of polished wood and down the wide curving staircase. French doors behind the staircase led to a walled private garden. The path wound away from the house; the garden was large by San Francisco standards. As we descended the three flagstone steps from the house to the garden, I could not see the end of the property or what lay beyond. I knew we were facing the Bay, and that the windows to Mr. Drucker's bedroom looked out over the garden and beyond to Sausalito and Tiburon.

The garden itself was based on Japanese traditions. To the left, as we entered the garden, was a sakura tree that was pruned to create a framework within its bare branches that led your eye to the beginning low waterfall of a koi stream. The stream meandered just off the main path for almost the entire length of the garden. At the sound of our voices exchanging a murmur of pleasantries, a rolling hum of energy and water began to come from just beyond the soft gurgle of the waterfall. It was the awakening interest of the koi, some quite large and all hungry for attention.

My arm began to sweat under the wrappings of DeeDee's arm and I could feel the now familiar buzz of a headache approaching. I disengaged myself from her and stepped off the formal graveled path into what appeared to be a natural passageway to the flowing water. There, by the edge of the larger stones that lined the stream, was a flat, ceramic covered dish. The movement of the koi became rolling as I approached. I have always loved koi. They seem the most joyously alive and social of creatures, while presenting perseverance and strength in adversity. In Japan, they symbolize longevity and wealth. They were almost standing erect in their watery home when I lifted the lid from the dish. Inside were kibbles. I picked up a handful and crouched by the edge of the pool. The fish slid over one another, taking bites of their food from my hand and arching in pleasure as I petted and crooned to them.

"Daddy used to speak to them in just that tone, but in Japanese. Do you think they understand you?"

DeeDee's voice came from behind me, still on the path. I turned my head to look at her and her brother standing now with his hand on her upper arm, as if afraid she would step off the path into territory unknown to either of them. Beyond them, I saw the large traditional Foo dogs found in certain temples flanking either side of the steps to the house. The buzz in my head stopped abruptly. In that moment, I made the conscious decision that I felt a tentative loyalty to the man upstairs in his death room and a distrust of both his children.

"No, I don't believe they can understand me." I turned back to the koi. "I don't speak Japanese after all, and it is unlikely that they are bilingual."

Only the elder koi and I knew that I was smiling. Mr. Drucker had been correct; it would be easier to hear Horace Jr. and his sister here in the garden. I stood, brushing the crumbs from my hands into the water, and replaced the cover on the feed dish.

"Is there perhaps somewhere we could sit?"

"Yes, oh yes, at the end of the path in the rhododendron patch. The view is unbelievable, and we will have privacy. Come on Hor; let's show Mrs. Mae the view."

DeeDee led us down the path, past lichen-covered stone lanterns and over a small wooden bridge. As we wound down the path, a widening came just beyond an ancient willow and I could see that the stream expanded its banks to create the illusion of a small placid lake. The softest of breezes rippled the mirror of the water. In the very center was a pagoda raised above the pond. In every direction from the pagoda were clumps of blue water iris and in the distance were two bronze statues of cranes poised to catch the fish dancing forever beyond their reach. On the far bank, elms cast shadows that played on a stone wall, the boundary of this small Eden. Ahead on the path and to the right of the pagoda, I could see a view of the entire northern expanse of the San Francisco Bay. This view began first with the Golden Gate Bridge, and I suspected ended, if one were in the pagoda itself, at the Berkeley–Emeryville coastline beyond Coit Tower.

I heard myself gasp. DeeDee paused in her run-on chatter, to which I then realized I had not been listening.

"What is this?" I asked.

"Daddy's shrine. Isn't it absurd? There is no way to get out to it without getting in the water, but it may be the best view in San Francisco. I can't understand why he designed the garden so that you can't get to the best spot."

"One of Father's little eccentricities one might say," Hor interjected.

"Yes, Daddy has some, uh, little eccentricities. Oh really, sometimes he can be so difficult."

I saw that DeeDee was on the verge of tears.

"Do you believe his dying is an example of him being difficult? It isn't, but it must be very painful for you."

My comfort level was rapidly decreasing and I again wondered why I wasn't in my office working on budget issues or lunching with a potential donor. We have people trained to work with the families; I'm not suited for comforting others.

"Oh, no, no his dying isn't what is difficult. OH! I don't mean that of course, but the way he is dying, his illness that is too much to… it is going to get out and then what will I say to my friends? I, I mean my family… this family… we have a position in society, in our church. It isn't like Daddy was a rock star or some other nouveau riche outrageous character. We aren't the Osmonds, after all!"

DeeDee's lower lip was quivering at this point, and I could see the tears welling up in her eyes.

"I believe my sister means the Osborns, but her point isn't far off the mark. I have businesses to run, and I depend on the reputation of my father as ruthless and my reputation as being like him. When it gets out that he is a damn queen I can't even begin to calculate the damage to our familial branding and market share.

"This is one of the subjects we are hoping to address with you today, Mrs. Mae. Why don't we sit down on the benches we'll find just a few more steps up the path.

"DeeDee, do pull yourself together. Your bridge club isn't going to ostracize you just yet."

I took a last glance at the pagoda in the middle of the pond, turned, and moved around the curve in the path.

The brother and sister walked together in front of me, Hor leaning down in a lifelong practiced slump in order to speak to his shorter sister as they walked.

DeeDee was one of those tiny women with round high-breasted hourglass figures who will morph into chunky if they do not spend every moment at maintaining their figure. I suspected she was a gym rat between bridge club, Botox treatments, and social events. Her hair seemed almost sable and swung from high on the back of her neck to fall in a straight geometric line along her jaw. As she walked, the pointed ends would brush up against her cheeks in a small caress. Her skin had a faint olive tint deepened by the sun. Her dark eyes, while very large and round, hinted of East Asia. They were framed in impossibly thick long lashes. Her makeup looked as if a professional had just done it. Red lips in a sculpted bow shape, perfect skin tones, and subtle eye color. She was dressed in designer casual day clothes of the sort one sees on matrons in fine resort spas. DeeDee managed to send a double message of bewildered innocence and sexuality ready to implode all wrapped in a conservative patrician lifestyle. It seemed to me that she had crafted herself. I was unable to decide which aspects of her were genuine and which were complete fabrications. Something told me it was possible that she was, in fact, the more complex of the two people walking in front of me.

We reached the end of the path. It opened into a small round area sheltered from behind by camellias and massed rhododendrons, and to the front by boulders placed against one another in a nonchalant Stonehenge. Curved stone benches defined half the circle looking out toward the rocks and the Bay spread before us.

Hor had taken the bench to my left looking back toward the house. DeeDee was on the edge of the bench to the right, facing more toward the Golden Gate Bridge and the Marin Headlands. I took the remaining bench in the center. Sitting, I realized that the boulders were not carelessly positioned at all. Directly in front of me, two rocks leaned together to form the illusion of a narrow cave opening through which I could see the San Francisco Marina's community of yachts. Looking up and through a notch formed at the top, the Sausalito Marina in the distance lay supported where the two rocks kissed.

"We'd like to discuss our father's illness with you," began Hor.

"Well, I may not be the right person for you to be talking to about our palliative care. I would be happy to set up a time for you to meet with Dr. Grove."

"You misunderstand, Mrs. Mae. It isn't the care or treatment we are concerned about. We are sure Father is receiving the very best of care from your organization. We are concerned about how the news that our father has a drug-resistant form of AIDS might leak into the press. It is only a matter of time before this becomes common knowledge. We would like to control the interpretation of that information. We are concerned about your relationship with him."

"As for being drug-resistant, I think Mr. Drucker's advanced age and that he carried HIV since at least 1986 can be attributed to the current batch of treatment cocktails not being effective.

AIDS, even in its more recent mutations, is still an illness that is ultimately fatal.

"Honestly, Mr. Drucker, your father looks far better than most of the advanced stage AIDS patients that I have seen. Whatever has made him strong enough to carry HIV all these years untreated is also acting to keep him strong as these final ravages of illness end his life."

"Yes, yes, we've been told all that by the doctors. The question is what we tell the press and our friends. What should Hor tell our... his... business partners? How do we explain Daddy having this AIDS? Where do we say he 'acquired' it in the first place?"

DeeDee had jumped in, and I turned to listen more closely to what she had to say.

"Daddy has told us, of course. Is it in your files? Do you yourself know? How he got AIDS, I mean. Do all your workers and volunteers know how he came to be dying of this horrible disease?"

"All that is in our file is that he found he was HIV positive in 1986 and that it has only been in the last six months that it has suddenly developed into AIDS. We have notes regarding the general medical concerns and the progression of the disease. We work closely with your father's physicians to offer him and you the best possible tailored services."

"Is it in your files how Daddy got AIDS?" she asked again.

"I remember our records briefly state that it is Mr. Drucker's belief that he attained HIV through unprotected homosexual practices occurring in the years from 1972 to 1982. Other than his own statement in our files, there is no other discussion of the causality of your father's illness.

'Frankly, even if there were more, I would not be at liberty to discuss our records with you without first attaining the senior Mr. Drucker's permission. I am sure if you just talk with your father…"

"Daddy won't listen to reason. We have, that is Hor has, a wonderful idea, or account really, about a blood transfusion Daddy could have received while traveling in Europe with Mommy."

I couldn't quite grasp what they were trying to get at with this conversation. My mind wouldn't wrap around it for a moment. They were upset about their father's apparent bisexuality, this much was clear. I just didn't understand why they were upset. San Francisco is well known for its gay communities. The concept of gay pride had been extended to the entire city; homosexuality and the embracing of alternative lifestyles was something that San Francisco's Chamber of Commerce almost used as their tourist slogan. Within the circles DeeDee and Hor traveled, a dinner party would not be complete without at least one happy, committed homosexual couple, and an unattached transgender as dinner partner to the host's depressed, divorced sister-in-law.

During the period of possible exposure that Mr. Drucker had provided to the doctors, the bathhouses of San Francisco had been the party sites du jour. Open sexuality was at its most heady in all aspects of San Francisco society. Stereotypes were being created and smashed as quickly as fashions changed. The Summer of

Love had come and gone. Mainstream society had embraced the ideas of free love, open relationships, recreational drugs, and hedonistic sensuality. The world looked to San Francisco as the trend-setting Sodom and Gomorrah urban landscape.

Men, even those just experimenting with their sexuality, would frequent the bathhouses along Market Street or in the Castro District looking for easy anonymous connections as often as those seeking love. Trendy, steamy, and catering to the sensuality of the times, the bathhouses accommodated all strata of San Francisco's experimental lifestyles. They reflected the heady freedom that the recent release from puritanical cultural constraints and the finding of community had fostered among the brilliant and beautiful across the United States. The world was still rushing to California, but in the seventies and early eighties, it was for the party, not the gold.

That the party was over was clear, but shouldn't shame over sexual orientation also be over. It seemed to me that puberty was no longer about discovering the opposite sex, now it was just about discovering sexuality. There are so many darker pieces of ourselves we must hide from others that it startled me when something as harmless as sexual orientations or practices was high on anyone's list of things unspoken.

"They did travel to Europe together in 1980. They were there for over three months. Daddy could have gotten sick, gone to a hospital, and been contaminated there couldn't he? Maybe not a transfusion, but maybe a needle from an IV or something could have contaminated him. You see then it wouldn't be his fault. It is so long ago there is no one for us to sue, no need to raise a ruckus. You see? You do see, don't you, Mrs. Mae?

"It is all just too embarrassing for us, and to think about poor Mommy! I mean wealthy men sometimes cheat on their wives but to also be a homosexual… what must she be thinking? I mean she is dead but perhaps she is in heaven or something and she would be upset if she did know. Oh, I just realized! Maybe Mommy did know! Poor Mommy. Oh dear, how hard for her to hide this and smile to her friends, our friends. Well, I just can't bear it at all, the scandal. Please Mrs. Mae, please you must help us, you see?"

As she spoke, her words pouring out of her in a cascade, DeeDee's eyes had again welled up with large glistening tears that gently navigated the maze of her lashes to fall in three drops to her cheeks and rest there like small gems. Behind me, I heard her brother mutter to himself.

"Unbelievable."

"I am still not clear what you want me to do. Are you saying your father, Mr. Drucker, contracted HIV during a hospital stay in Europe in 1980? Haven is not concerned with how our clients become ill. We are only concerned that their palliative care be the best possible and that this time of transition be as heightened and meaningful an experience as they or their families could desire. The only reason I have that statement in my files about Mr. Drucker's unprotected homosexual practices is because he placed it there in the form of a letter he had requested be attached. Really, this is a subject you and your family should discuss together with your father. I would be happy to arrange for one of our trained personnel to mediate the conversation if you like.

"If it is the press with whom you are concerned, I can assure you that none of the Haven staff, including myself, would ever speak to the press or anyone outside the family or our care team regarding any of our clients. If the press creates any story from your father's illness and death it will have no sources within Haven."

Hor shifted on the bench.

"You still misunderstand us, Mrs. Mae. We want your cooperation in confirming some version of the circumstances along the lines of those just narrated by my sister. I have arranged for the story to be 'leaked' shortly after the family makes an announcement that our father is ill and about to pass away. We are asking you to corroborate that 'leak.' I assure you it is for the good of the family and in the best interests of our father.

"It is my understanding that your organization may have a great deal to gain from my father's death. I would think you would want to take whatever steps you can to ensure that the benefit does not become inaccessible.

"As it stands now, our attorneys are already taking steps to block any interests outside the immediate family and family corporations from benefiting when my father passes away."

I stiffened as he spoke. Before I could say anything, DeeDee interjected.

"Oh but Mrs. Mae, we will try very hard to assure that Haven does receive a substantial bequeath. I mean, it might not be what Daddy has led you to expect, but still, we can be very generous. I mean, if we can just control the media information on Daddy's activities and illness then, well, if you are helping us that makes you almost one of the family. Doesn't it? You will help us, won't you?"

DeeDee leaned forward and grasped my hand with both of hers as she said this. I had been taking slow, deep breaths. My body wanted to leave them there at the end of the garden while it bolted for the house, but I held to the bench. I extricated my hand from DeeDee's grip. Hor sat watching me. I was looking through the gap in the boulders that gave the illusion of a cave or passageway to the marina. It felt as if I were moving in and through that passage to the moored vessels and back again to the garden. I had noticed a similar outcropping of boulders at the point that the river design of the pond widened to the small lake; it occurred to me to wonder if a similar visual message was contained in that arrangement. I don't know how long I sat there but I had learned long ago there was power in silence. When I felt I had cleared my thoughts, I spoke.

"Mr. Drucker, Miss Drucker, if the press or anyone other than someone authorized by your father questions me or anyone on my staff about your father's illness, treatment, or circumstances, we will state that all of our information on clients is confidential and we will refer the questioner back to your father or his designated spokesperson. This is how we handle all of our clients' privacy and it is how we will handle your father's. As for what Haven stands to benefit from your father's death…"

I left my thought unfinished. I stood, turning toward the house. I could see the Bay darkly reflected in the upstairs bedroom windows that spanned the house, the sails of boats dim stars on the glass canvas. There was no movement, no wavering of the image; it seemed a permanent rendering of the scene now behind me rather than a reflection.

"If you would like me to set up a time for one of our professionals to aid you and any other members of your family in conducting a constructive conversation with your father, please just let me know. I highly recommend that you utilize our expertise in this area before your father is no longer able or willing to communicate with you."

On my return walk to the house, I paused again near the island structure DeeDee had called her father's "shrine." If the water were shallow, one could wade to the shelter. It was impossible to tell how deep the pond was at this place. The way to know would be to enter the waters and move forward.

As I made my way back upstairs, I made a mental note to contact our attorneys and let them know about the potential problem with the Drucker offspring. Our attorneys could work with Mr. Drucker's attorneys while I maintained a relationship with Mr. Drucker and Haven continued to serve the family to the best of our program's abilities.

One of our hospice workers was just exiting Drucker's bedroom as I approached the door. He indicated that our client was awake and would welcome my company, so I entered, shutting the door behind me. I made my way over to the chair I previously occupied and sat down. Excepting a tidy stack of newspapers to the side of the bed, nothing in the room, including the patient, seemed to have altered during my time in the garden, though the glow filtering through the window coverings had changed in quality.

"I am pleased that you returned. Their foolishness did not disturb you? It is unimportant."

"No, Mr. Drucker, I enjoyed the opportunity to see your lovely garden and experience the outstanding view."

"Pull back the curtains and open the room to the sun. Turn your chair, experience the view from here. Your worker had been reading the obituaries to me. I am seeing who is going before me."

I did as he suggested. I noted that Hor and DeeDee were no longer visible in the garden.

The organizational policy is to sit waiting for the client to speak or indicate that conversation is welcome. We sat in peace for twenty minutes, during which time I was acutely aware of the man in the bed near me. The warm lowering beams streaming from the windows fell across him. When he began to speak it was as if the sound of his voice had already been present between us.

"My wife's name was Aoife, a-o-i-f-e. Her name means 'beauty.' She was beauty! When I created my garden, I worked at it until being in the garden I felt as I did when I looked at Aoife. All things beautiful in my vision of truth gain their status of beauty from Aoife and how I felt in her presence. I purchased this house for her after I stood in this room and looked out at the view of the Bay.

"DeeDee physically takes after her mother, though her beauty is superficial and contrived. Aoife awoke from her night's sleep more beautiful than the sunrise. She was a goddess, a warrior too! She was my ruling queen, my lover, and through it all, my friend.

"Aoife was small and exotic with eyes so large, dark, and deep it felt like falling into heaven to look into them. Her skin was soft; it was touching a cloud to stroke her arm. Everything about her was soft and quiet, earthy in the way of paradise, when you looked at her or touched her. It was deceptive, that softness. It hid a tiger, she was strong; her body was tightly muscled beneath the softness of her flesh. Her breasts rode high and proud on her ribcage, and her legs… her legs. She could grip me between her legs and toss me about; I was a kitten, a piece of wool, a toy. Her mind and soul had the strength of mythic heroes.

"My wife was raised on a small island off of Japan, but she was just minutely Japanese. Her lineage crossed every sea and resided in every continent. An orphan, she was raised first in a nunnery, then sold and trained to be a geisha. Her training had been specialized, very specialized.

"In 1944, I was a first lieutenant multi-engine pilot; as part of the Army Air Corps, I was in the Air Transport Command. I flew the hump, though of course, you wouldn't know what that means. I was also part of Operation Meetinghouse in 1945."

Here he stopped talking. The light had changed to the golden rose of late afternoon and the fog began to roll over the Golden Gate Bridge and Marin Headlands, as it does almost every evening. This was not the disruptive caustic client I had been led to expect. Sparkles square-danced at the edges of my vision, and I could smell gunpowder and gardenias.

We were breathing in unison. My vision had cleared a bit as he spoke again, continuing his story.

"I met Aoife in an unremarkable way, the way GIs always met geishas. She had studied Japanese rope tying, Shibari, a form of sexual bondage, and presented demonstrations of it as part of a party. I arranged a contract to meet with her every week for the months that I was stationed on the island base. At some point, I knew I could not leave Japan without her, that she would be with me the rest of my life; as it turns out, the rest of her life. She was not the meek Japanese girl; she was a tigress!

"I paid for her. That was the only way one could marry a geisha back then. I had to buy her from her geisha mother. I know that I paid too much and yet still I knew at the time she was worth a great deal. Her training in the ropes, her fiery nature, all these things added value. I was young. I knew I had the resources, and I knew I had to bring her with me back home to San Francisco. I made a show of negotiating but I would have paid anything rather than lose her. She told me once that she knew this but had said nothing to her geisha mother.

"She had such a powerful nature that once we arrived in San Francisco, she assimilated within the year. Her English was accented softly, without obvious origin. She created herself as the perfect Presidio Heights executive wife. She created herself as a willful dominatrix behind our bedroom doors. Once Hor was born, she became a mother whose son would be successful. To her, each role was a part of her real self and each was important to her. Most important to her was her sexual life. I would tease her that her sexual life was more to her than I was. She would respond with a wind chime laugh and seduce me on the spot wherever we were, whatever we were doing. I always followed where she led me. She is most certainly the only person, man or woman, I have ever followed. I did it with a will born of absolute trust and love. Aoife was my reason.

"She died in her sleep. She gave up her spirit. We never even knew of the cancer. No pain, no treatment or doctors, there was no suggestion of an illness. My belief is that she must have known, that she made some choice. It was her way of living, to know and make choices.

"One night after years together but long before the cancer was eating at her, as we lay spent from hours of sexual play and making love, she whispered to me that I was interested in men, that she would like to help me explore that interest. You see, she knew when I did not. She led, I followed; she led where I wanted to go.

"Do you know where you are going, Letty? Do you know where I am going? My Aoife is not here to lead me. Will you be able to lead me where I am going, Letty?"

IV

<u>Parinibbana Sutta</u>

"Do not be troubled, for this is the nature of life."

1/2/00

Hi LM,

My name is Alan. I read all of my supposed "matches" and yours is the only description that is really what I have been looking for. I think we may have described each other in our ideal matches. I am 48, married and not looking to leave my situation, but I would like to have a similar relationship to what you desire. I am 5' 11", medium build and have all my hair. I've been told I am particularly good looking, but it's kind of embarrassing to admit that in print. I live in Atherton and work in Palo Alto. I'm an insurance broker specializing in agricultural land, and I travel around the Bay Area quite a bit.

Would you like to talk some more (phone or e-mail?) or meet for a drink/coffee? My regular e-mail address is hobbs72@hotbot.com. I would love to hear from you if only to talk and see if we have some interest in each other.

Alan

1/4/00

Alan,

Well, we certainly do seem to be looking for similar things. We could set up a time to meet for coffee or a cocktail. I am happy to travel to you so why don't you suggest a time, day, venue, and we'll go from there. Afternoons are best for me. Could we put off meeting until the end of the month, I'm a little overwhelmed just now?

LM

1/20/00

Hope enough time has passed. We should get together if you can find the time. How does next Tuesday the 25th look? Maybe noon for lunch or 3 PM for a drink
Alan

1/20/00

Alan -

Tuesday around 3 ish would be fine for me. Do you know a good spot in the Stanford area? Let me know. BTW you may call me Lisa, everyone does.
LM

1/21/00

Hi Lisa,

We could meet at Moongold in Palo Alto. They have a nice bar. It's on El Camino Real, across from the northern end of the Stanford campus. Let me know if that works for you.
Alan

1/21/00

Alan,

Moongold at 3 P.M. on Tuesday the 25th
is perfect. See you next week. I'll be
wearing a red sweater and black skirt.
Looking forward to meeting you.
LM

Highway 280 is the freeway that passes
through Los Altos Hills into Palo Alto. The speed
limit in California is sixty-five, but if you aren't
going eighty on 280, someone is going to be
passing you and honking. The freeway crawls
through rolling hills that abut the Santa Cruz
Mountains. Those mountains rise, to the west,
covered with redwood trees.

I drove by meadows dotted with small herds
of cattle grazing, the grass, sun bleached gold,
shone in the sunlight with live oaks studding the
fields. It was hard to imagine that I was passing
through one of the most densely populated areas
in the United States.

The sky was blue but muted. Obscuring the mountains across the Bay to the east and on the distant horizon, smog added the effect of the atmospheric perspective found in early Italian Renaissance landscape paintings. The clouds were low wisps, streaks across the frame of the windshield as if someone's hand had swept the sky trying to erase the clouds.

Throughout Los Altos Hills are multimillion dollar homes, large houses owned by small families. The Stanford campus is on the east side of the highway, though no buildings are visible from the vantage of the freeway. It is the Stanford road that I took off the freeway. This road winds through the hills leading up and over, giving frequent views of the Bay. In the sky, airplanes lined up on their approach to the airport. Graceful curves brought me down into the more populous areas, toward El Camino Real. This is the land of the privileged intellectual. I continued the drop toward El Camino. Buildings housing various medical and technical research and development giants sit in the middle of their own parks. Once I reached El Camino, the landscape became the antithesis of the Palo Alto and Atherton area through which it slices. There are four lanes going in each direction. It is one strip mall or chain motel after another, interspersed with block buildings that house car dealerships, McDonalds, and seedy delicatessens. Elms, which surely must have a disease, line the street. Behind the sterile buildings, pines and firs rise above the flat roofs. Neon lights announce futon sales, dry cleaning, and adult videos. The traffic is thick with SUVs and large new Dodge pickups. It is the architectural landscape of generic America with the addition of a cornucopia of Korean restaurants.

Before starting from the office that day, I popped two painkillers. My doctor had run tests but found nothing to explain the headaches. He suggested I try doing yoga to relieve my stress and he wrote a prescription. Now nausea churned in my gut as the restaurant came into view.

The Moongold is set off the street to some extent. It is a building that reflects the country chic of the 1980s, with wood siding in a dusty gray blue. The restaurant proclaims itself in fat, rounded, gold-toned letters set on the side of the building, assuring patrons that prime rib and steaks are both available within its milieu.

The front entrance is in the center, with walkways leading from the left and right of the door to the parking lot on either side, which wraps around the back of the building. Other than a late model red Ford pickup with a camper shell and a beat-up white Chevy van, both parked toward the back, near the kitchen entrance, there were no other cars on the side where I pulled in. I parked a bit toward the rear of the lot. As I approached, I became aware that the windows on either side of the entrance could easily hide a watcher studying me and passing judgment. In my mind's eye, I saw the back of a man leaving a tip on the table and rushing past a startled bartender and out the back exit.

Once through the door, I allowed my eyes to adjust to the dimness. The interior walls were painted a sponged warm peach. Indirect lighting complemented the alabaster wall sconces and matching brass and alabaster fixtures hung every few feet over the peach colored marble bar top. The ceilings and bar were made of dark heavy wood. At the far end of the bar, a small aquarium held a selection of colorful tropical fish that seemed to swim in rhythm to the soft rock played low on the sound system. The place was deserted except for one lone patron, as a Hispanic barback and the bartender prepared for the five o'clock cocktail crowd and early diners.

I found Alan just to the left as I walked in, sitting with casual composure, watching the entrance with a glass of white wine in front of him. He had the beginnings of a receding hairline at his temples that gave the effect of having a large forehead. His silver hair parted on the side was in a tidy medium length conservative style. The moment our eyes met, I saw his cornflower blue eyes crinkle as his entire face spread into a bright welcoming smile. I instantly liked Alan. As I walked toward him, he stood and extended his hand. We shook hands, saying one another's name. He held my hand in his just a moment more than the handshake lasted; he released it as if freeing a small bird. He motioned for me to sit and asked if I knew what I would like to order.

"I'll have a glass of wine, the same as yours, please."

"Excellent! I took a chance and chose a bottle of wine for us."

He motioned to the bartender by raising his large balloon glass and waggling it just a bit. He set it down and reached across the table, once more capturing my hand in his. We smiled together, then he continued,

"I'm so nervous, I've been on pins and needles all day. Right now, at this moment, I'm suddenly OK. What about you? Are you OK?"

The bartender was in his late twenties and looked like he could easily be a Stanford PhD candidate working here just until he finished his thesis. He wore a button-down shirt in black, olive Dockers, and a watercolor tie. He sported a soul patch but was otherwise closely shaved. He smiled as he carried over the open bottle of wine.

Alan released my hand as the bartender poured my glass and set down the bottle, leaving us once more to ourselves. The color of the wine was a warm gold, like an afterglow. I took a small sip, and smiled my approval with a nod; it tasted of summer fields and walnuts. In return, I received another flash of Alan's even, white teeth as once more he smiled warmly and raised his glass, offering a small unspoken toast.

I took in my surroundings as the warmth spreading from the wine relaxed me. The table at which we sat, like those surrounding us, was round. Each table was covered with a white tablecloth and had a small, shaded candlestick. We were on the lower of two levels closest to the bar. The upper level, reached by two steps, contained a few larger tables to accommodate fewer intimate diners. The mirrored bar wall and the glass shelves sparkled.

"I am no longer nervous, but I was. Now I am just happy to be here and to be with you, sipping wine."

"I'm a bit of a wine lover but never a wine snob. This is from a favorite winery of mine located in the Santa Cruz Mountains—Red Hawk Canyon Wineries. Have you heard of it?"

"No, but that means nothing. I know if it's good when I taste it. This is very nice."

"It's a small winery. The owner is a client of mine. We met when we were both at UCSF working on our MBAs. He and his brother started it, the winery I mean, on property they inherited from their father. I helped them with some, uh, complications arising from their desire to turn it into a winery. I really like this Sauvignon blanc of theirs. It has won quite a few tastings. More importantly, you like it, so I guess my taste buds have been validated." He laughed softly at himself.

"The things that came up to delay our meeting? Have they all been worked out to your satisfaction?"

"Yes, I believe everything is on track now. Things come up and that is part of my job, providing the leadership to comfortably work through it with my board of directors. Do you know anything about the nonprofit world?"

"I am on the board of an organization here in Palo Alto, we serve women in recovery and their children. We run three transition houses and provide counseling and career help. I've been doing this for a few years and next year will be rotating off the board. I'm going to miss the satisfaction of knowing I am supporting these safe houses. I'm really proud of what we do."

We talked a bit more about what it means to serve the community. It wasn't long before it felt like we had been friends for years. Alan's long fingers would flick and play with his glass of wine, restless. When my wine would get low, he would refill both of our glasses without a break in the conversation. I appreciated that he listened carefully to what I said but never probed for more information about my work or organization than what I offered. His questions went to my perceptions and concerns more than to facts.

Alan talked about his childhood in the Los Altos Hills area and we exchanged stories about misbehaviors during Mass; he, as an altar boy at Sacred Heart in Los Altos, me as a member of the children's choir at St. Timothy's in Bakersfield. He had graduated from high school and gone no farther than San Francisco for college. Eventually, he ended up at Stanford to get his JD. Somewhere during those years, he and his high school sweetheart had gotten their real estate licenses and also got married to one another. He passed his bar on the first try and they purchased their house in Atherton the following month. They still lived in that house twenty-two years later, joined by their daughter and an English Springer Spaniel named Rogers. His real estate and legal backgrounds had served him well in his work as a large development and agricultural land insurance broker.

I shared my marriage to Peter with him and told him stories about Cain, my cat.

"He's black, white, and fluffy but underneath the fluff, he is one scrappy tom. His ear had been ripped so often it looks like it's fringed."

My earlier history, including the violent death of my first husband, remained as unspoken with him, as it had with everyone else in my life.

We sat for a few moments, sipping the last of our wine. A Sweet song had been playing over the sound system for the last five minutes. The chorus spoke to my heart. 'Love is like oxygen, too much you get high; not enough and you die.' The angle of the sun through the leaded glass windows of the pub had deepened the shadows around us, sharpening the edges of things still in the light.

"Why are you here today, Alan? I've told you about my circumstances, please won't you share yours with me?"

"I'm lonely. I'm just lonely. I couldn't love my wife more than I do, but she doesn't want me to touch her. It used to be different; I don't know what changed. I know she still loves me. I just don't know what to do differently. Last summer something happened to me, and I began to worry I would do something stupid and lose my family, maybe everything important to me.

"I like theater and have, off and on, been connected with community theater. This last summer we were doing a Neil Simon play—you know the one with the birthday party in New York? There was this young girl in the cast, very pretty. I don't think she was more than twenty. First, I noticed she was always near me when we would have a cast meeting or do a reading. She began to ask me things, I became like her mentor, but she was always so close. We would run lines together. Sometimes she would ask for a ride home but there would be other people. I started to think about her all the time. It became this distraction. Do you think she liked me? Do you think she was flirting?

"One night she got a ride home with me, it was just the two of us in the car. I felt like I could stop the car and reach over and hold her and kiss her and she would welcome that from me. She was twenty, maybe. I was so lonely, so sexually frustrated. I am so sexually frustrated. I thought if I kissed her, we would make love, have sex. Do you think she was flirting, always being near me?

Always getting in my car? She would touch me sometimes on the arm or shoulder when we were standing backstage talking.

"We were at a stop light, it was red, I mean. It turned green but I didn't move. We just sat there, just for a moment. I was so aware of her. She smelled like violets. Her hair seemed to glow. I could feel the heat off her body. She said my name real soft, just my name.

"I saw the green light. I saw my wife Bonnie's face. I heard my daughter, Anna Michelle's voice. Did this young woman want me? If I had reached across right then—I drove her home. Nothing happened.

"I was so frightened by that. From then on, I made a point of staying away from her, never being alone with her. I couldn't wait for the play to be done so I could escape. I was so threatened. No matter what her reaction, if I had kissed her, I could have ruined my marriage. I could have hurt a lot of people. But she was young, and I think she was flirting with me, with me! She was beautiful, very pretty, and I—I guess I should have been flattered, huh?

"I spent a lot of time thinking about that car ride home and what could have happened. I remained lonely and frustrated, but I knew that that wasn't the answer. So finally, I figured out I needed to find someone in circumstances like mine who had a lot to lose and understood my needs because they were her own. I've haunted these different websites for personals. When I read your posting, I just knew, and then when we exchanged emails, I felt hope building. Now I've heard your story, so much like mine, with your husband and I feel so, I don't know what I feel; it is just the absence of loneliness, I guess. I don't know what to call it. Just saying all this aloud, telling you about Bonnie not wanting to be touched and telling you about this girl at the theater. Suddenly I am not alone."

I had reached across the table and taken his hand, holding it securely now. Alan swallowed and shrugged, smiling tenderly.

"You're a very lovely woman. Thank you. Thank you for listening."

We talked for perhaps another hour. First about investing and the ups and downs of the stock market and the solid values and expenses of land investments in Northern California. It came out that Alan had season tickets and was a longtime and enthusiastic baseball fan. We were able to share memories of the Giants and Willie Mays; both of us had seen him hit home runs at Candlestick Park as children. In his excitement talking about the Giants, Alan forgot that we would never be public friends. He invited me to attend a game with him sometime; I let the invitation slide by without comment.

"I always take time off from work for the games at home. Never miss one. We have four seats on the third baseline, really great seats."

When we left, we walked out together and said goodbye in front of the pub, shaking hands warmly and promising to contact each other very soon. I noticed over Alan's shoulder that an old Volvo, parked next to a BMW, had joined those other few cars in the parking lot. A man in the driver's seat wearing a Hawaiian shirt wiped the ketchup from his stubble and gave me a nod before returning to his burger and fries. I turned and walked away from Alan, toward where I had left my car. I felt him still standing where I left him, watching me. As I entered the parking area where my car was located, I couldn't help but notice that his eyes were following me with approval and desire on his face. I gave him a wave and he turned around and walked in the other direction toward his BMW.

1/25/00

Dear Lisa,

It was great to meet you today. Fridays are usually my best day. This Friday looks pretty good in the afternoon. I checked out the Santa Clara Marriott and it's pretty centrally located. We could meet at 1:30-2 pm for a late lunch.

The Marriott is located at 2700 Province College Blvd., which is right off Great

America Blvd., just off 101. How does that look for you? If not, maybe an alternate day or location. Got my presentation done and get to travel to beautiful Martinez tomorrow.
Alan

1/25/00

Alan -

Friday this week is impossible for me. Next week most weekdays are fine I believe.

The location is fine as well, but I did have an alternative thought and looked up the URL before getting your message. It is a B&B in San Sergio and I believe the link below is that place.

The reason I am suggesting it is because it is about as out of the way as we can get. My understanding from the pictures is that it isn't an over-the-top frilly country decor otherwise I wouldn't suggest it. To be perfectly honest I think I would be more comfortable in a place, a bit more removed from "real life" than in a corporate hotel setting.

http://www.goingto.com/sansergio.htm

I now feel like I am being demanding but would you please consider the alternative and if the travel time and cost aren't very different would you consider this option. I was quite taken with you today and felt far more comfortable than I expected.

Lisa

1/26/00

Lisa

I like the Kingston. The description is pretty appropriate, don't you think? Next Wednesday is my best day, as the others have scheduling conflicts to be able to block out sufficient time. I don't consider knowing what you want to be demanding at all. Cost difference is a non-issue.

Alan

PS: By the way, the feeling was mutual.

1/26/00

Alan -

Please go ahead and make Wednesday plans. I must admit I am feeling -- well, nervous isn't quite right the word but perhaps it is the sense that something I've only thought about is really happening.
I expect you may be having similar thoughts or feelings, so I am comfortable expressing this.
I am looking forward to seeing you again.
Lisa

1/27/00

Lisa,

We have confirmation from Kingston del Mar for Wednesday. Check in time is 3 PM, but she said we can come earlier. How about 2:00?
I assume you will be coming from the North, so when you get to San Sergio you should turn left by the lighthouse on Seal Point Rd., and it's the 1st driveway (on the left I think).

Anyway, there will be a sign, and our room will have my last name on it and will be unlocked. Apparently, we don't even need to check in. How cool is that?

See you Wednesday.

Alan

That Wednesday, I found myself driving on the Pacific Coast Highway, going to meet Alan. The ocean was a still, dark power, fury waiting to awaken, matching my mood. Century barns stood to the west, planks all gap toothed, harvesting the wind, whistling while they worked, were set in the painfully green meadows cloaking cliffs that fall to the sea. The earth below the shallow roots is unstable; it is all eternal, it is all temporary.

Breaks in the rocks and cliffs' edges revealed clean sand beaches where transient hands had built driftwood temples to unknown idols. I traveled through this landscape as if transported to myth, reality only a distant concept.

The backs of my hands holding the steering wheel were beginning to show age. The skin was thinner, a layer of crepe laying textural claim. The hills and farms rolling out this coastal stretch were cracked and broken in seemingly random patterns. For a moment, I was driving through the highly magnified coastal ridgeback of my own hands, my eyes returned to the backlit sky with no landscape beneath it.

A swollen San Sergio Creek fed its insatiable mother, as rounding a curve and sweeping down and up the lighthouse appeared, pretending to still brush the horizon of the sea, it steered the elephant seals to their own liaisons on the shores, pointing the way for the gray whales.

The lighthouse alerted me, edges seemed sharper; my foggy mythology was gone as I watched for the left turn onto the dirt road. It curled through a motley assortment of friendly ranch dogs that followed behind until I parked. I wondered at myself, the person taking these steps, as I walked past the chuffing horses lining up at the fence that followed my path. I found the key and welcoming note under the woven grass mat, and let myself into the cottage, leaving the dogs to chase down the road again, tails high.

I settled in, set the scene, and waited. I was as still as the falcon, which I could see, in an updraft below the cottage, who had no present agenda. She just waited for movement in the field, now stripped of artichokes but still a harbor for grounded creatures, a home for her prey.

I stood, turning toward the sound when I heard him at the door. He came past the threshold leading from the bedroom to the kitchen and his eyes found mine right away. We smiled. He had taken his shoes off at the entry. Barefoot, he held a bottle of wine in one hand and a box of chocolate truffles in the other, lifting them up as offerings. We met in the kitchen where he noticed the wine I had opened and the glasses ready to be filled.

"But I brought Joseph Schmidt truffles with my wine," he laughed, setting both the truffles and the bottle down on the counter next to the glasses. We stood face to face only inches apart.

"This place is just perfect, and the view is so beautiful," I said.

"You are beautiful."

Saying those words, he took my face in his hands and kissed me gently, lingering, his lips brushing mine, his hands increasing their pressure. He kissed my eyelids delicately and released me.

"Shall I pour your wine?"

He was blushing as he took refuge in what he knew, pouring the wine, handing my glass to me. I moved to the loveseat that served as a couch in the middle section of our suite and he followed, sitting next to me. We offered one another a silent toast and tasted the wine. Indicating the classical music that was playing on the radio, Alan told me he had been listening to that very station as he drove to meet me. He said it comforted him that we had both been listening to Liszt's Liebestraum Number Three. I had finished my glass of wine quickly—out of nervousness, I suppose—and so had he. He asked me if I would like him to refill my glass, but I shook my head, setting my glass down on the end table. He reached across me, carefully setting his glass down next to mine, and then sat back up.

Gazing out at the ocean and lighthouse, his hands on his knees, there was an awkward moment.

"The view…"

His arms were around me and we were kissing, deeply. It felt like drowning and just as I began to imperceptibly struggle, he began to stroke my shoulders and arms, kissing my neck, my cheeks, sipping in my scent, touching my hair. I found myself holding him and kissing him wherever my lips could find him.

He pulled us both to our feet, still kissing me, caressing my head and hair, tipping my head back. He kissed the hollow of my collarbone, making the smallest sobbing sound. The wine had made me a little dizzy and the passion I felt from him, and in me, was overwhelming. We held each other from falling. His hands found their way under my blouse, pressing into the small of my back as he continued to cover my neck and shoulders in kisses, always coming back to find my lips.

We stumbled a bit and I found we were near the plate window looking out over the meadow to the cliffs that fell in steps to the ocean and the lighthouse. We paused, taking in the view of the rising gray Pacific Ocean as it spent itself on the distant rocks. Slowly with a gentleness that suggested I might flee or simply turn to a shimmer of falling dust, he undid the three buttons on my blouse, discovering, as he did, that I wore nothing underneath. Before he could pull it open to expose me, I took his shoulders in my hands and with intense pressure, turned him away from me to face the window. Pressing my groin against his buttocks, I pulled my blouse open and leaned into his back. I started at the top of his shirt and when all the buttons were undone, I raised myself from his back enough to slip his shirt off and set it over the back of a nearby chair, my own falling to the floor behind us. I nibbled his back and neck, my tongue searching out first one ear and then the other, my mouth creating a whispering current before moving on. All the while my hands swept his chest, pressed, gripping through the material of his pants, teasing his nipples, and working his belt, and then his pants' zipper, open. I reached using care not to scratch him accidentally, easing my hand into his pants. His stomach was hard as my palm slid against his bare flesh. He pulsed under my hand and moaned again, so faintly. I molded myself to him, our bodies in full contact, my breasts rubbing his back. He held us both up, using his hands pressed against the glass; we were rising and falling as I continued to stroke him. I felt rather than heard him struggling to speak.

"I want to see you. I want to know your body. Let me take you to bed. God, please."

I gently lifted myself from him and stood just off to the right side looking straight into the window glass. He lifted his head and our eyes met in the reflection. I stood in my black stiletto pumps and reached around with both of my hands to unzip the back of my skirt. This movement raised my breasts and with awareness I allowed my skirt to fall. I steadied myself by placing my left hand on his right bicep and stepped out of the skirt pooled at my feet. I could see my body reflected back at me. High round full breasts, nipples erect, a somewhat thickened but still slim waist, my skin so pale it seemed transparent in the reflection. The black of my stockings, garter belt, and lace panties seemed to unnaturally lengthen me. Fascinated with my own reflection, I let my arms fall to my sides. Alan hadn't moved, as fascinated with my reflection as I.

"You can tell yourself whatever you want to tell yourself, we all do," he said.

"We are creatures of rationalizations and fantasy, aren't we?"

In that moment, I grew shy and vulnerable. Alan recognized this and moving his eyes away from the reflection, the fantasy of me, he turned to the solid reality of me. He removed his slacks, placing them, in their turn, on the back of the chair. With a single step, his right arm embracing and supporting me, his left hand cupping first one breast and then the other in sacramental offering to himself, he sucked and kissed my nipples. There was no haste in his movements, only veneration, and this he proved further by steadily moving down my body with kisses until he knelt before me, slowly removing my panties, his hands traveling down my legs with them until they were forgotten.

He spread my legs a bit more and holding me, he kissed the softness of my belly, the inside of my thighs, and I felt disconnected from myself. I became a baby bird held in his hands, helpless, but unafraid. His hands teasing the softness they found below my belly, I watched as he selected one of the gray pubic hairs that had appeared recently and pulled it straight, separating it from the remaining lushness and just gazing. He looked up at my face and smiled that boy's smile with his crinkled bright blue eyes. In one movement, he gave me a final kiss just below my belly button and stood, taking my hand and leading me to the bed.

He sat me on the edge of the bed, quickly replenished his glass of wine, and brought it to me, first taking a sip himself. I drank the wine, watching him as he pulled off his shorts and stood before me, erect, beautiful, no longer young but not yet old. I offered him the wine. Taking the glass, he again took a sip and set it to the side. With great reverence, he had me lay back on the bed, pulling my butt to the very edge. Again, he knelt down and with deliberation, he removed my pumps. He began licking and kissing my thighs just above my stockings, his fingers fiddling a bit with the garters, bit by bit moving up my legs, parting them ever wider to expose the soft fragrant folds now flowing with my desire. It was only a moment later, as he reached his destination, that I became only sensation. Lost in the tremors that coursed through me, dancing glimmers all around me; nothing existed for me except his tongue, his breath, and the control of his hands.

I don't know how much longer it was before I lay panting, trying to slow my heart. Alan undid the garters and rolled my stockings down and off my legs. At his command, I pushed my belly upward so he could undo the garter belt. That too, found its way to the floor. Now I was naked on the bed.

"Move over so that I may cover you with the comforter and lay next to you. I want to hold you. I want to make love to you."

Alan retrieved the chocolates while I slid to the far side of the bed. He crawled in next to me, pulling the comforter over the both of us. For a few minutes, we just lay together, my head resting in the hollow of his neck, his arms around me.

"Life is really all we have. I remember reading something by Rilke that 'Love and Death are the two greatest gifts that are passed on to us, and usually they are passed on unopened.' I feel that I am just beginning to figure out how to unwrap the gift of life.

"You are so beautiful to me. I can't understand how your husband could ignore you."

Alan had relaxed into a contemplative mood. I let my fingers explore the palm of his hand while we talked, and he began to knead my arm, finding sore tendons and knotted muscles.

"I understand almost nothing. Lately, when I think I know something I get this headache, and then in no time I can't concentrate or think about anything. All my knowing evaporates; I never get to be right anymore. I don't know. I don't understand how your wife can reject you. So here we are, two worthy people, worthy of physical love, worthy of all that life has to offer."

His massage moved to the back of my neck, and he sat up looking at me. Both his hands began to work the tension in my neck, and he came onto his knees straddling me as I looked up at him. His eyes followed his movements as he now massaged my breasts, my sides and ribcage, and my arms, often coming back to my breasts. When I tried to reach up to him, he would shake his head.

"No, not yet. Not yet."

I was being adored, worshipped. There is no other word for the experience. His face suggested that what he was seeing was a miracle, a vision. I reminded myself that he was seeing me. I felt my starved soul respond to this adoration. He touched my cheek with the tip of one finger, lifting a tear and placing it on his tongue and I knew that I had started crying.

"Open up to me. You may be feeling what I am feeling, how am I to know? I know real estate law and insurance; these are not the dominions of feeling or self-expression. Help me understand by talking to me. I want us to be one hundred percent genuine with one another.

"I happen to believe that each person that comes into our life is someone the universe has given to us because we have a lesson to learn from that person. It may be only for a moment or maybe a short while or it may be for a lifetime but there they are, until we learn the lesson they have to teach us. You and I do not yet know the reason or lessons that we will teach one another but I think it is abundantly clear that something is there. I can tell you that I am exceedingly good at uncompromising empowerment and deep emotional support."

I felt my mind quiet to match the relaxation I felt in my body. Alan and I were in perfect sync, in the moment. I felt that I could talk to him without violence or fear.

"Isn't it odd how everything can change in an instant? If we know anything, it's that we know nothing. No matter how creative one tries to be in order to make things right, what will be is going to pop to the surface. Trying to make things right is like trying to hold a beach ball underwater. Yet I still don't know what we have other than trying to figure it out and make it work whatever it may be in our life in a given moment.

"Sometimes there are big things, world-shaking things that occur to rock our realities, but more often than not, it's a small personal thing that acts as the defining moment.

"I began this year with the idea of taking the pressure off of my relationship. I decided I'd take my sexuality and needs into my own hands and do whatever I had to do to let him off the sensual and sexual hook. So, I put a posting up and connected with a few men. Beyond the connecting, the twenty or more responses every day to the posting was a type of mending for a sexual ego that had been flayed into ribbons.

"The landscape has shifted again. I don't wish to be an emotionally unavailable woman seeking only sexual satisfaction and companionship. I want to manifest my own aspect of that beach ball metaphor and once more have a loving partnership in which to grow old, sensual, and deeply full of gentle adventure.

"I've really felt that the reduction in my own tension levels and the heightening of my activity without waiting for my husband to choose to participate would improve his and my relationship.

"Maybe it has. Maybe the removal of the pressure will allow him to pop to the surface like that metaphorical beach ball and find the courage to finally express his own dissatisfaction with the status quo.

"It isn't enough for me to love him—he must love himself and he doesn't seem to be able to do that.

"I don't know what the reason or the answer is. I am not even sure of the question. An improvement in the relationship must be defined as each member of the relationship feeling better about themselves and the other. No specific picture can be painted that looks like that. It will always be a surprise.

"Am I worrying about the wrong things?"

Alan continued rubbing my upper body as I spoke, following his movements with his eyes. He had his own ideas to share.

"For me, marriage is entirely spiritual, mental, and from the heart, and the legal certificate has only an economic relevance for the protection of spouses and children. I love my wife and my daughter. But certainly, I deserve my own happiness. I would prefer to find that happiness at home but if it is withheld, what is my obligation?

"The silly notion that a person stays with another person for any reason other than the desire to stay with them is simply composed of the lies we each choose to tell ourselves. There is no right time, no time when the kid is grown, or the economy recovered, or the illness healed.

"Those are just stories. As long as we remain with our partners, we are safe. We risk no vulnerability of being emotionally available to joy or pain, none of the uncomfortable feelings that come with self-fulfillment and healing. You and I know better than many people that the pain one knows is far less scary than anything unknown. Each time we stop our stories and take a step into the unknown, we act with courage, and regardless of the details of the outcome, we achieve some degree of enlightenment.

"You may now think I am being harsh or judgmental, but I am not. I am only suggesting that we are human in our frailties and nature. We, all of us, do these things."

His hands rested on my belly, still, as we each dwelt in our own thoughts for a moment. Then I responded.

"This is an entirely true statement, however, if one is truly not in marriage then there is no need to hide one's actions. To say one is not married, but to neglect to inform the other member of the marriage contract of that fact, is to be lying to at least one someone about something.

"If you had asked me not long ago what I thought of men who 'cheated' on their wives, you would have found a low tolerance. It is only in my own recent history that I have come to understand the break of trust that can occur in a relationship, the frustrations and hole in the soul that can develop when a part of one's life is being denied because of a choice to remain true to a commitment that might be best let go.

"If you approached me and said you wanted a relationship to usurp the role of your wife in your life, I wouldn't give you the time of day.

"I will do nothing that takes something away from another woman. I will do nothing that hurts another woman. These are absolutes for me.

"Why is it OK to be with a married man? Because if your wife truly does not desire to go down the path you need for yourself, then pressure can be removed from the relationship by not denying yourself or pressuring her. It can be a win/win/win. Life is too fleeting to not grasp the moment, the energy, and the spirit offered to us.

"I don't want to take you away from your wife or impact your relationship except in positive ways. If what we do together aids you or me in finding our individual ways into our best futures, then that is a wonderful bonus but not an objective."

"The Beatles said it best: 'The love you take is equal to the love you make.' "

He murmured this into my hair and with this, our conversation ended. He entered me and we had a lingering, slow intercourse punctuated by intense but tranquil orgasms. The late afternoon sun sent a warm golden glow through the window to bathe us as once more we lay in one another's arms in harmony. He talked about his daughter, Anna Michelle, who was graduating from high school in the spring. I shared with him my concerns for my daughter, Jennifer.

"She seems so angry. Since she became a teenager, she has been aggressively competitive. Now that she is in LA and twenty-four years old, I am not sure she has any friends left… no one can withstand her need to win. Her aggression seems to serve her in her career, though. She has become the most successful of my kids in terms of earning a living. She works as a financial broker specializing in health care and related services. She is the middle child, the one I am least connected to now that they are adults."

Alan fed me a chocolate.

"My girl will always be her daddy's girl. Maybe the dad always gets the girls or maybe it's just my wife's coldness to us both that drives her to me. Is your daughter closer to your husband?"

I thought about that. Did Peter communicate with Jennifer at a deeper level than he did with the boys or me? What about Jennifer, what was her perception? Maybe I could talk with her about her dad and gain some insight without giving her a hint of the distance that had grown between him and me.

As I thought about this, I became aware that Alan had recovered from our earlier lovemaking. This awareness changed the path of my own thoughts and I let him know that it was his turn to receive.

I took my time, working my way over his entire body with my hands and mouth, teasing every sensitive spot until ultimately there was only one place left unkissed on his body and it was there that I focused. As I dwelled on consuming Alan, I watched his skin flush, his eyes defocused becoming a blue so intense as to seem ethereal. I felt his pulse in my mouth, tasted first the mild salt of his skin, then the richer salt of his orgasm, his body shuddering with his release.

The sun had lowered to the point that it seemed to approach the sea. We knew that our time was drawing to a close. The open wine had been finished.

Alan got up from our nest and went into the bathroom. Shortly thereafter I heard the sound of the shower. I knocked softly on the door and entered, joining him. Beginning with his hair, I washed him using a natural sponge, scented soap, and my hands. I worked my way down his body, cleansing him, and in the act also cleansing myself. When we stepped out of the shower, I gently dried him following the same head to toe pattern as before. We kissed once on the lips and without a word went into separate rooms and dressed.

We were like a couple that had traveled together forever as we inspected the room, gathering our things and tidying as we went. Finally, just by the door we held each other again, kissed softly, and in unison murmured, "Thank you."

I watched from the entry as he got in his car and pulled down the dirt road. I returned to my own car and followed, each of us returning to our real lives.

2/2/00

Thank you.

LM

2/2/00

You're welcome. And thank you.

Alan

2/4/00

Alan -

Were you thinking about getting together
again anytime soon?

Lisa

2/5/00

Lisa,

Have been doing a great deal of thinking
about us this past week. First of all, it was
wonderful. I hope you felt the same way.
My anticipation of it was exceeded only by
the experience itself. My dilemma now is that
though this is what I thought I'd been looking
for, for so long, I'm no longer sure. I guess
it's a twist on "be careful what you wish or..."
Part of me wants to see you right away; the
other part of me is now stuck in uncertainty.
Maybe it's an attack of conscience I felt
would never occur, I just don't know.
I know you have been searching for a long
time for someone, and I worry that you may
think I've taken advantage of your situation. I

just didn't think I would have such feelings of ambivalence. I really thought I would feel differently.

At my age I should be more sure of my feelings.

So what to do now? I would like to see you again and talk in person, but it will need to be after next week. Perhaps the week of the 11th? What do you think?

Alan

2/6/00

Alan -

What do I think? I think you are a good man and that your wife is very lucky. I think we had a beautiful experience together.

I also think that everything you're feeling is real and natural and a good truth.

I don't know what you have tried with your wife ... but if I may?

Have you tried having an afternoon sneak away with her? Like we had?

I mean the whole thing from planning it,
so no one knows but the two of you.
Planning it someplace completely different
from where the two of you usually meet or
go.
Do you watch her walk away the way you
watched me walk away the day we first
met in person?
It was that which got me to our seaside
nest.
When was the last time you just leaned
into her neck and shoulder, inhaled and
told her how wonderful she smelled?
If she is my age there are some truths
about women that don't seem to be
spoken.
We feel more powerful and energetic than
we ever have but somewhere on our
bodies something is hurting and we are
very tired. We can't understand how we
can be both ways at once.
Men aren't looking at us the way they used
to and we notice that.

We want to be acknowledged, desired, and remembered. We want to be recognized and that is the hardest thing for a man to do.

Between now and Easter try to think about and watch your wife in the little things. Look at what she does -- not at work or with the kid so much but just in her daily patterns and routines. After she flosses her teeth does she throw the floss away in the basket or just set it down somewhere? Does she always set the dinner table with napkins or placemats for dinner? Is her car floor a mess or neat as a pin? Is there a turn of speech that is unique to her? Does she write poetry that no one reads or keep a journal?

Now write her a letter in your own hand on lovely paper and tell her that you notice these things and that these little things are the touchstones of your days together. That her presence is what keeps the world real for you, what gets you out of bed in the morning. Let her know that all of your many accomplishments in the world pale next to the fact that you somehow have managed to have her in your life for so many years.

I promise you'll get some results with this. If it is a completely foreign thing for you to do just tell her that recent events in the news got you thinking.

Meanwhile, I am available to talk or get together. I will not contact you out of respect for your feelings and circumstances.

You are a very good man, and your wife is very lucky.

You know, what's happened here is that you have been reborn.

LM.

V

<u>Parinibbana Sutta</u>
"Diligently practicing right effort, you must seek liberation immediately."

I clicked send on my final email to Alan. I harbored the fantasy that our encounter and my counsel would result in him and his wife finding their way back to one another. I longed for the fantasy that somehow our encounter would help my husband, Peter, and me to find one another again.

I took a chance by sending it from my own computer. Prior exchanges, I had picked random spots in San Francisco and visited public libraries in a widening circle around that spot to use their computers for all my communications with men. Using the false identities given to me by that young client from several years ago, I always used a different library card. I felt the risk of using my own computer, just this once, was a calculated one since I was using the wireless service I quietly accessed from a nearby neighbor. It wasn't as if anything unexpected had happened or would be happening to Alan.

It was dusk. I love this time of evening because the light is like candles, soft and a bit rosy, even in winter. It is a light that is kind to women and memories. I rose from my makeshift desk in the family room after shutting down the computer and stood in the almost dark for a moment, listening to my house. Through the sliding glass doors leading to the backyard, I could see the three olive trees, one for each child, each lit by small spotlights Peter had installed.

When Jennifer was born, Peter had taken Zack out to the backyard and planted the first of the trees. I remembered so clearly, Peter explaining to Zack that the small stick they were placing on that day would one day produce fruit. He cautioned him that the fruit would be bitter to eat, but that the two of them could work together to make the harvested fruit taste yummy.

That night, they had opened a can of black olives and stuck one on each of their fingers, roaring with laughter as they popped an olive-dressed fingertip into a mouth only to have the finger reappear denuded of its olive raiment. I remember Jennifer on my breast as I watched their antics and wondered about the future of this child whose birth tree bore bitter fruit.

When Ian was born, the second tree was planted and because it was a particularly cold winter, both saplings were wrapped in burlap bags for protection. This time, Peter had Zack and the not-so-very-helpful toddler Jennie as his helpmates. Peter told the children the story of Minerva and Neptune.

"Zeus chose the olive, but a horse would have been better," Zack had declared, establishing his role as the arbiter of taste and opinion within our little tribe. Again, that evening the familial correct consumption of black olives was enacted. Again, I held my newborn to my breast, but this time, I remember staring out the glass doors at the sack wrapped trees, the laughter and giggles behind me, apart from this new baby and me. The two trees, bitter witnesses to our lives, disturbed me. Were they guardians of principle or prophets of doom? I shook my head to clear it of such thoughts; these were surely the mental postpartum ramblings of a sleep deprived new mother.

On his next birthday, Zack had asked why he had no tree. That afternoon, he and Peter arrived from the nursery with Zack's 'very own' olive tree. Zack shared with me what he had learned on their father-son outing, while Peter planted the tree and the other two children napped. He told me that this tree was younger than he was because, while the trees can grow anywhere, olive trees did best when planted very young. He told me that even if something harms or damages an olive tree, the roots rarely die and they usually grow good new suckers.

"Mom, olive trees live forever but not as long as redwoods," he told me.

That night, olives danced on all fingers but mine. Even little Ian had olives placed on his fingers though he was still a baby and could not eat them.

"Mommy don't like olives… they always taste bitter to her," Zack explained to the baby Ian.

Zack's small tree stood a bit off from the other two because of the way the bedding in the yard was configured. Together, the three made a triangle if looked at from one perspective, but that night, from my view out the glass doors, Zack's seemed separate, and it caught the moonlight in a way that the other two did not. In that moment, I named his tree Peace, Jennifer's was Witness, and Ian's tree was Light.

Over the years, these thoughts returned repeatedly. I have never felt comfortable with the olive trees in our backyard.

My disquieting reverie was broken by the sound of the front door opening and by Cain rousing himself from his couch spot with that languishing disdain evident in cats when displaying their special blend of intense interest and abject boredom. Peter was home.

I glanced at the computer, assuring myself that I had shut down all but the desktop screen as Peter entered the family room, piling his coat and books on the couch and gathering up Cain as he moved toward me. Smiling, I stood open, facing him.

"Hi, sweetheart, how was your day?"

Would he come up to me? Hug me? Maybe give me a small kiss? But no, he simply stopped short of me stroking the cat in his arms.

"The usual, I have some stuff I need to do tonight, when will dinner be ready?"

The body memory of my time with Alan made this ritual dismissal hurt less. Still, the pain was recorded in some ledger kept on my spirit, even as I smiled and moved through the remainder of our evening routine. Peter went upstairs to his office to, as he put it, unwind after his day, and I began preparing dinner in the kitchen. When a brief time later we sat across from one another, eating, our conversation carefully stayed on the mundane of everyday, like two strangers sharing time at a roadside café simply to avoid the act of dining in silence. While I cleaned up, he returned to his office, closing the door.

When I shut off the light in the kitchen, I stood for a moment, my eyes shut. I suppose a sigh escaped as I walked up the stairs. Peter's office was just to the left at the top of the stairs. The room had once been Ian's bedroom but when Zack had gone off to college, Ian had seen it as his right to claim his brother's larger room as his own. I had converted the space abandoned by my youngest son into a retreat and office for Peter and surprised him with it on his birthday that year. Now he rarely emerged from his hole when he was home. I began to knock on the door, but experience told me he would complain that I had disturbed his train of thought, so I opened my fist and placed my palm on the door, whispering.

"I love you. I'm sorry."

I moved on down the hall and entered Jennie's room, which had become our guest room but retained most of its personality as her space. The ambient light from the hall provided enough illumination that I could sit on her bed and allow the objects of the room to guide my thoughts. How could I assure myself that my daughter never found herself as painfully alone as I found myself? Was she different enough that her pains would be foreign to me?

One corner of the room held floor to ceiling shelves full of the achievement awards she had received through high school. In the attic, I knew there was a box that contained the recognition certificates that she had collected since she was in preschool. She had packed them up herself and asked me to save them for her when she was fifteen years old. Jennie had always enthusiastically entered into any activity that she thought had an element of competition. When she didn't excel at sports, she still continued to train but not to compete. Right up until college, she had sought out every speech or essay contest, math competition, and science fair. Jennie realized at a very young age that it wasn't enough to have the best idea or do the best work; execution and style, she said, always carried the day. She was aggressive with both her brothers, but they adored her. Ian would always squelch his usual artistic inclinations to help her design and execute displays for the competitions that looked like professional marketing booths at a trade fair. She would enlist Zack's expertise as a presenter when rehearsing for a speech or debate. The three of them united in an effort to prove that she was the best at whatever she tackled.

I remember, when she was twelve years old, she sat in the kitchen watching me. She announced that she had decided to be the most influential girl in her class.

"Most popular, you mean."

"No, I meant most influential. Like, I am popular but not the most popular, you know. I want to have influence and that requires respect, like people respect you, Mom."

It was in this decision coming from her that I at last had a use and value to her developing teenage heart. I was enlisted as coach and mentor in the art of leadership. Flattered, I had hidden my own feelings of inadequacy in this area.

Now, out of college with a BA in finance and a broker's license at the age of twenty-four, Jennie lives in Los Angeles and is a successful financial investments advisor specializing in health care and related services. She no longer seemed to need my advice or her brothers' support.

I knew that she worked hard and had no deep personal relationships. She rarely called or emailed, and she almost never visited us. I wondered if she was happy, without trying to ask myself the question: Was anyone, anywhere, happy?

I felt engulfed in darkness though nothing had changed from the time I sat down.

I hadn't heard from Zack, though I had been expecting to receive an email from him. I looked over at the phone sitting by the bedside. The "kids' line," we called it. We had put in a second line for the kids when they had all been teenagers. Later, we used it as a connecting line for the internet. Since we had had cable installed for our internet connections, because it only ran upstairs in the kids' bedrooms, we never used this line. I decided I would call Jennie and Zack and just chat with them. Perhaps it would raise my flagging spirits. I reached across, picked up the receiver, and heard a woman's voice!

I turned the receiver up to face me as if I could see who was talking by looking at the source of the sound. I could hear her; she was moaning, going on about her nipples being pinched. No, it wasn't her nipples; it was his nipples! She was talking about clamping his nipples. My mind would not work. All I could think was how filthy and how funny it sounded. She was over the top with her language. I heard Peter heavily expel air and groan in the affirmative. I almost laughed aloud and then it clicked. The same moment that I realized this strange voice was having phone sex with my husband, a searing jab of pain struck directly between my eyes, knocking me back on the bed. I felt the weight of the words on my chest like the playwright was using me for a chair while composing his comic tragedy. The phone rested in my hand, limp beside me; the voices became enflamed and rough.

"Aaaah, aaaah, yes, are they tight? Do they pinch?"

"Ooh, yes, uh-huh."

"Uh-huh, yea, squirm baby; you're a real baaad boy. Mama doesn't let you get away with being a bad boy. Noooo, baby, I'm gonna punish your ass now, yes baby, that's what mama wants, bend over, spread your cheeks, you bad, bad boy, do like mama tells you."

"Yes oh, mama."

"Yea that's it, bend lower, yea, mmmph, I'm grabbing your balls now. My hand is reaching between your legs and grabbing your balls; yea can you feel mama squeeze?"

"Uh-huh"

"Uh-huh, yea like that, yea it's good isn't it, bad boy? You have that enema mama told you to have ready?"

I don't know how long I lay there. I could hear the voice but could no longer comprehend the words. When I opened my eyes, the world had become indistinct, and sepia toned. I didn't hear Peter do more than moan once they had started the enema. Using exceeding care, more because I was unsure of my own ability to command my body than from a need to be undetected, I replaced the receiver on its cradle. Standing, still with extreme care, I moved out of the room to the hallway just outside Peter's office door. I had no plan; I didn't seem to have any thought at all. I felt limp and tightly wound all at the same time. I just stood there.

Something brushed against my ankle. Looking down, I saw Cain twining around my feet and between my legs in his characteristic figure eight. As he passed, I hooked him on the toe of my shoe and lifted my knee. He hung, draped across my foot, relaxed. I lifted my knee a bit higher, looking down the stairs in front of me, swinging my foot to gently rock Cain. The vice around my head tightened for a moment, he began to purr. I looked down again and saw Cain still draped across my raised foot, his head turned so that one eye trained on my face. When our eyes met, his purr became a roar of self-satisfaction bolstered by trust. My foot swung a little higher in its arch. His eye held mine, but he remained relaxed and confident.

I raised my knee a bit higher and used my hand flat against Peter's door to balance myself. With the other hand, I reached for Cain and scooped him up to my shoulder. I turned and went down the hall to my bed where we fell asleep curled against one another, one of us still purring.

I awoke when Peter finally came to bed. He did not touch me while getting under the covers. He had been in bed next to me for so many years I still knew his presence even when he wasn't with me.

"Peter," I spoke quietly, "It is never the right time to talk to you. You know I love you. You know I have never said 'no' to you. I want us to talk to one another. I want you to desire me again. If there is anything I can do to help make that happen, will you let me know what it is? I am so incredibly sad, so lonely, and so disappointed when I think about us now. Please won't you help me connect with you? Please won't you come out of the seclusion in your office and be with me in the evening?"

He held his breath. There was no movement, then finally, his familiar weary sigh.

"There is nothing wrong; I still desire you, I'm just tired. Go to sleep."

Again, we lay in silence. I could feel his gradual relaxing; the change meant he was easing into sleep. My headache pounded in a samba rhythm. It hurt more to close my eyes and so they remained wide open.

"I tried to call Jennie and Zack tonight on the kids' phone, but the line was in use."

The pounding slowed. I felt a flutter as if a bird had just left my center to fly out an open window. I felt the movement of the sheets as Peter swung his feet to the floor and sat up. He plucked Cain from where he was curled atop my hip and began to pet him. A moment later he stood and, carrying Cain, he left the bedroom. I began to weep, but eventually my eyes closed and without realizing it was occurring, I fell soundly asleep.

VI

<u>Parinibbana Sutta</u>

"Within the light of wisdom, destroy the darkness of ignorance."

My life was a silence so profound that the only sound I could hear, and rarely, was in my mind: my own voice in third person singular.

My headache was with me night and day, but I used the business to push the throbbing into the background. My hours grew longer at the office in my attempt to fill what felt like a dark wound in my side. Since overhearing the conversation between Peter and the telephone sex worker, my home had become a cold and empty place; maybe it had been that way before. We didn't even pretend to be OK anymore. I was feeling alone and trapped most of the time, only by concentrating on my work was I able to push the pain into a small walnut shaped knot at the base of my skull.

The world had turned a swirling foggy gray to match my pain. Rain regularly soaked the hills of Northern California, just enough to keep geologists and meteorologists standing on the overbuilt summits, waiting for the inevitable mudslide. We Californians are always waiting for the earth to move.

It wasn't long before the emails and telephone calls were flying between the younger Druckers' attorneys and Haven's attorneys. DeeDee and Horace Jr. had taken my responses as blocks to their agenda, as I had expected. The morning that I was first to meet with Alan, Haven had been served with notice of an impending lawsuit alleging fraud and coercion in the case of Mr. Drucker's bequest. That morning, after our initial meeting with the corporation's attorneys, I told them to handle it all. I was trying to concentrate my efforts on developing deeper relationships with our remaining funders and strategizing with my board and development staff on broadening our current base of funders. Times were hard. I felt my skills should be used where they were best suited; let our attorneys use their skills where they were best suited.

In subsequent conversations, Mr. Drucker and I had reached an understanding. He understood that I would honor his request for my time if he would respect a schedule that allowed me to fulfill my duties as an executive director. He and I agreed that any bequest or donation to Haven on his part was to remain completely separate from our services to him, including my participation. I shared my experience with the identity thief during the beginning of Haven's Street Youth program, explaining that there had been precedent for my sitting with clients.

Nancy reported that Mr. Drucker had mellowed in his treatment of our volunteers and staff since my first visit. It seemed that he could as easily charm his caregivers as bring them to bitter tears. His health was holding; the doctors remained noncommittal, unable to predict the progress of his deterioration. A schedule had been established for my visits with Mr. Drucker based on his most alert and awake period of the afternoon.

"Witches! All of you are witches without spell books. Get out of here and leave me alone. Go practice your black arts on someone who doesn't know you're incompetent!"

I heard his voice chasing the nurse and doctor as they came down the stairs to where I was shaking the rain from my hair and handing my coat to one of Mr. Drucker's several aged retainers. Sying or Lei or Long, I could not keep it straight which one was which. The nurse disappeared into the hall leading to the kitchen while the doctor and I shook hands. I knew him from various conferences and fundraising events. Here on a house call was a physician always found in the lists of top doctors that local magazines are so fond of publishing, and he was being turned out and berated by his longtime patient. After our brief exchange, I headed up, reaching the third step before I heard Drucker's voice again.

"Tell that uniformed witch-bitch to stay out of my room until you leave."

I glanced at Lei-Sying-Long and received a slight head ducking as acknowledgment that he would pass the message along before I continued up the stairs. As always, the light was subdued in Drucker's bedroom, the curtains pulled back to reveal his garden and view. I settled into the chair by the bed without a word, the pain a vice on my soul.

"You are a witch too! You... you are the most deceitful person who dares cross into my circle of death."

"Mr. Drucker, you seem to be feeling energetic this afternoon."

"Your headache? It is still with you, am I right? It comes from practicing magic without any idea of its power. I can offer you spells and incantations if you will learn them."

"Are we all witches who come to visit you, Mr. Drucker?"

"Horace Cosgrove Drucker, THE THIRD! I know who the hell I am. Do you know who you are? No! You don't. Call me Cos, or if you someday like me, call me Cosi-san. I call my son Hor, as you may have noticed, it drives him nuts. An excellent result for such a small word, don't you think? He will be the ruler of the family when I am gone; he rules our business concerns now. Perhaps I make him feel insignificant, perhaps he is. An insignificant ruler, well now, who among us can say otherwise about ourselves and tell the truth, we are all insignificant rulers of our domains. Each of us is a pharaoh, each a slave. Call me Cos. I name you whatever I wish, don't I, Ms. Mae, sometimes Letty," here he paused, "or sometimes Lisa?

"Do you want to learn the power of your magic, Letty Mae? It is what I have to offer today."

"I will call you Cos, if you will please be nicer to your health care providers and my staff people. I will listen to you and your tales of magic since you have so much to say today. I will listen."

Together we watched the waters of the Bay define the infinites of gray. A benefit of these visits was that I relaxed, and the pain became as remote as the world outside the room.

"Your headache?"

"Not so bad. Your room and garden seem to relieve the pressure."

"You don't think it is my company that offers you relief? Who am I? What sort of person?"

I had discovered that he did not require quick answers, that he preferred I take his questions seriously and consider them first. I tried out his name, but it came with difficulty, awkward on my tongue.

"Cos… I don't know who you are, but I believe our visits are teaching me that. You are not to me what you have the reputation of being to others. Do you treat me differently? I am always on the verge of crying so perhaps making me cry would not be such fun for you. You notice that I am in pain when others don't see it at all. That happens with our hospice clients, their own fragility helps them see it in others, I suppose. You seem to use your ability to see the weakness in others as fodder for torment. You have a reputation for finding entertainment in emotionally tormenting others. What sort of person are you? A powerful one who is used to getting his own way? Does it matter what I think? I am not here to judge you. I am here because you demanded it, and it is in the best interests of my organization.

"No, that isn't true. It was the reason I came the first time, but now I come because I find a few moments of peace in this room and because I look forward to your stories."

"There was truth in your reply. Not very tactful of you."

"You already know, why would I deny what you already know to be true? Anyway, you have a reputation for attacking people who are polite and tactful. I am sure I will set myself up enough without trying; I might as well be honest with you."

"I don't think everyone perceives me as a tormentor. I will let you be the judge."

"I am not here to judge."

We lapsed into a comfortable silence, and then I asked, "Aren't you giving magic lessons today?"

"Prop me up more, there are pillows on the floor over here, use those."

I moved around his bed and picked up the two pillows lying there. Sitting on the bed, I slipped my arm behind him and lifted his weightless trunk, placing the fat pillows behind and leaning him down into them as I slid my arm away. His large hand grasped my arm as I began to stand, our eyes met. His watery eyes held me, so pale now that they seemed to have only light but no color. We sat in stillness, the blood traveling through his tissue-thin flesh was a stream of life circling around my wrist. I lowered my eyes after a moment, searching the room for something to rest on, some object to present itself as worth a second look but found nothing, ultimately having to return to that light, his stare, and blushing under the scrutiny. A smug smile, and then he released me as he adjusted his red patterned silk kimono.

"Go back to your chair. I look like a Dalmatian under this dressing gown, but my face has been spared that one ravage. You had best let that nurse know she will need to provide me with my shot soon and I need a diaper change. You don't fidget when I touch you. Aren't you afraid?"

"You will not be the death of me," I replied.

I smiled at him, now secure once more in my customary chair after using the intercom to request the nurse.

"Virginia Woolf wrote 'Nobody sees any one as he is… They see a whole, they see all sorts of things, they see themselves… One must follow hints, not exactly what is said, nor yet entirely what is done.' Do you know her work, Letty?"

"I am not so literary. I've never read Virginia Woolf. What book is it from?"

"The point is not the citing, nor even if I have gotten it exactly, the point is the meaning, the understanding behind the words.

"I once had a pastor at our church tell me something during a conversation that greatly affected me, I had him write it down. One day, Aoife found it stuck in the pages of a book she was reading. These words had a strong impact on her, and she tied it to everything we did. It was during this period that she and I began to explore the tantric."

"We aren't going to be exploring your memories of orgies past, are we? I don't think I am the right person for this conversation. Really, don't you have deeper concerns, pleasanter, more pedestrian social interactions, spiritual ruminations?"

I shifted uncomfortably in the chair, but he ignored me and continued.

"Tantric practice is only about group sex when American men bastardize it into a word that translates to 'anything goes.' No, tantric practice is spiritual, and it is physical and, yes, it is sexual at a remarkably elevated level. Now be quiet, I am teaching you magic, you should pay attention, after all, compassion is entirely a mutually beneficial exchange."

There followed a long period after this comment during which the nurse came in and administered Cos's palliative care. She flashed me a look, questioning his passiveness and acquiescence during her ministrations. I could only shrug. When she left, his voice slid into the room as almost a whisper.

"You know these people don't get it. They want peace and beauty in my death. There may be that, but it is still a messy business at best. This is not a tranquil time and mine was not an outwardly tranquil life. I have no control; I have vomited so much I feel internally like a single raw patch of bleeding tissue. The pain, what is left of the diarrhea, the anal tumors are almost welcome signs of life. Birth is messy and beautiful, so is death. Your job here today, and until I am clinically dead, is to see the mess as beauty and remind me. I am alive. I am dead. Can you be my pool of tranquility if I help you find it for yourself? Can you remind me that I have as much control as I ever had, only the illusions have disappeared? This is why you are here; you are going to become my hands, my will. You will be my last vestige of control."

"I will… I will stay the evening if you like. I am listening."

"My next great adventure, I don't want to go without saying goodbye but to whom do I bid my farewell? DeeDee and Hor are my children, and the truth is I love them for who they are and who they can never be, but they have been only a piece of my life. Certainly, I have never felt alone while I was alive but now that I am dead but not yet gone, I feel alone with no one to whom to bid farewell.

"Yes, stay. Stay; learn about magic. What did you ask me before about my spiritual ruminations? You know my family were founders of the Presbyterian Church, St. Broderick's, here in Presidio Heights? I haven't been to services there in years. It is important to DeeDee and Hor, so I have consented to their holding a service there for me. My wife and I practiced Zen, and as we matured, we discovered tantric yoga to augment our practice. The practice, what a wonderful concept that is, practice law, practice medicine, practice being fully in the moment. Zen Buddhism is the intent and desire to be fully aware, fully in the moment. It is practice; only the Buddha has reached full enlightenment. In the tradition, Christ was a Buddha, Muhammed was a Buddha, other great teachers, teachers of peace, have been Buddha regardless of the religions that followed after their teachings. I longed for the mystic, though I am not meant to be Buddha this time round.

"Open the drawer and hand me my cards."

I opened his bedside drawer as he indicated and found on top of what seemed a bundle of dark velvet, a deck of large tarot cards, well worn from years of fingering and the laying on of hands. I passed them to him, closing the drawer. He manipulated the cards as he continued to speak. Through the window, I could see a gardener quietly at work weeding near the edge of the pond near the pagoda. He was taking advantage of the moist earth and the break in the weather.

"The mystic. In the study of tantric practices, you learn to worship the god in everyone. When you choose to approach a person sexually you do it with absolute reverence. In the moment you are fully engaged and committed to loving the divine in that individual.

"Have you ever had that, Letty? That reverence?"

The palms of my hands rubbed the mahogany armrests of the chair. I spoke slowly, carefully.

"I… I think that, yes, I have very recently experienced what you are saying."

He nodded, as if confirming what he already knew, then continued.

"Tantric sex provides for a deeper experience. Tantra is about the trinity of the divine. Mind, body, spirit. It is in the embrace of all three that we are able to recognize and experience the divine in ourselves and in our partner. This is the expansion of the mind that goes beyond creativity into the realm of the fully realized being.

"The books speak of touch and emotion as a unified experience in order for tantra qualities to occur. I believe fully that the deepest level of being occurs only when first one unites the trinity in oneself and the universe, this is the Buddhist quality of being, and unites with the unique trinity of the loved one. It must be a loved one. The holy transcending tantric experience only arrives with the full connection: mind, you have a common goal, common belief, abiding respect for the other's rational processes; body, you each touch, physically worship, and have reverence and care of the other's physical needs; spirit, this is the realm to which you bring romance, wonder, and intuition.

"Trinity is an immensely powerful notion and the trinity as one is ultimately a tantra experience. The male—mind, the female—body, the sex enchantment, creation of love—spirit, and what you have is one hell of an experience because suddenly you are sitting in the divine inside and out.

"I think that is why being present at the birth of a child, especially as the father or mother, is such a powerful experience. By being present I don't just mean physically but rather fully present and in the moment. That child, new to the world, in that moment of birth, is conceived in love by those present. They all know in that moment the transcendental unity I've just described, and of which volumes are written. In that moment, divinity is all in all and the participants are overwhelmed and recreated in the very embodiment of god.

"It sounds so simplistic. Simple is not wrong. In fact, I firmly believe it is almost always right. I know that Buddhist teachings are simple, and yet often so hard for the mind to grasp because of the simplicity.

"I think that in order to achieve what is described as sex enchantment requires great focused caring, time, and some specific techniques.

"I think that to achieve the fully divine or mind-blowing levels of experience one needs to perceive the real and still see it as divine. We can call this true love if you like. I call it Aoife."

On his lap, in a reversed pyramid, he had dealt a number of the tarot cards face up. The remainder of the deck he now placed carefully to his side. His hands passed sensually over the faces showing and he tapped one near the top left side with the nail of his index finger. The tapping made a clicking noise as we both exhaled. I leaned in to see a naked man facing backward atop a large white horse with a flowing mane and tail. A woman wearing a blue dress, her hair falling in waves to her ankles, was leading the horse. The man was blindfolded, his wrists loosely bound behind his back.

"There is a cheaper version of this sexual enchantment. It is thought that all sex acts are intended to lead to creation. The most important psycho-physiological event in the life of a human being is an orgasm. Oral sex cannot lead to the creation of a human life so to what sort of creation can it lead? Sex magic is the art of utilizing sexual experience for the concrete materialization of desire. You use the technique of oral sex and in that moment of orgasm, that most powerful of moments, it is possible to manifest what is most wanted. In a concrete manner, you can literally wish your dreams to come true.

"You've heard of speaking what you want into the universe? I think that this cliché of new age thinking is a dilution of the powerful nature of sexual incantation."

He gathered up the cards, shuffling them into the deck as he went.

"Letty, now you have had your magic lesson. These cards were yours, but they are also mine. This deck, I have had it so long that my very essence is embedded in the fabric of the cards. Any time I do a layout, it is my reading as much as that of the person whose life I am trying to read. You and I especially are tied together in our futures.

"I am a bit worn out now. I don't want you to go but I think I shall take a warm drugged nap. You may use my study for a bit if you want to check your office phone or your email. The other witch can sit outside the door and listen to my distressed breathing. But for the moment, please sit here until I am asleep."

He closed his eyes and I turned to watch the wind combing the treetops where the fog clung as if in fear of falling and disappearing. It trembled and seemed to shimmer even as the oncoming evening brushed aside the melancholy dullness of the day, opening holes in the clouds to let fingers of sunlight filter down to touch the waters of the Bay, the final stroke by a farewell sun lingering, hidden behind the banks of fog and the Golden Gate. I felt drained and overflowing all in a circle. I longed to retreat, but when I thought of retreat the only place I was able to conjure was right where I sat. A few minutes later, I heard the shallow rattle of his chest which meant he was sleeping. I got up, suddenly homesick for all my children, and slipped out of the room. Downstairs in the kitchen, I snagged a glass of merlot and asked the evening nurse just coming on duty to call me from the study upstairs the moment our patient awoke. The cook and I decided he could serve me dinner on a tray when I rejoined Cos.

The study was two walls, floor to ceiling, of books, many of them collector items. The other walls were a deep green and indirect lighting dispelled all but the most artful shadows. Facing the door to the study was a heavy teak desk complemented by the teak of the bookshelves, door, and moldings. There was little artwork in this room, but tucked amongst the books I noticed tiny colorfully enameled bottles with Asian design themes. The desktop itself was clear other than a telephone, notepad, and fountain pen on one side, and a laptop resting on the opposite corner. I moved behind the desk, clicking on the floor lamp to concentrate light on the work area before relaxing into the Queen Anne chair and turning to the computer.

It was only moments before I was pulling up my email messages. I was so relieved and excited I almost cried when I saw that one was from Zack!

2/7/00

Hey Mom,

Sorry I haven't called or written. I have just been swamped since the move to Houston. My new apartment is small but in a great complex. There are mostly young singles living here. The facilities include a gym and pool, but they also have a large social room with lots of events to encourage mixing and mingling. The truth is it reminds me a lot of some of the retirement communities I visit when I meet clients at their homes.

So far, I am pleased with how the company operates and the job is going well. Having to drive around to meet with those families I am counseling makes it easier to get to know the city.

You asked about my job. I think I fell into this because of you. I seem to have an ability to discuss the issues that come up for our families with more ease than some of our counselors who are way senior to me.

As a community counselor, for ELL (Eternal Life Limited), I have the responsibility of helping families understand the benefits of pre-arrangement. Essentially, I sell a concept. That is, helping them get all the paperwork, details, and permanent decisions that need to be made when someone dies completed in advance of need. In this case need = when a death has occurred. As simple as the paperwork and questions and decisions seem to answer today, they will be difficult for their loved ones to answer in the event of death.

Talking about cemetery and funeral arrangements means that we have to admit we are going to die. This is something most people don't want to do, as you are very aware. What we have to do is find ways to prospect; find people who don't have pre-arrangements and are willing to listen to what we have to say. We do that through different marketing strategies. The first is telephone prospecting.

I will grab a phone book. Or I grab a Polk Directory which is a phone book designed for sales and marketing with a section listing retired people and homeowners, sections sorted by telephone prefix, and sections sorted by street addresses. The script I use goes a little something like this:

"Hello, Mr. Jones? This is Zack Mae calling from Lone State Memorial Parks, and we are trying to locate folks who have not yet received a personal planning guide from us. Have you received one of those from us yet? (If they say yes, I will ask how long ago they made arrangements and offer to come by and update their records to make sure everything is taken care of. If they say no…)

"Our Considerate Commemoration Personal Planning Guide is a special book designed to organize all the information that is needed at the time of death. It answers questions, like what benefits you'll be entitled to, what paperwork is necessary, and it even helps with the permanent decisions that need to be made at that time. It is my job as a community counselor here to make sure you get a copy of this book. What we usually try to do is find a time when we can sit with you and go through the book, that way we can answer whatever questions you might have about it. Would an afternoon or evening be better for you?"

In the appointments, I will go through the personal planning guide with the family and get them involved in my presentation by asking questions about their personal experiences. Trying to get them to think about what it is going to be like when one of them dies. But delicately. Carefully. I don't want them to cry. I don't want them to feel like one of them did die. I just want them to feel a little bit of what it would be like. (If you like, I will send you one of the planning guides so you can kinda get an idea of the presentations.)

Anyway, that is what I do. I get paid on commission but that works for me since I really get how this is a big service and I really like talking with people.

There are several financial and emotional benefits for the families inside this concept of pre-arrangement. If someone makes an initial investment today, they can freeze the price of their arrangements. Historically, cemetery and funeral arrangements triple in cost every 5 to 10 years. Another reason is Customized Terms. If people wait for an "At-Need" situation, when someone has already died, the cemetery bill has to be paid within 24 to 48 hours. Emotional reasons are, for one, peace of mind. Knowing this is taken care of and that their children won't have to worry about it. Another is the fact that couples will be able to make these decisions together. 85% of the time it's the husbands who pass away before the wives. Too often we make these arrangements with just one, and we prefer to do it with both. There's a little saying in our business: If every wife knew what every widow knows, every one of them would pre-arrange.

Guess what you and Dad are getting for Xmas?

Hey, thanks for sending me those sheets and towels. They were delivered a few days after I got here. Anne thinks they look great in the new place. Oh, Anne is this girl at my apartment complex I've been hanging out with. I sold her and her roommate both prearrangement plans.

Anne and I are planning a ski trip up to New Mexico.

In April I am running the ELL booth at the County Fair. We will have a pretty big space in order to accommodate the displays and tables for sitting and working with on-duty councilors. I got us assigned to a spot near the corn dog stand so foot traffic should be good, and the resulting heartburn might spur the idea of prearrangement seeming timely. HA HA

OK well I'll try and call soon and write more.

Say Hi to Dad,

Luv yaw,

Zack

Anne? My mother's radar was pinging and all else became insignificant. How long would it be before I was a grandmother? Would I have to travel all the way to Texas to see my grandchildren? I reread the bit about this Anne person, then shook my head, laughing at my own silliness. I seemed to be having some problems with keeping things in perspective lately. It felt good to be concerned about motherly things; it felt easy and natural. I closed Zack's email and immediately noticed one from Ian, my youngest.

2/7/00

Mom, I am coming home for a while. I am taking a leave of absence from school. They said no problem. Don't worry. I am traveling with my friend, Todd. We will leave here at the start of Spring Break. We are stopping in Salt Lake for a few days and then I'll be home. I'll call when we get close. We're driving. The show was successful, I guess. I love you mom.

Ian

Ian was coming home with a friend named Todd! Again, my mother's radar was pinging, this time in earnest. I reached over and switched off the lights, sat back in the chair staring at the computer screen. Ian coming home was not that unusual, nor was the short email full of unstated meaning. Bringing a friend home, however, was unusual. He had not mentioned anything about his social life since he left for college. All his communication was about art, politics, or money. Ian had been happy in high school in his role as an artist and mild activist.

His friends were the friends I would have chosen for him, and we never had any problems with drugs. The only thing that had ever made me wonder was that Ian just didn't seem to care about dating. I sighed but it sounded like someone else. I smiled and relaxed a bit more, thinking happily of a few weeks from now when I would be wrapping my arms around my baby and be startled to find a man. It happened every time we hugged in the last few years with both my boys, but especially Ian. Finally, he was bringing home a friend. I smiled, knowing I would like Todd if Ian liked him.

My thoughts traveled back to Zack. I reread his email. He was happy and becoming successful. He would likely be in this business for the rest of his life; it was how he envisioned and executed his role in the world: steady, committed, and happy. If this new young woman was whom he was dating now, she must fit into that vision he has for himself. The time was right, he was at the point in his life that he would choose a wife who would be his wife for all his life. Zack had been a girl magnet since he was a little boy and had grown up assuming that this was the level of popularity everyone experienced. He didn't work at his social life the way Jennie did, nor did he fill a special niche as Ian did, he just lived; work, friends, and adventure came to him. Zack had experienced the most difficult early years of all my children, and yet I worried about him least. My perfectly normal child, an open book of emotional stability, I didn't understand him at all, but I loved him completely.

There was a soft knock on the door; the night nurse poked her head in. Mr. Drucker was awake, and alert. Would I care to join him for dinner?

VII
<u>Parinibbana Sutta</u>
"Nothing is secure."

The drapes were drawn, the room more brightly lit than I had seen before, every lamp blazed, along with the indirect lighting and spotlights on the artwork. A fire burned in the recessed fireplace nestled in the far corner. A tray had been set up near the chair in which I customarily sat. Drucker had been changed into a black kimono patterned with red and green dragons. His sheets and comforter were folded down to just cover his knees and lower legs, the bed and pillows had been arranged so that he was nearly in a full upright sitting position. He smiled, scrutinizing me as I came in and took my seat.

The nurse was instructed to inform Cook I was ready for my dinner and to wait at her station outside the room until she was called. I felt his eyes evaluating me as I took in the room in its evening dress. The huff and sizzle of the fire, his moist gurgle of shallow air in and out, my even breathing broken by regular deeper inhalation verging on sighs letting out tension with each exhale, these were the dialogue of the moment.

The muffled rattle of a cart and Sying-Lei-Long—I knew it was a different person from earlier that day though what the differences were, I could not say—entered with my dinner and using a practiced subtlety, served my dinner, and after mumbling assurances and thanks, he was gone. Cos nodded to me to eat, smiling with encouragement.

The meal was outstanding. I found that I was hungrier than I had been in ages, but I took my time. I knew I was eating for both myself and for Cos. My enjoyment and my ability to savor each taste and texture was a gift to him. He could no longer sit down to a meal like the one before me, though at one time it would have been common fare for him.

There was a small loaf of fresh San Francisco bread and warm whipped butter in a small tureen. A Napa Valley white wine had been decanted. A green chili cream soup began the meal. It was the end of crab season so, unsurprisingly, fresh crab simply prepared was the center of the meal. The cook had offered it hot, shelled, and flaked in a feathery pastry nest. Asparagus delicately steamed in a savory bath complemented the crab. A butter lettuce, goat cheese, and apple salad prepared me for the single serving of lemon cheesecake, which finished the meal. Each separate aroma would meld with the others, then separate again to create a fugue of delicious scents.

It was no trouble to finish every morsel. I felt the strange sensation of happiness moving through my body.

"Shall I tell you a story while I eat? I saw something on the street the other day. I just remembered. Would you like to hear about it?"

He nodded, watching my every movement. I reached back to the person I had been for my children. I would come home and tell them a bedtime story made up from some event or something I had seen during my day. I wondered if I could still do that trick so many years later.

"It was one of those days in San Francisco. A day where the sunshine has taken up residence as if night will never come. There was a breeze at my back as I walked down the street.

"I already had my latte. Still, I pass the coffee shop on my way to and from where I park my car and my office. The sidewalk in front as I approached had all the usual people and dogs lounging on or near the benches. They are usually there at that time of day discussing events and solving all the ills of the world."

I surprised myself by changing into my version of doggy voices at this point.

"'I don't know, Rufus, I know we are supposed to be color blind but I gots to tell you that I am a traditionalist. I like my fireplugs yellow or white.'

'I know what you mean, Fangila, I feel so self-conscious when the fireplug is painted as a rainbow.'

"Spike, the bulldog, chimed in with 'I tell you what, it is just wrong, wrong, wrong to lift a leg on a red, white, and blue plug! Those public works fellas have just ruindt it for me. And now there are those little fences around the trees, what is this city coming to? I askt you!' "

I took encouragement at this point in my story from the fact that Cos was smiling broadly.

"It made me smile to hear these dogs. I was happy that others were taking responsibility for world affairs so I could just enjoy my day. Then I saw him down at the end of the block! He was heading toward me, and we would cross paths right in the midst of the café sidewalk crowd.

"He was no more than five feet tall and in his mid-forties. He was Hispanic with dark hair that had a forelock falling just to the top of one brown eye. Do you know how I mean? In his arms, he carried a large wooden tray, perhaps four-foot square, and on it were bobblehead dogs of every breed. There were Beagles and Bassets, Goldens and Greyhounds, Rots and Dobermans. The tray was alive with bobblehead dogs all facing toward me; bibble, bobble, they came down the street.

"He drew closer to the café, as did I from the opposite side. Slowly, one by one, the conversations stopped, human and canine, and attention was turned toward this small señor and his tray of dogs. Bibbledy bop, wriggly bobble.

"Dogs who had been lying by their human friends were now sitting up at attention. The humans were on the edges of their bench seats, leaning just slightly forward. I found I had stopped on the edge of the crowd, waiting to watch the entrance of Senhor Doggy into this group of caffeinated residents in this, our urban village.

"He stopped before the first couple resting with a small white Scotty between their chairs. He indicated a small sign in the mouth of one especially charming Lab. His wares were for sale at the nominal price of a single five-dollar bill per pup, or so proclaimed the Lab with a nod of his head directed toward the gentlemanly couple.

"The men and their Scotty consulted, and I approached to listen."

Emboldened by my earlier success, I deepened my voice, also adding a lilt, to emulate the two men speaking.

" 'Should we?' questioned the first man.

'How can we not?' answered the second.

'But what will we have? Just a tacky kitsch.'

'Yes, but how can we not?'

'Shouldn't separate a litter,' suggested Scotty at their feet.

"The men shared a moment in each other's eyes. One man reached for his wallet as the other's hand dropped to rest on the soft back of the Scotty. A five dollar bill was laid beneath a bobbleheaded black Scotty.

'No, no,' protested the couple to Senor Doggy, 'We don't want one—we want them to all stay together, that is just for visiting with us today.'

"They waved the tray and vendor away. I stepped aside but one of the men looked at me and said, 'Together they are special, apart they are nothing.'

"I couldn't have agreed more and apparently others felt the same way. One person from each grouping of human and canine placed five dollars under his or her bobbleheaded dog of choice but no one removed a single wiggly pup from the tray. As Senor Doggy and his tray of canines passed beyond the café crowd, I, too, turned and traveled on my way.

"One of the reasons I love the Bay Area is that the people here often recognize how unique and special life can be on a sunny sidewalk."

I stopped, suddenly shy. Cos began to chuckle and clap, animated in a fashion he had not been at any time before in my presence. I grinned directly at him, rather pleased and surprised at myself.

"Delightful, to be reminded of life! Thank you. I find you are more than I suspected. Some weight has been lifted from you… some pain is gone. I take it you had positive news of some sort?"

"I had emails from my two boys. One of them is in Texas and the other at school in Chicago. The one at school is coming home soon."

"You have two children, as do I. How old are they?"

"I have three children, a girl and two boys, all grown. The youngest, Ian, is in college. They all live too far away and I miss them. I… Ian… uh, dinner was wonderful, thank you so much for the excellent meal. You are feeling strong this evening?"

"Evenings are often better for me, and sleep only comes in spurts throughout the day and night. What were you going to say? Why did you stop? You aren't going to begin to play games with me, are you?

"I see you are relaxed, more at ease. I am in the mood to talk so it is of no use, your deciding not to. Tell me what you were thinking. It has to do with your son coming home from college, Ian, did you say?"

He smiled at me gently.

"Ian. He has taken a leave of absence from school, which I guess begins directly after the end of spring break. I don't know what that is about, but he said not to worry. He is coming home for spring break, maybe longer, I don't know. He is driving from Chicago with a friend of his, Todd, who I have never met or heard of before. They are stopping in Salt Lake for a few days and on to here. I am guessing that Salt Lake is Todd's hometown, otherwise, why would they be going there?"

"But it isn't the leave of absence or the drive that has you concerned, is it?"

"No, no… I think, I guess I almost hope, I mean I don't know. I have no real reason to think so, but I think he, Ian, is coming home to tell his father and me that he is gay. I think maybe this is his 'coming out' trip with this boy Todd. Maybe they are both 'coming out' to their families, first in Salt Lake and here."

"Does this possibility disturb you?"

"No, no you don't understand, I am hoping this is what he is going to say, it would explain so much. Plus, if he could just come out instead of hiding this, he will have a chance at finding a strong, solid relationship that can last a lifetime."

"You are very much the romantic, aren't you? You believe in love. Is your marriage so fulfilling, so happy that you want and expect the same for your own children or do you simply believe in the fairy tale?"

I took a sip of wine and thought about his question.

"It isn't a fairytale, is it? I have listened to you talk about Aoife… didn't you live the fairy tale? Wasn't she that happy, fulfilling, and even romantic love of your life? Why shouldn't I want my children to have the comfort of such a union?

"Our family, we keep such distances and yet we are remarkably close. We can talk about death or politics or even religion, but we hide our true selves from one another. We never speak of personal troubles or share our hopes and dreams other than at a superficial level. I don't understand why that is. Ian knows that I, we, would have no issue with his being gay or anything he might naturally be or anything he might choose for himself, for that matter, that makes him happy. He knows that, I am sure. All the kids do. Yet they keep such a distance. They all do!"

I leaned forward in my seat. The sudden shrillness of my own voice startled me into silence; Cos's voice entered that silence, controlled, not soothing.

"Oh, but now you are returning to your former melancholy mood. Please let us retain our dinner temperament. Shall I do the talking while you gather yourself?"

I nodded. There is a reason I stay in the office and others sit at bedsides. There is a reason that my family keeps its mouth shut, while I stew or spew. The truths might be too startling to face but they are still present, secrets simmering just below awareness, some as mundane as Ian's sexual orientation, some as complex as Peter's masochistic fetish, some as dangerous as a map to hell. A moment later, Cos continued in the same controlled tone.

"I am pleased that you shared. Don't be embarrassed, I asked because I wanted to know. I am never just being polite or making conversation, I don't have such wasteful habits, as you know.

"Shall we talk about me now? Shall I tell you my secrets?"

Again, I nodded, brought back to the moment by my own curiosity.

"Will you tell me about who you are? When did you know you were gay?"

"Bi, not gay. I became sexually active later than most by today's standards. I absolutely had sexual feelings, certainly around the time of puberty but it was masturbation, no actual sex with anybody."

"Not until much later, actually it was in high school when I was maybe seventeen or eighteen years old. I didn't really have intercourse until I was twenty-two years old. Aoife was my first. Most of the sexual activity I had when I was seventeen or eighteen was about masturbation or mutual fantasy, not really sexual intercourse."

"Aoife was your first? Does that mean your primary sexual partners have been… "

"Yes, male I suppose, but Aoife was and remains my primary sexual partner, and my love. I simply had sex with more men than women but not more often. Do you understand? Since I found myself to be HIV positive, I have had sexual intercourse with no one. Once Aoife was gone, my practices, my play, became exclusively male. If I didn't have HIV, that might have—would have—been different. I prefer sexual intercourse with women and sexual play with men.

"I have had an extraordinarily complex life. I came out to myself that I was bisexual only after Aoife pointed it out to me, as I have told you. These were turbulent times for me. I was traveling from one country to another on business. I had diversified the family's holdings, and I had complex family relationships. Sex was the last thing on my mind really, except when it came to my Aoife. I had many more important things to worry about, so it never came up until after she brought it up. You know I was free to do as I please—I could do whatever I wanted.

"We began to play, Aoife and I. There was no disease, and there were no restrictions. It was a sexual renaissance for everyone in San Francisco, if not the nation. Public bathhouses were abundant, clubs with private rooms, there was an 'anything goes' party every night. Aoife and I would find these beautiful young men in their twenties and they would be overwhelmed by our physical beauty, our resources, our access to drugs, and our skills. Aoife would play at bondage using her remarkable skills at *Kinbaku-bi* and I would have the sexual pleasure of both a beautiful young stranger and my extraordinary exotic wife. We never repeated a game; there was always a new boy willing to play with us. Always, we could find new environments and scenarios, thanks to my money. We never brought our toys home.

"One night, in retrospect I know exactly the moment, I took a boy with AIDS. I don't think he knew himself. We didn't know at the time. The disease itself was only becoming known, no one had heard of HIV or AIDS though people were starting to get sick and die. A short while later, they called it GRID. I was never able to find the boy again; we didn't know his real name, you see. By the time I discovered I was HIV positive, it is likely he was already dead, it was so quick in those days.

"When rumors did begin to hit the streets and we realized there was this horrid killer wiping out the gay community, we stopped our play.

"When testing became available, Aoife and I both went in and were tested. The tests were very poor. It took a long time, and really, you needed to have AIDS, not HIV, to be detected. Still, the threat was there and though we both seemed healthy, we knew we must be more cautious. This is when we started to explore tantric yoga and sexual practices. This is when we began to realize our spiritual natures, you understand.

"Every time my doctors felt they had an improved test for HIV, we would go in and be tested. There were fewer and fewer parties, bathhouses and clubs began to disappear. Parts of the city, like the Castro, were in constant mourning. The time had changed; everyone was starting to look for meaning.

"One day we got the call from my physician, you know him, spoke with him earlier today? I had tested positive for HIV… Aoife was not infected. She remained uninfected.

"Yet my dear Aoife died. I lost her, but I continued to live with HIV and never became symptomatic.

"It was after my test came back positive that I started my new play, the play that has become my art, the play that has made the years without Aoife more bearable. Are you ready for my secret, Lisa? Do you want to know?"

"Letty, I am Letty. Yes, tell me."

"It was basically something I was always very curious about. That I thought was kind of fun, but in a way, kind of an attraction–repulsion thing. For instance, I would see kids being smacked when I was really young, and I would be afraid of that because it never happened in my family. I wouldn't like it but at the same time, I had a friend, you know, some visiting third cousin when I was about five or six, one day for no reason at all while we were playing, and I just spanked him, and I liked doing it. After that single episode, I didn't really have a lot of opportunities, but it would come out when I was a preteen, and I would play with children belonging to friends of the family and it would come up. I would do it and it was something I would enjoy as play, but I never actually wanted to hurt them. It was something I would do, that's all."

I was stunned. His voice had changed as he told me his history, and I could hear the little boy that he had once been.

"But you didn't perceive it as a sexual thing at that age? It was just something you would do that was fun? We are talking about spanking?"

"Yes, we are talking about spanking—not the first time you have thought of this subject, is it? To answer your question, no, it was later, around puberty I think, that I found myself sexually aroused while thinking about spanking or even reading about it. When I was a child, I used to read a lot. So, reading something like Tom Sawyer, I would think 'Oh, that's interesting!' And I would find myself sexually aroused."

I was having trouble processing what I was hearing. I felt a nervous giggle escape as I asked for clarification.

"There is spanking in Tom Sawyer?! Were you spanked as a child?"

"No, I told you, not at all. My parents were very liberal people, but they also had nannies and tutors for me, so they never felt overwhelmed and I never gave anyone cause to punish me. My nanny would sometimes be pushed when a friend and I would fight. To separate us, she might smack us just to get our attention, you know, and because she was frustrated. 'Losing her wits,' she would have said. It was more like she needed to separate us two; it would be a smack and then 'I am out of my wits!' Didn't you ever reach behind the front seat while you were driving to whack your kids?"

"They just laughed at me when I tried to do that. This attraction for you started when you were young. But it didn't become sexual for you until general sexual feelings started coming up. It doesn't sound like you had yet identified it with sexuality."

"It was not necessarily a sexual feeling, but more like a fun thing to do. It was a way of bonding. Bonding with another person in a way that was more intimate than just playing Cowboys and Indians.

"What I came to realize after several years of actually practicing the art of spanking, is that when I am doing it, it is erotic because it involves tangential things I like. When you are gay or bisexual or whatever, there are things that one likes on the other person's body. The male rear end is something that I find attractive, the shape. I like touching it or pinching it. This is something I find attractive and sexually arousing. So…

"I've never admitted it before, but what I like is the drama of sex. It is the drama, the passion, but I don't really like hurting people. I have difficulty with that; I am not a violent person. It is a different way of being in total control of somebody. It is very primal, something left from the cave ages, establishing your dominance, your territory."

"Are you always the dominant partner in your relationships?"

"Yes, of course I am. Aoife was an equal partner, we took turns in all things, you might say, but to the world, certainly I was the dominant one. I am always the predator, even now in my feeble way."

"In the spanking, are you always the spanker?"

"Yes, absolutely. Well, if I were healthy and if Aoife were still here, I might have been willing to experiment as a bottom... Pleasing someone I deeply care about, that turns me on. It would have had to have been somebody I respected and knew, even loved. There are not that many people I have known who would fall into that category—none, in fact, that I can think of. Only Aoife. I suppose I am definitely the type of person who is the driver, the top. I don't think most people know what they're doing or know what it's about."

Cos laughed at his own small joke, but my mind was jumping from one thought to the next. I had lost my bearings and felt a bit like I was getting my bearings all at the same time. Are these some of the things Peter would be saying to me if he were to open his heart to me? I wanted to know all I could. I felt like I had to know, to push on until the world made sense to me.

"Did you use your bare hands? Is there art and technique?"

"Oh, assuredly, art and technique! You always have to respect a person's core. I always respect people's boundaries, where they are comfortable. I would never meet with somebody who doesn't know what they are getting into, and I believe when I first establish a meeting with somebody, I can pretty much screen if they are bullshitting me or not. The more I talk to them, the clearer it becomes. They might say, 'What do you do?' and I would say, 'What do you like?' and they say, getting excited, 'Whatever, whatever! I don't care, I don't care.' I know they are not serious about it. But if they say, 'Well, I am afraid of this and I would never like to have that, or welts on my skin, or I am concerned about noise, or whatever.' When I know they are serious, I respect their concerns. That's what I like. I can work with what they like if they are specific to a certain point.

"My own personal preference is for a hairbrush. I have one that is perfect for the job. It is teak with soft sable bristles. The handgrip is a good fit for my hand and the base is broad and flat. All the edges are rounded, and the length of the base is five inches. It is the most versatile of tools and has been with me for many, many years. Using my bare hand was always very sensual; after that, I like to improvise with whatever I can find, like my belt if I am wearing it or if they have a good soft leather shoe laying around, I will use that. Some people are extremely specific regarding their fetishes, and I wanted to please them, after all. Paddles and brushes, those are apparently an American thing. People have a whole variety of things they like to use. Like I said, my preference is my hand or my brush.

"Other implements are made out of wood or leather. The shapes are often like a Ping-Pong paddle or something you find in a sports store. Yes, people have very specific things they like.

"I personally like to lay the person over my lap. So, if they like something big like a fraternity paddle, it is difficult for me to use."

"Because of the length?"

"It is too long. Something like a huge shaving strap, I won't be able to use while they are across my lap. I like the closeness of the body on me."

"Does that create a more intimate experience?"

"For me, yes, I believe so. Some people are more into other stuff. For instance, you need to be very skillful with a leather strap or belt. If it wraps around, it hurts like hell. You have to know what you're doing, and you have to have very good eye–hand coordination. Tennis players use the same coordination, you understand? That way you will actually hit your target.

"You never hit close to the tailbone, or below the fatty part of the buttock, it is too close to the genitals, and that is dangerous.

"Reedy things made of wood are the British preference; those English love canes and things like that. Those are too narrow and can cut the skin, so I don't particularly like them. Some people like them, but for myself, I like my brush or something small that I can manage well. I was very skillful with my belt if I folded it twice and depending on how I actually held it."

"Did you have a belt that you wear specifically for these experiences?"

"No, but I always wore fine Italian leather belts that are small and supple and have a small square buckle. They are not dangerous because I could always hold the buckle in the palm of my hand. My belts were always a bit wider than current fashion calls for because if it is a thin leather belt, you have that problem of cutting the flesh if it hits sideways. Something wider is better.

"I used to be online in bulletin boards that would post a photo of just my belly and crotch area. I was holding in my hands my wonderful brush. I used to get quite a few responses to that photo! Even from people who are not into the fetish, you know? Constant comment and constant interest, it is kind of interesting what turns people on. I couldn't hide my age in a photo. My face wasn't there yet, people would be extremely interested.

"I have always guarded my privacy and the privacy of my family. To this moment you are the only person who knows this about me. I'm not ashamed of it. Certainly not! But if I can talk candidly about it, I am also delving into the private life of the person with whom I am communicating, your private life. We are having a very intimate conversation here at my deathbed, you and I."

"Yes, yes, I am aware of that. It sounds like that photo might have brought up, even for those persons not into the fetish, a lot of fantasy."

"Absolutely."

"This is an art form for you? As an art form, would this hold appeal for even people who are curiosity seekers or who might want to experience it for one time?"

He took a moment to seriously consider my question.

"Especially if you are talking about an art, as opposed to sexual education, or it could even be both. It may attract people who are generally open-minded, if you are around art circles, or perhaps people who are attracted to the unusual but inexperienced. It is hard to narrow it down like that because in my experience, there has been such a wide variety of people.

"People who generally identify themselves as heterosexual; people who are older and never developed this particular interest until very much later. On the other side are the people who are young, and this just happens to be something that attracts them. What I usually find out is that people who are into this are not necessarily people who fit into little pigeonholes. I mean you might hear people say, 'Oh, it is like leather,' whatever that means, well, I know what that means but it's the whole getup—leather and so on, more like the slave and Master thing. A lot of what I have noticed in my experience is that people who are not really very into that still like the kinkiness of the spanking, no type, no pigeonholes."

"You're saying that spanking is very separate from the S&M, bondage groups or styles. Spanking seems to be simpler."

"Yes! To me, more elegant—you don't need anything except your hand or brush, no equipment is required, no getup. It opens a lot of flexibility, for instance, if you are a Master in sadomasochism, but you don't do certain things if you are not a real Master. You can take on a lot of fantasy roles with spanking, people are into a lot of that; I am, myself. You can be a daddy, police, soldier, teacher, uncle, whatever. It is just up to your imagination. For me, it is more about the art form, like you said. Performance art. I am giving a bit of who I am away, but I am an artist. That is what an artist does isn't it, gives a bit of themself away?

"I didn't do it just for my pleasure or gratification, I took pride in how I was doing it. I developed my form so that it wasn't just whacking someone on the ass but was actually able to fill the fantasy perfectly for each person with whom I had an encounter. I am the best at what I did."

In silence, we smiled, he lost in memory. I thought about being the best at what one does.

In the pause, I pictured Peter standing with Cain in his arms and I wished for a moment he was in the room with us, sharing his thoughts and desires. But in the same thought was the realization that he would never be able to do that, not with me. We would always have a silence between us. Maybe, though, it didn't need to be an unhappy silence. Maybe if I just stuck it out, I could find a way to… I didn't know what.

Cos continued.

"I would never allow just anybody to play with me. I got the quality playmates. And as far as availability, I have—or rather had—a life. There is a culture around this fetish; I couldn't be everything to everybody. Like any other culture, there are various levels and aspects so even if there were someone I would love to play with, but they wanted something I cannot give… well, I wouldn't be able to play with them. For instance, if they really wanted to be dominated or degraded, or to be abused, I couldn't do it, but it is within the context of a spanking fetish. I know others who honestly believe they are punishing someone when they are spanking. They genuinely believe they are in control of the person's life. You can look in the personals and you will find them saying 'I offer true guidance to people.'

"Who the hell are they!? To give guidance to anyone? They are only offering control. And sometimes that is what someone is asking for. I had this young man that I loved playing with, but I made it clear he was not my friend. Friends let friends get away with things and that was not my role.

"He would tell me that he loved me and I would say, 'No, you do not love me; you love the idea of me but you don't know me as a person, you don't even know my last name, you don't even know if the name I gave is my real name.' I developed my skill and became like a chameleon. I seemed so real… I could be that particular thing or person at that particular moment for the one who was my playmate, my toy. This aspect turns me on in a way that is profound.

"I become the villain of the story. Everybody loves the villain! You understand?

"I am a nice person—polite, caring—but for half an hour I can be a complete asshole. I am mean and merciless. And that's fine fun. It is taking myself out of myself, and it is part of myself also. I am a good villain and if it gets that person open, it's a great experience, it's like being a lawyer or an actor, and I am talking about being a lawyer because that is one of the things that I know. When you are out there and delivering in court, you do it because you want to win, you don't want to settle.

"Now, I am a passive villain, waiting for victims to cross my threshold and enter my room. My villainy rests on the vulnerable emotional realities of the people who come to my bedside. Still, ultimately, they are able to open up to themselves and for them, on reflection, it is a wonderful experience.

"An actor is composing a whole psyche, a whole character—so it is an art. This is my art."

"How did you connect with someone for this kind of practice, this spanking?"

"How did I meet them?"

"Yes."

"Right, it's a very interesting question.

"I was specific about what I was looking for. I stressed that it was not sexual because a lot of times when I say it is sexual, it opens a can of worms. It opens them to a lot of interpretation, as if I should be open to this, that, or the other thing, by association I am open to this intention, occurrence, or other obsession. And I had the wildest requests, that's what I am saying, like people were asking me to do the weirdest things to them.

"Oh my god, it was wild! I had to say no, so I learned to say this is nonsexual but, of course, it is, and after the spanking, masturbation is fine, of course. That is how I would post to filter people out. I never approached someone at a club after the internet became widely used. I loved being online and there are websites. It's like I said—there is a whole culture. I used to have personal ads and online services with a profile, and I always stated the purpose was to party. For a while, before the internet, I had a newspaper ad in one of the weeklies."

He stopped; all the energy suddenly gone.

"Letty, I believe I have excited myself and stirred internal functions better left alone. I am suddenly quite worn out and I believe that unless you intend to take on the messier duties, we should perhaps call the nurse."

All that had been said since dinner had stunned me, but I managed to go to the door and softly call in the nurse. As she reached the bed, Cos began retching. We both lifted him from the bed. She murmured comforting platitudes as we carried him to the large bathroom suite. I left, to afford them privacy; even so, I could hear the painful nausea overtaking the old man's body.

I went to the window and looked out across the blankness of the Bay to the lights of Tiburon. I kept hearing Peter and the telephone dominatrix replaying under all Cos had said about his spanking practices. Secret lives, do we all have them? Are we all charades of normality, good at business, fine parents, and responsible community members?

The strangled vomiting had slowed; I could faintly hear Cos gasping as he struggled for breath.

Moe had struggled for breath.

My head burst. The blackness of the view flashed into white light, it felt like a fork was thrust deep into the back of my neck at the base of my skull. I collapsed forward, bumping my nose on the window and crumbling to the floor. I could hear a running shower, there was blood and water swirling across tiles and down the drain. The body, carefully casual as it lay face down in the water.

I must have cried out because the next thing I was aware of were the hands of Sying—yes, it was Sying—lifting me into my chair and placing a cold towel across my forehead. He was chattering in Chinese; I could hear other voices, but I was afraid to open my eyes to that blinding white agony. Finally, I heard Cos's voice coming from the bed.

"Let her be now. She will be fine… all she needs is a moment's peace. As do I, let us rest. Tell them to go, Ms. Mae!"

"Please. Yes, I will be fine, fine, just a headache."

A darkening and hush, the waves of pain ebbed like a receding tide.

I don't know how long I sat there but eventually, I realized that Cos had picked up the thread of our conversation and was speaking again. I was able to cautiously remove the damp towel from my face and open my eyes as he continued. The drugs he had been given seemed to have moved him directly into his memories.

"It's just really weird, people would find me, it's like a cosmic something, I have no idea.

"I was walking home from an early breakfast on Lombard. This man approaches me. I am thinking he will be asking directions, instead, he just comes up and says hello. I ask him, 'How can I help you?' and he says, 'I am on my walk of shame; I was out clubbing all night. I am going home but I've been a bad boy.' I thought, 'Oh god no,' but as I am talking about it with him, I discover he is totally into a daddy–son relationship fantasy, and he is asking me if I live nearby. As I said before, I never brought anyone home or revealed my identity, so I just tell him, 'I am not going to take you home and have sex with you.' It was almost as if this person knew me, as if he knew I could be his daddy. It was very spooky."

"Did things like that happen frequently?"

"No, but other things happened. For instance, I was speaking at a conference and there was this handsome couple, they suggested we share a cab back to the hotel with the materials from their presentation, including this long rod. We were all to attend a dinner at the hotel. In order to fit inside, I held the rod in the front seat with me. It was Halloween. The taxi driver was very personable and probably gay—he was wearing a boa—and he asks, 'So what is that for?' and they say, 'Oh, he is our teacher. When we are bad, he spanks us.'"

Cos broke into a fit of coughing laughter, and I joined in the absurd humor of the situation.

"Well, it's true…"

"Halloween in San Francisco, everything is true," I responded.

"Yes, well, that is—"

I couldn't help but interrupt him.

"I just don't understand why the person whom you are spanking finds it erotic? What do you think it is about the actual feeling of you hitting their flesh that they find erotic?"

"Some people love pain. From what I read, chemically, pain and pleasure are registered at the same level."

"We just had a study presented to us that suggests the place in the brain that experiences pleasure also experiences pain. That is why sometimes people find pleasurable activities painful, and why those in pain often lose their desire for pleasurable things like eating or intercourse. I guess the reverse could be true, that some people experience pain as a pleasurable sensation. This means that when you are spanking, you cause pain?"

"Oh, of course. Not always, it might be the whole setting and tension leading up to it. The anticipation, the role around the spanking, the drama. That gets me off! Some people might get it from the setting, some people might actually like the sensation. That is my interpretation. It is a release. We all have lives. These are usually people who are extremely smart or extremely handsome, often very political. It gives them a chance, that's how I see it, to not be in the driver's seat. Someone else is just taking control, even if only for fifteen minutes. The bottom always has the real control though, always. It is never, ever the top, no matter what anyone may tell you. If the bottom does not allow it, want it, you are just playing with yourself. It only works when the bottom is going along with it. It is always the bottom who has control. It is the release, the serving yourself on a silver platter, which is fun, it is vulnerable yet controlled fun like being on a roller coaster. You feel that you are flying; you feel that you are about to fall but you're not—you're strapped, safe. Some people love the idea of an ethnic difference. It adds something extra for them as a total turn on. Some people like the emotional idea of being kept close; men aren't supposed to cry or be vulnerable so when you are actually being played with like that, and can cry, it is like whatever they were holding in can be let go. It is very therapeutic. I am not claiming that I was doing anything of service for them, but I do believe that all of this, that sex and sexual fetishes, is therapeutic."

Was this what Peter needed? Was it therapeutic for him to interact with some stranger on the telephone?

"When you are in the act, can you describe for me the actions of the other person?"

"It is never, and this is what I pride myself on, it is never the same, not ever. I used and read the person's body language. And I read the person's spoken language and his personality; I worked with it. Again, we talked beforehand.

"I liked to undress them slowly, not just boom here we are naked, but I liked to do it myself. So, I take them and move their body where and how I want it. I might actually undress them, or I might direct them on how to undress, piece by piece. I control them, their body. Even before we met, I would tell them what I wanted them to wear. Physically, they are somewhere because I told them. I would tell them to be somewhere at a specific time and I made them wait for me. It is all for fun. Though one time I had a beautiful young boy, I think he was twenty-five, I loved playing with him! I had him wait for me at an empty apartment, but I couldn't get in because it was a gated community and I had forgotten to bring the code with me.

"I just wanted to discover him somewhere. We had great play, anyway. I loved the curves of his body. If I put him over my knee, I cannot really see the curves from my view, in this respect that position doesn't work for me. At some point, since I have control, I can have them move as I talk to them. This particular boy wanted to see himself. The apartment I had chosen had a huge mirror. That play was very erotic for me! It worked really well for both of us.

"There is another young man I played with who was so memorable, I am giving you examples, you understand, he liked a long, long session. It was difficult for me to sit in a chair for so long a period. I put him over the bed to accommodate his desire. In this position, I could go on for perhaps an hour, a complete hour whacking his sweet bottom. That is a long time with a wooden hairbrush. And he would love it! I would ask him… I never asked, 'Are you OK?' but I would say, 'Can you take it harder?' or 'If you can take it harder, put your ass up' or 'If you want it more, move your ass.' The dear boy, he would actually raise himself if he wanted more or not, you know, or if he wanted it harder. This is how I read him and his movements. This boy could really take it and we often went for more than an hour. I was genuinely surprised every time. He and I played two or three times, maybe more. He loved it."

"Was that exciting for you the whole time?"

"Oh, yes, it was! I was so excited. I am excited now just remembering the sound of the brush on his flesh. I was totally turned on the whole time. Absolutely! One of the things I always asked the men was to never ever drink or do drugs before they saw me. Not while they were with me, either, because that prevents them from thinking clearly. I learned this to my own downfall. I haven't drunk or done drugs myself for years because it inhibits my ability to think clearly. I was afraid I would just whack them until I killed them or severely injured them. I feared I might do something else that wasn't safe for them, like engage in actual intercourse."

"It doesn't sound to me like you want to truly hurt them."

"No, no, no, but again if he can take it… and if he can, um, if he is getting off from it by all means…"

"Now if someone were, uh, across your lap, they would not be masturbating while you are doing it… I find this so hard to understand, just the whole thing, you see. But I want to understand."

"Right."

"But that does occur, doesn't it? The masturbation?"

"It occurs. Sometimes they will rub themselves against me. That's what gets them off. The whole struggling part… it turns me on that they struggle."

"So, it works both ways?"

"Yes, that they are rubbing against me and struggling stimulates me, but it's not the motion that is… it is the whole thing that is setting us off, it is the concept. The reaction, if I am just smacking someone until they are unconscious and they are not moving, I am not getting any response; I hate it. I might as well be slapping my pillow, you know. If they are working with me… that is getting me off. If they are struggling and I have to restrain them, restraining their arm or their waist or even their neck. When they struggle like that, I know they are appreciating what I am doing for them. Like this one young man… this is an interesting story, he had this fantasy that he wanted to be a secretary, so we went into an office I rented for the night. He comes by late at night and we start playing from the beginning as we had talked about before. It is kind of tricky because we are playing our roles, you know—he was supposed to have a report ready and didn't deliver on time and I am going to have to punish him: either I am going to fire him, or I am going to spank him, right? He has to pick. I take him into my office, and I start whacking him. At first, he was just lying there, and he says, 'Fuck this' and tries to get up. For a moment, I thought he wasn't playing but I, well, how do I know? I had to make a call, so I just whacked him harder—he was smaller than I am—and put him back on the desk but I went slower, at a slower pace, and he started to enjoy the whole thing. If he couldn't take anymore, I wouldn't have done it. I wouldn't restrain him against his will, but it was about just reading him."

"And if you are in a role…"

"A role, exactly. If I am in a role, I must read him and stay in the role, 'No you get back down, you were late with the report.' I wouldn't want to do it if he didn't want it, so it takes a lot of power and concentration. It takes self awareness, knowing what I am capable of doing and what I want to do, and secondly knowing exactly what the guy's limits are and if they have ever done this sort of thing before. This boy had never done it before. He had never played out his fantasies. I was able to give him that gift. It is all about communication.

"Beyond the mechanics, when it works it's, it's so good, so sexy. I am remembering this other man, an older man, he was hot—great ass, totally into the action. I actually did put him over my lap for a little while because that is what turns me on. He whimpered—he was actually afraid of me, he didn't want to tell me he had carpal tunnel syndrome so he couldn't support his own weight. He couldn't hold himself; after a bit, I thought it out, I realized he was uncomfortable in that position, on my lap. That's why he was whimpering. I just lifted him, put him on the couch, and we continued our play. It wasn't until later that he told me he had carpal tunnel syndrome. But he was enjoying himself. We are all complex people—I am including myself—so how you work with the person, like having sex, is never the same."

"Did you spank Aoife?"

"No, I didn't spank her. I adored her. I would never lift my hand to her. Ever! Oh, I did a few times when I was first exploring this new play! After HIV, do you understand? But she told me she was not into it, and I respected that. It didn't really fit with our tantric focus, anyway, and the idea of punishing her, it didn't really appeal at any level."

"It sounds like where the relationship involves love, there is a willingness to forgo curtain pastimes."

"Where the relationship involves love, there is a willingness to include certain pastimes as well, Letty."

"And you wouldn't have intercourse with these play partners?"

"No, no. I may consider masturbation of me. I may consider it if they wanted to. Or if they want me to insert something into their anus, you know, but never myself. I might do that but... never myself."

"Never yourself. You wouldn't insert yourself?"

"Right. It is a great plaything that, spanking, but with HIV, well, play is good because it is safe. You don't exchange fluids. People don't understand it, even gay men who have been playing forever, San Francisco you'd think that we should know better but... For instance, when I am on an online service and they look at my photo and they go, 'Oooh, you are into spanking?' and I would say, 'Uh, yes.' They would ask, 'And what else?' That is always the second question. I always answer, 'What else do you have in mind?' If they said something like, 'Water sports!' I had to go, 'No, sorry.' I mean, I am willing to do some things that naturally lead from one to the other, Point A to Point B, you know? But often they want to go from Point A to Point X. That's a little too wild and not something that I would be willing to offer them. I would never put myself or another at risk."

"Is there something that occurs in your fantasy that never occurred in reality?"

"Of course, but I am such a lucky person that I can tell you I live my fantasies. I don't consider myself so unusual, my fantasies are pretty commonplace; I just had the resources to make them happen, but some, maybe not. For instance, I would fantasize about having a boy for an entire week. But my lifestyle, my schedule, was such that I couldn't manage that. There are things I would have done, but how could I have my anonymity and fulfill these fantasies? It is that certain environments are not available for my play but other than that, I really don't think there are things that I haven't done that I... of course, I like beautiful attractive people, but I also like different boy types. The variety or looks aren't that important to me, but I might see someone on the street and fantasize about them. I might never know them, though, so not everything is possible.

"The first person I ever met who was into spanking, I was nineteen and he was fifty-five. Big age difference! I was so young! I would tell people he was my friend, and they would gasp, 'But, he is so old!' He was an officer, outranking me. This was overseas.

"But to have someone so sexually positive and having him share his experience with me. I remember him so well, and all we did. He was amazing! He introduced me to Aoife by hiring her house for a group of us. He introduced me to many erotic things through his conversation and our adventures but we, he and I, never did anything sexual. He told me that when he was in military college everyone was doing it, spanking, but they didn't think of it as a sexual thing. I hadn't experienced hazing, but I think he was talking about something different and darker. His was the ritualized hazing that you find in fraternities, deeply sensual and deeply blocked psychologically.

"You know there is a company here in the Bay Area, they produce erotic muscle videos and at one point, they had an entire division dedicated to spanking. They used to hold parties, video release parties. I remember one party held at this club in SoMa. It is a very hard sex and leather place. It is very tough but interesting. It is not exactly the best place for video viewing because it has slings and medical tables, dental chairs—a place you might want to go with some horsewhips in hand. This scene is all about physical punishment. They are as hard as you can get. They have these little rooms where you can go and people, if they want to play, they just approach you and you go at it."

"Do you go into a private room? Did you do this?"

"No, it is all semi-public. You have this whole trio of excitement in that it is semi-public, and a stranger, and punishment. If you want to do something more private, you just arrange to go someplace with the person. It is a fascinating spot and I have met interesting people there, mostly in their thirties and forties. But every now and then, you see someone younger, they sort of stumble in, it is always interesting to see how they react. There is always a crowd there and sometimes it is just men present for the theater of the scene. The video parties are advertised in gay magazines and at certain shops. They are very popular, but they don't draw such a large crowd at places like that as they once did.

"There is a whole culture around this—that's what I am trying to show you. There are people at these parties that I wouldn't have played with otherwise because I wouldn't trust them in a private setting."

"It doesn't sound like there is anything local that caters to the more specific play of spanking. What about uh, heterosexual spanking?"

"There are clubs more geared to gentle games. That is where stuff like heterosexual spanking might happen. People dress for the parts."

"Like fetish wear?"

"Yes, people have become a little more open about this. There was one woman, I think I read it in the New Yorker, who admitted she liked getting spanked but other than that… I don't really see spanking otherwise as a specific thing that gets mentioned, especially between males, gay, bi, or heterosexual. There are a few media producers, but really, not an area or place that people can go to meet one another."

"Only online or maybe telephone sex lines?" I could hear the voice from the phone demanding obedience from my husband. I felt like I had to know more.

"It is odd to me," I mused, "that it seems like spanking's a subject that has a certain taboo attached to it while other things—more extreme things—don't have that taboo. By the time you are doing the extreme, anything goes, I guess. It is sad that most people can't talk about these things easily."

Cos looked at me intently, I could see a question in his eyes but then he lowered his gaze and continued.

"Yes, because by the time someone reaches that level, well… you know some big queen that doesn't have a day job, no problem, but spanking a person who might have a job or career or family and spanking just isn't... it is maybe just a spice in their life, maybe they do it once or a few times and that is it. They aren't going to talk about this or change their lives. They enjoy it, but they might not do it again, ever. It was hot while it lasted. That is what happens with some people with whom I've played.

"I was thinking that there was something maybe wrong with me when I was eleven or twelve. When I was introduced to all the sensual and sexual possibilities later, I understood that there was nothing wrong with me. Spanking was just a practice I enjoyed, like other things in my life. A spice."

VIII
<u>Parinibbana Sutta</u>
"Everything in this life is precarious."

1/3/00

Marty –

Thank you for replying to my post.

I, too, am new to this medium. In addition,

through the end of this month I am

overwhelmingly busy with personal and

business concerns. I will not be able to

make plans until the first of next month.

I look forward to hearing from you and

learning more.

LM

2/6/00

Marty –

I am now more available. We can perhaps

plan a meeting?

LM

2/7/00

Hello LM,

Sure, let's find time for a chat…and a visit if

it seems like fun…

I'm at 408-555-0174, my cell. Sometimes it's

off for meetings during the day. Good times

to chat are normally in the evening between 8

and 10 PM. Most often I hear it ringing at

home.

Let's use our intuition…why not? Maybe

intuition will make the right connections…I

look forward to talking with you!

Marty

2/8/00

Marty –

After much wavering I have acknowledged to myself that I am a bit shy of calling you. After hello what do we say?

I am not usually shy, but I have my moments and I guess this is one of them. I am wondering if you would be willing to take a leap of faith and come to the City to meet me for a drink? Maybe on Friday evening after work? If we hit it off, we can take it from there. If you are willing and able to do this let me know what time and I will figure out a quiet place where we can meet.

LM

2/9/00

Hello LM,

First, thank you for your note letting me know how you feel…and that you feel shy…its nice to hear what your feelings are…and its…well normal! Now you know how guys feel about calling a woman…

But I am a good conversationalist …all that's going to happen is that we are going to visit about one thing after the other…there is no rush, no right way to meet...its just visiting a lot of times while walking in the same direction. The crucial point is having enough trust and safety to feel comfortable to say what is on one's mind and in one's heart…

Where about in the city do you live, what neighborhood? I used to live in Saint Francis Woods and know the City fairly well…

I suspect that we will get together for a drink in the city, but I don't know how you can find a drinking place that is quiet! Anyway, take a deep breath and remember that I am easy to chat with and I'll be responsible for that!

I'm thinking this weekend?

Call me at 408 555 0174, push the buttons and I'll do the rest…

Cheers,

Marty

2/10/00

Marty –

I spent all day yesterday dealing with a particularly difficult client and his family. I just got home and am absolutely whipped.

As for finding a drinking place that is quiet, I am a true babe in the woods even in my own stomping grounds. However, I did think of a place I haven't been for a long time! One of my favorite restaurants is The International Film House on Potrero Hill. They have a bar on the street in front of the restaurant.

Have you been there? You can sit outside under heaters and watch a movie. The food is California French chic.

We can't get together this weekend, but we will get together soon, perhaps a Friday would work for you?

LM

2/11/00

Wow, LM,

A client and his family…I thought I had it tough with clients only!

The Film House sounds ok if its not too cold out…I recall the city being chilled all the time with foggy chilly air…in which case could we go inside?

However, I'm a film lover, especially foreign film, been watching a lot in this past year. Last year I went to Bollywood (India) and Russia a couple of times. Love those foreign flicks!

Hmmm, time on Friday…well, next week, the AM is booked up with telecons, but after 12 is OK. If you get my recording it means I am in a meeting and I'll call back. It's late and I'm bushed so I'm going to sign off now.

Cheers,

Marty

2/12/00

Marty –

Yes, of course we can go inside, the bar is inside anyway.

I woke up this morning with an incredible headache and my entire body hurts. It hurts to speak out loud. Don't know what kind of virus gives a headache like this. I am still hoping this is just fatigue.

LM

2/13/00

Hi LM,

Sorry to hear you feel ill!

Visualize sending that person's energy out of your space, let a "rose" sweep around your body collecting that and all the other person's energy over and over.

Picture the rose filling up, then throw it out the window with a firecracker attached! Let it blow up- to release everyone's energy…to go back to them…

You get your own, they get their own. Very useful for getting other persons energy out of your system.

Don't know what it does for germs but its great for the person's energy!

Let's get together on Saturday for sure. I'll look forward to your call, knowing if you don't speak it's your Charlie Chaplin silent movie disguise. Very clever…

Cheers,

Marty

2/15/00

Marty –

I have been to the doctor since our last communication, but they have found no reason for this ongoing headache. It comes in waves and often is barely there. I am under strict orders to take it easy. That isn't something I am particularly good at doing. We shall see. I am pleased with your suggestion but already have plans for Saturday, so we wouldn't have been able to get together regardless. Perhaps we could stay with our plan to meet on a Friday, but maybe next week?

LM

2/15/00

Hi LM,

Sorry you are still suffering but I'm glad you went to the docs. Did they give you drugs? Its good to save your strength and recover when faced with such a tough malady…!

Let me figure out some good times to meet. First, I'll check to see how your recovery is coming.

R-e-s-t ! This is good!

See ya,

Marty

2/16/00

Marty –

Feeling fine. They really don't know what is causing the headache and other symptoms. I am eagerly awaiting a time and place that we can get together. Looks like Monday or Tuesday of next week are full for me. The remainder of the week, I am available during the day as well as the evening so if you want to meet in San Francisco some afternoon….

LM

2/17/00

Hi LM,

Glad to hear that you are feeling better. Let's plan on Wednesday. We can have coffee and go for a walk. You know that a little relaxation and play regenerates the creative mind and allows for new ways of viewing issues and problems. There is truth to the cliché.

"all work and no play makes Jack a dull boy."

Very good.

Marty

2/18/00

Marty –

I am looking forward to meeting you in person.

I am not unlike an overcharged electrical circuit sexually. I hope to find a regular and enthusiastic lover to catch up on all the sensual and sexual moments I have missed in the last few years. In the best sense of the word, I want to be a courtesan for the pleasure of being possessed and yet free. I want to explore my fantasies and those of my lover, create an oasis of comfort and relaxation, and build a friendship without sticky strings that intertwine the lives of the people involved. I will be thinking of you and looking forward to our time together on Wednesday.

LM

2/18/00

Dear LM

Thank you for your very nice and open letter. Very interesting…I am perhaps one of the few men around who appreciates the true courtesan!

Its true…there's something about Courtesans that just warms the soul…I suspect it comes from past lives where this was an important part of my life…well, I told you that once before…in Venice, I believe it was! Late 1600's?

I have no desire to possess anyone right now. I am fairly stressed on the business side of things. In fact, I am possessed by this business! So "sticky strings" just aren't my thing right now. ☺

Its freeing to let go of all the "stuff" of life every now and then…so in some way it could be good for you…I've let go of a lot of things in order to focus on this business.

…the thought that comes to mind about the headache from which you have suffered is what energy is there, perhaps unspoken…that is/was ready for expression?…to be said, and released?

Perhaps it would be good to say whatever needs to be said so that its not all backed up causing an illness there…just a thought…could be nothing related at all… Take care…

Marty

3/19/00

Marty –

I don't know if you would mind changing the location for our meeting and walk. Where the International Film House is located isn't a great area for enjoyable walking. I have a suggestion. We could meet at Café Copine located on Gough Street near the metaphysical bookstore. It might be a fun neighborhood to explore together.

If you have another place in mind just let me know. I will be available on the telephone most of tomorrow.

I am looking forward to meeting you in person. Since you suggested a walk, I am planning on wearing jeans and being fairly casual and comfortable. I hope you have the opportunity to be the same.

LM

I took the train into the City and the light rail down Market Street until I reached Gough Avenue.

The café was not far from the symphony hall. The musicians, done with their rehearsal, passed me carrying their instruments in beaten black cases down the street to the cheaper parking lots where their cars waited. This time of day, walking from the Muni stop, the only music was the twenty-first-century urban symphony of jackhammers, heavy traffic, distant sirens, and the brakes of buses.

Redevelopment has created apartment complexes set side by side with the multiple-flat late Victorians. In that neighborhood, old and new wear subtle rainbow colors.

Once I arrived at the café, I was able to settle into a postage stamp-sized round table and tiny slatted folding chair just outside the café door. The café owner delivered my macchiato in a tiny white china cup, the dab of whipped cream an artful island floating on top. From a nearby table, the wind brought the smell of cigarettes being smoked in my direction, but somehow it wasn't unpleasant with the dark espresso taste that lived on my tongue after my first sip.

The wind additionally carried the joyous voices of children in the play yard of the French American School located just behind the Café Copine. The joy of their games was made more musical by the accents and foreign words.

I watched for Marty but saw instead a bowlegged young French nanny in a pink pencil skirt escorting her small twin charges down the sidewalk toward Hayes Street. She was dispersing chocolate treats from a local chocolatier as she walked.

Would he know me? Would I know him?

An attractive man in a green Honda stopped in traffic and stared at me. When our eyes met, we smiled, but I knew it wasn't Marty.

I glanced up at the tightly trimmed trees that lined the sidewalk, watching the wind. There, directly above me where the branches had been cut back forming curling fingers, in the palm of this tree hand, nestled a small owl. Hidden, guarded, she waited for dusk to arrive and her hunting to begin.

Inside the café, the owner embarked upon a short argument with an employee in French. I wondered if a more romantic urban setting could be found in all of San Francisco in which to meet a lover for the first time.

His approach, when he finally arrived, was not the Parisian swagger of an unconstructed suit but the own-the-sidewalk stride of a homegrown American boy. He marched into this small slice of Europe neighborhood, a rowdy American army of one. The very air seemed to move out of his way as if the atmosphere could not stand the demands his energy placed on it.

He reached my table, and as he said hello, he bent down and gave me a kiss on the forehead.

"LM, the traffic, the parking, but here I am. I made it and I'm here, just a bit late, but here. I knew it was you. Listen, I've got to use the facilities, I'll be right back. Wait here, I'll be back. Right back."

Abruptly, he turned and went into the café. I hadn't said a word. He looked a bit like a thin Hugh Grant, but I wasn't sure how much of that impression was due to his actually looking like Hugh Grant or his affecting to look like Hugh Grant. He wore Dockers and a polo shirt, but they didn't fit quite correctly on his frame. I had noticed that the shirt had that washed-once-too-often quality about it.

He returned and stood, pulling on one earlobe and staring at the sediment in my cup. His blue eyes squinted, his sunglasses resting just above his eyebrows where they remained for the entire time we spent at Café Copine.

"I'm going to get something. I'm getting something to drink. I'm getting a drink, hold on."

Once more he had turned and gone inside, and I was again left sitting at the table on the sidewalk in stunned wonder with only the muddy dregs of an espresso. Moments later, he settled himself into his chair with his latte and a small croissant. He crossed his legs at the knee, leaning the small chair back onto its rear legs with a push of his left foot.

"Intuition. I believe in intuition. Intuition will make the right connections. Am I right? That is why I am trying this online dating service." He shrugged.

"I live on my cell, except for meetings. I mean I answer that cell even at home at night. I answer that cell anytime because I live on that cell. If I can get a woman, if I can get a woman or anyone, if I can get anyone to call me on that cell, I can sell them on me. That's why you didn't have to worry about calling me or wondering what to say. No need to worry when you're having a conversation with me. I know how to carry on a conversation."

Holding his palm out facing me, his hand still close to his chest, he took a breath.

"I can sell anything, but it is always me they are buying. When I worked for an international HR services company—I told you about the company I worked for, right? When I worked for them, I lived in Saint Francis Woods. Are we near there? No, we're not near there. To get there, we'd need to drive up and over the hill at the end of Market Street and that isn't near here. I had this girlfriend that lived with me. This girlfriend had a body. She had a body, a body that just got noticed. She was like white chocolate, smooth and sweet, but it didn't work out. She was too needy, and I had people to talk to, deals to make, you know?"

Chocolate, now there was something onto which I could grab. Maybe we could head towards that chocolatier I knew was at the corner of Hayes and Gough and Marty would offer to treat me. I waited until I could find an opening, suggesting if he were done with his coffee, perhaps we could walk up to Hayes Street and see what there was to see.

"We could just stroll and window shop. I understand there are some interesting galleries and stores."

We stood and I slipped my jacket on after waiting only a moment to see if Marty would help me with it. A chill had been added to the wind on Gough and I tugged at my sleeves, bringing them down around my hands. We walked side by side, not touching, Marty keeping up his end of the conversation. It felt like I had no end to the conversation to keep up; he was fine on his own.

"Have you been in this neighborhood before?" I asked. "I mean when you lived in the city?"

"No, I don't remember ever being down here. Maybe for lunch or something, but I don't remember being here. I could have been here and just not remember.

"Say, you know, I was pretty impressed with your posting and emails. You could write a book about how to meet men doing that. What you should do is write a book. What you should do is write a book on how to meet men. Have you met a lot of men through your posting? I've gone out with a few women through mine. Amazing that I've found the time, seeing how all my time is with the business. Maybe if my business doesn't work out, I could write the book instead of you?

"There was this guy I read about. Have you heard of him? He wrote a book. A book on how to get women. He was this guy in New York. An average New York guy, not bad-looking, not too good-looking, just an average guy but he worked as a photographer's assistant or something. Something with a camera and models. So, he always had gorgeous models around him. Beautiful women. So, he thought he'd just ask them what attracted them to a guy. What a guy could do or say to attract them. Well, what happened is they all wanted to talk to him. So, he carries his little notebook around all the time. Wherever he goes, there is the notebook in his pocket. Right there with him all the time, you know. Whenever he sees a beautiful woman, he pulls out his notebook and asks the question."

We walked right past the chocolatier even though I had pointed it out, and now I was taking some deep calming breaths in front of a shoe store full of trendy Italian footwear for men. Breathing had become a survival habit for me. Marty stopped his story long enough to peer into the window and I asked, "So, what did this guy learn from asking his question?"

"He wrote a book about it. What he learned was to carry around that notebook and ask the question. He made a lot of money. Then they made a movie out of the book, about him writing the book, and he made even more on the movie. So, what you should do is write a book, a book about meeting men, a how-to book."

"I think I've heard that story before, maybe it is like an urban myth."

"No, not this guy, this New York guy, this guy wrote this book and had a movie made about it, and that is what you should do."

"Well, it's an idea," I mused, "and if I ever decide to change careers, I will certainly consider it as an option. Don't you think that maybe what worked for him was that he was listening?"

We had moved a bit farther down the street and I found myself resting my forehead on the cool glass of a window behind which lovely and colorful art glass pieces were displayed. I could feel the headache growing and the colors of the glass seemed to be coming from me. I straightened up and walked into the gallery, surrounding myself with the luminosity and color of the glass objects.

Inside the store, I asked the clerk if she had any Chihuly. The gallery was divided in two, between art prints and art glass. Marty moved to the wall that held Vargas prints.

"I've seen these before," Marty said as if to suggest his having recognized this art set him apart from others or validated his existence.

He moved from print to print, talking about each portrait's attributes in terms of what he found sexy, pulling at his ear, always in motion. There was no Chihuly here, another disappointment to add to the day's mounting disappointments. I was thirsty and hungry and wondered at this man's emptiness. How could anyone talk so much and say so little?

He cornered the gallery staff person and began telling them, "What you should do…"

I stayed with the art glass and the shimmering colors. I swam through their colors, floating on his words without listening; the store was an aquarium, the glass lining the shelves the tropical fish. Just for an instant, everything was beautiful, liquid, and pain-free. When I walked out of the shop, he followed.

As we moved back outside, passing a bar, the open doors sent out the voice of Janis Joplin, "Though I've looked everywhere, and I can't find me anybody to love, to feel my care."

We walked on for the moment without talking and I filled my lungs with oxygen that only moments before had seemed unavailable. As we continued moving down Hayes Street, Marty again began to talk, holding his hand to the top of his head as if he were keeping a hat from blowing away in the wind. His voice sounded like his emails.

"You own a dog? I had a dog once. Are you a dog person? You can learn a lot from a dog. You ignore a dog; a dog leaves you alone, goes away but not too far. When you are ready you just shift around a little bit, the dog comes over and wants to know what he can do for you, tells you that you are a wonderful person. You ignore a person; a person bothers you for a while and then leaves you alone, goes away, really away. You can cry out and call, but no one will come. You're the same person but no one is there to tell you about how wonderful you are. My dog is gone."

He paused a moment and looked at me for what felt like the first time. Abruptly, he crossed Laguna Street, tossing behind him the statement that he was hungry.

Kuchenkrakle, a traditional German *wirtshaus* on the corner of Hayes and Laguna, had their menu posted on the door of their restaurant.

Marty headed directly up to it and read it to himself.

"I have to watch every penny right now. Haven't paid myself in weeks. Everything is going to the business, all my energy, everything. I can't waste a dime. Tight budget. Have you eaten here before? Is it any good?"

"I've never had a meal here, but friends have told me it is very good and has hearty food," I replied.

"It looks like they have soup. Bread probably comes with the soup. You want a cup, or uh, a bowl of soup? I could buy you a bowl of soup. Tight budget, watching my money, I want to eat though, so we could go in here. You want a bowl of soup?"

I smiled; things might not be so bad after all. Maybe he was just nervous or preoccupied by his business worries. Maybe some food would help, and I was willing to order a minimal amount in order to spare him the cost. I thought I might even be willing to treat if we began to connect a bit more. I would wait and see. Meanwhile, I thought having something to eat might mitigate the growing headache, and perhaps mitigate my general irritation with Marty's voice.

I caught the door, holding it open for myself after he let it go, having gone through. At that moment, out of the corner of my eye, I noticed a tall middle-aged man wearing a Hawaiian shirt leaning up against an old Volvo. For the briefest of moments, we locked eyes and he smiled. He was familiar, as though I had seen him before, something about his smile… I was being followed!

Inside the restaurant, the decor was traditionally spartan, the crowd boisterous. We were seated at the end of a large oak plank table. Marty prattled on, his hand to his mouth, one finger going up his face, his thumb holding his head up while his elbow rested on the table.

"Hey, they have soup. You're going to have soup, right? *Kürbissuppe*, hmmm. You want this soup. Have the soup.

"Did I tell you I went to India last year? I went to India on a spiritual journey. Can you imagine that? Me on a spiritual journey, but there I was. Of course, I have business there also. That is where we have our manufacturing unit. I visited Russia a couple of times last year also, looking for engineers that will work for less than the greedy SOBs in Silicon Valley. Even the Indians are getting too greedy. I can tell you all about India, and Russia too. I traveled in Germany last year. I was in Germany on business, but I went to beer halls, and I can tell you all about Germany also. Don't ask me about how greedy the Germans are. Just don't ask. Don't ask."

When the server came to us, setting down two glasses of water, I obliged and ordered a bowl of *Kürbissuppe*. Marty quizzed the server on the various German beers available, settling on a dark rich brew. He ordered the *Entrecote vom Grill mit Zweibel Soße, Bratkartoffeln un Tomaten Salat.* As she left, he reminded her to bring me some bread with my soup. I had an inner flash of annoyance; my arm did an involuntary jerk, knocking against my glass of water, which I caught before it had completely fallen over. Even with my catch, water sloshed out and across the corner of the table, mostly missing Marty's lap but still managing to get his right leg a little wet.

"Jeez!" His face contorted in disgust and just as quickly recomposed itself. His beer arrived and the flow of words resumed.

"What I learned in India is to visualize what you want to achieve. That's the spiritual part, visualization. So, I visualize my success when I am in a telecom and then I sell.

"Of course, spiritual only goes so far and then you have to let real science take over. Real science, that is how things work, am I right? You know what I mean? You can visualize but you have to have reality to back it up. Am I right?

"I'm right. I know. I learned this in India and in Russia. I knew it before."

He shrugged and pushed his sunglasses up onto his brow above his eyes, as our orders were put in front of us.

"This economy, though, is tough now. I don't have the product, and I've got delivery dates coming up that we may not meet. I have to work round the clock. I have to work at selling the idea of waiting for the product to my customers. I work all the time. It is my discipline, my meditation, I learned that in India when I was there this year."

While he ate his meal, I listened to his concerns about his business.

He was CEO of a dotcom with one product concept in the business-to-business sector having to do with HR compliance. The product was not yet shippable. He came from a sales background and had engineers working for him on the product. His role was to bring in the venture capitalists and sell the product that did not yet exist in a beta model. He had done just that and now had delivery dates coming at the end of the month but no product to deliver. The money his customers paid for the product had been spent and it seemed that everything was unraveling for him as quickly as he talked.

I had to give him credit for still being in operation at all. It had only been months before that most of the dotcoms in Silicon Valley had suddenly disappeared as if they had never existed. However, it was clear that Marty's time was up shortly, and everything would end for him. It didn't seem that he would have anything for which to live if his business failed. To me, it was obvious that the business and his life were indeed failing.

This date was concluded, although not over, by the end of the meal. I knew that he did not feel we had connected. On this one thing, we fully agreed. I discovered that I disliked being sexually discounted by this virtual stranger more than I disliked being sexually ignored by my husband Peter. Peter, at least, listened to me and allowed me the opportunity to talk. True, he often didn't hear what I was saying, but at least he listened.

I thought of my two encounters with Alan, his consideration, and his depth of feeling; the contrasting desperation and frantic need to control being exhibited by Marty became more pitiful.

My head pounded and I felt an anger bubbling in me as I stared at the bread I had crumbled into my empty soup bowl while he had eaten his rib eye and the rest of his meal.

When we left the cool darkness of the restaurant and entered the brightness of the late afternoon summer sun, the anger broke through as a solid thought and a decision for action. Rejection is nature's way of saying, "Fuck you." Marty's life might be pointless, but he was a man who had agreed to meet based on a desire for a sexual encounter. Earlier, he had followed me out the door of the gallery; I knew he could be led. There was a way I could help him, and that way lay through my initiating a sexual connection.

There was no sign of the Volvo or its driver as we retraced our steps back toward our starting point.

"This is my car. I need to get going. I have to work. I have to head home and work. Busy," he announced as we came to a late model taupe Oldsmobile on Gough. We had retraced our route, though on the opposite side of Hayes from before, and were back near the Café Copine on Gough. We stood facing one another for a moment on the sidewalk. I kept my hands inside my jacket sleeves, gripping the ends of the sleeves tightly. I took the smallest step toward him but still did not touch him. The air had continued to cool but the sun still warmed my back as we stood there.

"I came on public transportation, remember? I will need to walk up to Market to catch a bus to take me to the train."

I took a deep cleansing breath and continued.

"Thank you for the soup. I am sure your business concerns will turn out well. You seem to have thought of everything and certainly have the ability to turn it all around. If anyone can make a success of it, you are the one. It is clear that your travels to India and all your experiences have given you great insight into how things should be."

A look of confusion crossed his face, and just as quickly, was hidden. I looked down the street toward Market Street, with just the smallest hint of a sigh. My concentration on what I was doing and on Marty was so complete that for a moment,

I did not notice the headache. I looked back at Marty, directly into his eyes, and smiled.

"Uh, would you like a ride up to Market? Or, uh, a ride to the train station? I could take you to the train station if you want. What you should do is let me take you to the station."

"Thank you, I'd like you to take me." I leaned into him but did not move.

He popped around the back of his car, opening his door, and was almost sliding in before he noticed that I still hadn't moved. He stopped part way into his seat and looked at me over the roof of the car; I did nothing more than glide my hands deeper into my jacket pockets and smile again at him. He came back around the car and opened my door for me. I carefully slid into the seat, assiduously not removing my hands from my pockets. I took care that I did not catch my clothes on his car door. He again circled the car and slid into the driver's seat.

As he turned away from me to put his seat belt on, I reached for him and placed my hand on his leg where the water had splashed on him. I rubbed down to his knee and back up with great gentleness.

"Are you dry now?" I asked calmly. "I am so sorry that the water got knocked over."

I continued to slide my hand on his leg with just a bit more pressure.

"I am going down the peninsula. I guess there isn't any reason I couldn't give you a ride home. Do you want a ride home? You could use a—"

"Yes, please." I interrupted him for the first time. "I'd like you to take me."

I could see the sign for the metaphysical bookstore over Marty's shoulder and a conversation I had had with Horace came to my mind. I kept my voice low and soothing, as if I were talking with a client.

"Do you remember why we were meeting? What it was we really wanted to happen today? I find you exciting. I have something to tell you. Have you ever heard of sex magic? It has to do with creating the answer to a material problem. The concept relies on the idea that sexual intercourse results in creation. When a physical child is not the result or point of sexual intimacy, there is the possibility of another type of child, the magic child. When one has physical sex, especially oral sex, the issue, or magic child of the intercourse, relates to the physical world. This uses the sex act to create a moment of clarity in which the answers to concrete questions can be discovered. Creativity and inspiration are the result.

"I think that with concentration, which would require mostly silence so that we can both focus, you and I could fill our needs. I believe that if you concentrate, and at the very moment of your climax, you focus fully on what you want to happen, perhaps the success of your business. I know that your business holds great concern for you. If you can make that focused wish at just that moment, then a magic child will be created that will answer your deepest desire.

"I have an idea how to heighten the experience for both of us. I know a place. Will you let me show you the place? It isn't out of your way home. Why don't we take a little while to see if we can create a magic child that grants your deepest wishes?"

As I talked, I continued to gently massage his thigh and had moved up so that my hand now rested on his crotch. I was applying pressure to his cock with the tips of my fingers, I could feel him beginning to respond. Looking at him, I could see that his eyes had become bluer, and his skin tone had paled. The most significant indication that he was going to follow my directions was his ongoing silence.

"Shall we go?" I asked, pointedly looking at his key in the ignition.

Off of 101, near Candlestick Ball Park, the Bayshore Highway leads up San Bruno Mountain on Guadalupe Canyon Drive. Suddenly, we found ourselves rising, the stadium receding as the car climbed over thirteen hundred feet. San Francisco was replaced by the sage and yarrow scrub hills of golden California. On the road, we passed the roadkill of the day: opossum and skunk.

To the right, far below the wide sweeping road on which we traveled, was the Cow Palace, and to the left, Brisbane was nestled in the green valley linking and separating the two parallel ridges.

Climbing toward the radio towers, the reception on the car radio got fuzzy, distorted; he didn't lower the volume, distracted by my hand working his now rock-hard penis.

"Turn right here," I instructed.

We pulled into the county park's empty parking lot. The sun was low in the afternoon sky, but we still had several hours of light.

"I want to show you my courtesan aspect," I purred, leaning into him, and followed my statement with a sweep of my tongue along the outline of his ear.

"Will you walk up the trail with me? It isn't far."

He got out, and again I waited until he had circled the car and opened the door for me.

We took the Summit Loop trail, gently ascending through the grove of eucalyptus. As we emerged from the trees, a top-knotted California quail paused in the trail and looked directly at me.

I stopped and turned, placing my hand on Marty's chest.

"Shhh, can you see the quail in the road behind me?

I slipped my hand under the front of his shirt; the other found his crotch again.

"Is it still there?"

I gently bit his neck. I could see the distant city shining in the afternoon light. It was important to me that there be no witnesses to our actions.

A bit farther up, the trail turned away from the Bay and the view changed. The trail here was edged on one side by a steep ravine; erosion had washed away the scrub in certain places, but it thickened again at the bottom of the ravine, becoming what appeared to be an impregnable mass. On the other side of the trail was a hill moving up and away from us.

This mountain ridge was a remnant of what was the natural ecology of northern San Mateo County. It is composed of solid rock with a thin veneer of ground soil. The plant life clings tenaciously, reaching into small cracks within the rock face, holding on and occasionally breaking off larger and smaller pieces of the ridge face.

I stopped Marty again and indicated a sheltered area on the side of the trail that was created by this slow process of wildflowers breaking granite. He seemed to suddenly come out of his reverie and understand that this was where we'd been heading. In one movement, I backed into the shelter, kneeling and pulling him in by unbuttoning his jeans and lowering the zipper to expose him.

He bent down toward me to kiss but I pressed him back with both of my hands flat on his chest, taking him into my mouth. He didn't protest; his hands rested on my shoulders until it was done.

I had him relax, sitting between my legs and using my body as a chair back. We sat watching the fog move slowly inland from the Pacific Ocean, approaching the mountain like a predatory animal. I waited until Marty's breathing indicated he had fallen into a post-coital sleep and carefully maneuver him to pillow his head on one of the many rocks that lay within the sheltered area.

It took some time to extricate myself. I carefully wiped his neck, ear, and hands to make him comfortable. The fog rested on the edge of the ravine's far side, the afternoon light appearing to come from below. I knew it was time to go home. There would be rain in the evening.

Rolling him over didn't take any more effort than moving a client. I did one final police of the trail, shelter, and nearby area before walking down the hill to the parking lot and the street. I thought about calling a cab on my cell phone but decided that the walk down the hill into Colma would be pleasant. From there, I would take BART into San Francisco and the train home.

It was the first time in weeks that my headache had almost gone away. It felt good, and I thought I smelled roses.

IX
<u>Parinibbana Sutta</u>
"Always wholeheartedly seek the way of liberation."

I had received a call from Ian the night before; he and Todd were in Reno for that night and would be coming in the next afternoon. Days before, I prepared both Ian's room and Jennie's room, our designated guest room, for their arrival.

I shared Ian's email with Peter by forwarding it to him the morning after I received it. He and I still weren't saying much to one another, no more than was necessary for polite passing in the house, though he had inquired if I knew why Ian decided to take a leave of absence from college and wondered whether he would be living with us during his time off. I told him honestly that I did not know the answers to either of these questions, but that I was taking Ian's statement not to worry on faith. I had suggested that there might be another item on Ian's agenda.

"Agenda? He has an agenda?"

"I don't mean that exactly, Peter, it is just that I think he might want to tell us something important that is separate from the reason he is taking a leave of absence, that's all. I… I will sound very silly if it turns out I am wrong, but I think that this Todd may be, uh, may be Ian's partner, his boyfriend, you understand?"

"Are you saying Ian is homosexual?"

"I am saying that I think there is a strong possibility that he is, yes. I don't know."

"How long have you known he is gay?"

"Peter, I just said I don't know! I could be completely off base. But haven't you ever thought about it? I mean, he didn't date though he was popular with both the boys and the girls in his class. Didn't you wonder? Haven't you ever talked to him, man to man?"

"We were very forthcoming with the children. We both spoke to them and educated them on sexual matters."

"I know, I know, but isn't it strange, I don't think I ever went past the talk that starts when two people care about each other… you know what I mean? I never talked to any of them about, uh, well, about practices not so well, I don't know what to call it… not so missionary."

"What are you talking about? Missionary? We talked openly in this house with the children, we talked to them about safe sex and drugs and tolerance, we had discussions about politics at the dinner table and accepted all their ideas, and we encouraged debate. Are you saying I didn't do my job as a father? That I should have sat down 'uno a uno' and talked about how to be homosexual?"

"No, Peter, or maybe yes… oh, please, I just mean that it is one thing to teach children to be accepting of, say, people who are gay, and another thing to teach them what it really means to be gay. I don't mean just the mechanics of it, but the implications, the cultural challenges. There is so much they must deal with daily: the stigmas, hatred, discrimination, all that.

"You are a good father—the kids, all of them, could not have a better dad. Please, this isn't about our parenting, I was just thinking, that is all. I was thinking that no one ever talks to their kids about alternate lifestyles, what they are, and what the people who live them face in our society. We never talk about accepting our own personal inclinations though they might be different from the standard model, that it is OK to talk to family about personal inclinations, choices, and concerns, that… that… not just about being gay or straight but all the places in between, all the preferences or natural inclinations."

"Oh, I see; this is really about me. You don't know anything! You are wrong, what you think is wrong! I am not going to have this conversation with you."

"Peter, I… it isn't about you or me, I am just saying, I am trying to say that all of us, a family, should be able to teach and talk and accept one another's life choices and that still, no matter what, we…"

Peter had left the room and was up the stairs and in his office, the door slamming shut.

"… still love each other completely."

Our one real conversation in months hadn't gone particularly well. I just buried myself in my work and in preparing a welcoming home for Ian and his friend. I planned his favorite meals and stocked those snacks and drinks that he had favored last summer, hoping his tastes hadn't changed too much.

I removed the telephones in Jennie's and the boys' rooms. I knew that the boys almost exclusively used their cell phones and wouldn't miss it. I just didn't want to take a chance of Todd or Ian overhearing any conversations, like I had.

Spring had unexpectedly come into our garden in the form of bulbs shooting up their green leaves around the bases of the olive trees, but other than the early dandelions by our front door and some paperwhites along the edges of the driveway, no blooms had yet appeared. The weather had warmed, we saw the sun more than rain now; the evening fog stayed steeped, just lipping the tops of the coastal range.

My mood had generally lifted, but I credited my time sitting with Cos more than the freshening weather. He was having more frequent bad days, and his periods of energy were shortening. The doctors assured his family and Haven that he was stable. The fact was he should already be dead, but he just wasn't. His constitution continued to battle the ravages of AIDS. It was age and his inability to move around much that was doing the most psychological damage. Arthritis had curled his feet and knees so that he couldn't stand. Cataracts had begun forming, which thwarted the impact of his dimming vision induced by the disease. Morphine dosages had been increased to the maximum allowed levels. All this, yet his bedside was the place I was most relaxed and happy. Cos himself seemed content, dimly watching the progress of his cherry trees as they prepared to blossom, and his garden came slowly and brightly alive below him.

It was March and my youngest was coming home!

I heard the sound of their tires on the driveway and was at the door by the time they were getting out of the car. Ian wrapped his arms tightly around me in a hug, all smiles, youth, and good health. He had filled out but still retained the look of a boy acting the part of a man. Over his shoulder, I smiled a greeting to Todd, who stood back and a little apart from us. Behind me, I heard Peter. Ian released me to embrace his dad. I stepped forward, extending my hand to our guest.

Todd was shorter and more broadly built than Ian. Where Ian was lean, his muscles ropey and long, Todd had the build of someone who took his weight workouts seriously. His orange T-shirt molded to his bulldog chest and his upper arms stretched the fabric of the short sleeves. As he stepped up to shake my hand, I saw that his bandy legs carried him in a slight swagger not unlike a rodeo rider just thrown from a bronco. He had a shock of bright yellow hair gelled to attention. His handshake was firm and confident, his smile toothy and genuine, but in his green eyes, there was hesitancy. I liked him right away. He was bright to Ian's drab, solid to Ian's ethereal. If his personality met the promise of his appearance, I thought he would be a wonderful friend, if not lover, for Ian. I waved them into the house.

"Please, please come in. Ian, you look wonderful! I've been so looking forward to your visit, your stay. Come into the kitchen, all of you. Todd, can I get you something to drink?"

"Mom, we're tired, Todd especially. I want to get our stuff before we sit down."

"I'll get the bags, E—you sit with your folks. Mrs. Mae, I'd love a Coke if you have one. Where should I put our stuff?"

"Call me Letty, everyone does. I prepared the guest room and Ian's room upstairs. Ian, you can show Todd the rooms and you two can settle in however you are most comfortable."

Todd shot me a smile, this time one that included his eyes, as he left to retrieve their gear.

Peter had brought Cokes for the boys and himself and set them down at the kitchen table where Ian had arranged himself with a weary sigh. I sat down between them, reaching out and holding Ian's hand, at which he smiled indulgently. His other hand traced the lines of the mandala that had been shallowly carved into the surface of the wooden table.

"Did we ever punish you for defacing the kitchen table?"

"You and Mom never punished me for any artistic project, surprises and destruction included, unless you count making me varnish and seal this table after I was done."

Hearing Todd come in with their bags, Ian grabbed a soda for Todd and went to show him upstairs and get settled. Peter sat at the table, sipping his drink. I looked at him, but it seemed we had no words, nothing to say to one another. I got up to fill the kettle with water to make myself tea, and as the water ran, I felt tears filling my eyes and tried to will them away; I had no reason to cry. I heard the scrape of Peter's chair as he got up. As he walked behind me on his way out of the kitchen, he reached out and briefly touched my shoulder. In the touch, I felt his apology. The tears quietly won out, but no one knew I cried because I was alone with the water overflowing the kettle, sunshine flooding the kitchen.

Ian returned to the kitchen, hugging me again from behind and immediately noticing I was distressed. I turned off the water, putting the lid on the kettle, and moved from his arms to the stove to put it on the heat. To his questioning glance, I said, "No, nothing, just being a mom, I guess. Really, I am just so pleased you are here."

"Making tea? May I have some, Coke doesn't do it for me right now."

I nodded my assent and retrieved two cups from the cupboard.

"Where's Dad? I want to talk to both of you."

"I think he is upstairs in his office. You can get him, and the tea will be ready soon. Do you want milk in yours?"

"Yeah, thanks."

He went to the foot of the stairs and shouted up to Peter. Yes, the house had been very silent without the kids. Maybe Peter and I had never talked, maybe all the conversation had been the three kids and their friends, loud and frantically alive with childhood, puberty, and later, with that raucous serge of approaching adulthood before leaving for college. Maybe the silence had always been in our house, simply disguised by the noise.

I brought the tea to the table where Ian was already sitting as Peter joined us. It was all suddenly very solemn. Ian and I blew on our teas. I swiped at a moisture ring made by the cup on the table. Ian added more sugar to his tea, the spoon doing all the talking as it clicked against the side of the cup. We sat until I felt a smile building in me. I looked at Peter and saw that his smile was already forming, which made mine race for first place. In a moment, we were both giggling while Ian looked at us with that expression all kids have when they think their parents have crossed into full insanity.

"What?"

"Your mom and I feel like we are awaiting sentence after having been found guilty, it is all just so serious and important, and yet we have no idea why. Perhaps you could tell us why you're home on your spring break instead of partying wherever kids party on spring break in Chicago. Didn't you go to New Orleans last year? I guess we want to know why we have been so honored by you and your friend with this visit."

"Oh."

"Ian, your dad and I are both sitting here, listening. Are we waiting for something? Are we waiting for Todd to join us?"

"He's asleep, tired from the drive."

Again, he stirred his tea—the cup the bell jar, the spoon the clapper, calling us to hear the news; he placed the spoon to the side and took a sip of tea. Finally, he placed the cup back down on the table.

"I want you to know that I am gay."

There it was. My son was finally opening up to us! I had anticipated this conversation, played it over in my mind, rehearsed the best possible responses, and now in the moment, found I didn't know what to do or say. Peter spoke up and it was one of those instances that reminds you why you love someone, which puts a seal on any long suffering because small, good things can easily remove the big bad things. It was a moment that brings the vow of "for better or for worse" into sharp understanding. We were suddenly in the "better" as Peter smoothly engaged.

"And?"

"No 'and,' just that: I'm gay."

"Does this have anything to do with why you have chosen to take a leave of absence from college without talking to your mother or me about the decision?"

"Uh, no, that is something else, but I thought…"

"We can see that this is particularly important to you. Your mom will say more, I am sure, but I want you to know we, both of us, appreciate your desire to share this with us, but we're your parents and frankly, we'd like it if all you kids shared more of who you are, and what your lives are now that you live away from home. Is it too much to ask? How long have you recognized that you're gay? I mean, that isn't important, but it hurts your mom that you couldn't tell her, couldn't talk to us about this when you were first figuring it out. It hurts us to think about you or your brother and sister going through tough things, tough times, without asking us to participate, if not help. I mean, we're family for crissake, we love you, all of you. Do you think it is easy for your mom with all of you away? Do you think it is easy for either of us, alone in this house without the three of you? Wait until you're a parent!"

"Shit."

"Son, your mom and I love you. There are no conditions on that… it's just something you'll have to live with your entire life, sort of like being gay. I suggest you embrace the idea fully."

Ian and I sat, stunned. Peter had delivered his speech almost without breath. As far as I was concerned, it was just about perfect. How Ian felt about it, I couldn't guess at that point, but I thought it was my turn to ask a few questions.

"Todd is your boyfriend?"

"Yeah."

"How serious is it? Did you bring him home with you as support or to plan a wedding?"

"Support, boyfriend, uh, no ceremony is planned."

"Do you think you will find someone to marry someday? Do you want to, I mean?"

"Yeah, I do."

"And children, do you think someday if you find the right man, you will want to have children?"

"Yes, Mom, I do."

"How long have you known you are gay?"

"I guess I became sure during my last year of high school, but it wasn't until I went to Chicago that I, uh… had any real experiences, any chance to explore what it meant to me."

"Do your brother and sister know?"

"No."

"How do you want your dad and I to manage this? Do you want us to be tacit or do you want us to be open with it? How 'out' do you want to be?"

"Completely out."

"What about Jennie and Zack, then?"

"I'd like you guys to arrange a conference call for tomorrow or whenever everyone can be on the telephone together. Would that be OK? I can tell them, and we'll all be together, in a way.

"Dad can give his speech to them."

"I don't understand why people have to announce they're gay, but they don't have to announce they are straight. Maybe there should be a requirement or a ceremony like a bar mitzvah or confirmation. It would be a rite of passage or maybe a requirement before you can graduate high school, like volunteer work is sometimes. It would be that sometime between the ages of fifteen and eighteen, each person would have to come out as straight, bi, or gay. A Declare Your Sexual Orientation rite of passage."

"You have the weirdest ideas, Mom."

Peter was chuckling as he stood up.

"Well, I, for one, am announcing that I am straight, and I am going straight up to my office to see if I can get hold of Jennie and Zack to schedule that call you want. Call me when dinner is ready or for any other revelations. I am particularly interested in this leave of absence thing. You stay here and chat with your mom."

I warmed our tea and then we sat, looking at the tabletop.

When he was in ninth grade, Ian had saved his allowance for two weeks and bought himself a set of small wood carving tools. Months passed before he even opened the package. One night, apparently right after Peter and I had gone to bed, he came downstairs and spent an entire night with the wood carving tools and one of my favorite paring knives, working on the table.

At that time, Jennie had recently begun running early every morning. It eventually became a routine that stayed with her, evolving into one of her passions. In fact, she placed in a marathon last year, receiving a ribbon that she promptly sent home to be added to her other awards. That particular morning, as had become her habit, she was the first among us dressed and downstairs. Before heading for her run, she came into the kitchen to grab a bottle of water and found her brother on top of the table, working feverishly on a mandala he was carving into its surface.

She tells us that he didn't even look up and that other than coming closer to see what he was doing, she did not disturb him. She got it into her head to forego her run and returned upstairs to wake Zack. The two of them managed to cajole and harass Peter and me out of bed, dressed, and into the family car without ever entering the kitchen. They told some confused story about Ian waiting for us at our favorite breakfast restaurant. They assured us that this was a gift from the three of them to us for some occasion, I can't remember what they settled on, to show us how much they appreciated us. By the time we had our coffee and ordered breakfast, a new story had been devised about Ian maybe being at the wrong restaurant. They assured us we needn't pick him up, that it was close enough to his school to walk and he had already started. I think both Peter and I knew at this point that Ian was somewhere doing something that we would put a stop to if we only knew what it was and where he was. We had learned that the kids never protected one another if one of them was contemplating what parents and police would consider actual dangerous or criminal behavior. Zack and Jennie were both old enough then to discern what Peter and I would consider dangerous. I believed they understood the police's idea of criminal too. I wasn't that convinced they completely understood my idea of criminal.

Their story ran on frantically, assuring us that Ian's wish was for us to have our breakfast treat at the restaurant and go on to work from there. He was sorry to miss sharing it with us, but he had made the mistake, after all. Resigned, we ate our meal, dropped the kids off at the high school, and assured them we were going straight to the train station where I would drop Peter off for his commute and I was going to be in meetings all day, but they could call me if anything came up.

Two blocks later, we did a U-turn and headed home. We talked it over and decided Ian must be at home or there would be no need to get us out of the house. We reasoned that he was doing an art project, since he was almost always working on an art project, and that we might not initially approve of some aspect of the work.

Entering the kitchen, we saw Ian bent over the table, wearing flannel pajama bottoms and an SFMOMA T-shirt.

I don't remember if Peter or I said anything, but I do remember my rapid series of impressions, a crowd of ghosts in a panic, running, passing through me, each a rush of cold, on their way to oblivion.

At first, all I saw was the table, hacked and gouged. It wasn't an expensive table but it was good solid maple. I knew the dents Jennie made by banging her toddler cup to Grover's singing. I knew the scratches Zack had caused while working on his Pinewood Derby car. There was a deep hammer dent on one end, where a little Ian had first banged his head on the edge when running from under the table in a game of hide and seek. He had left the room crying, then returned with his father's hammer and simply hit the offending table back. In the middle of the place setting area typically used by Peter, a darkened ring forever reminded me of his taking care of things while I was sick with the flu when the kids were still at a highly demanding age. He had set down a hot pot of macaroni and cheese from which he had been serving the kids, leaving it there for several minutes because he had heard my call from upstairs. I treasured each mark; each, a piece of history, would jog my memory and bring a wistful smile.

In those first moments, watching my son straighten from his task and turn to acknowledge our presence, all I could see was the willful destruction of these memory love notes.

Ian grinned and said good morning.

Now, eight years later, we were sitting at the same table. The mandala he had been carving that day was a series of rings moving from the center of the table to the edges where parts of the final two rings were cut off by the rectangular nature of the table itself. The rings are sectioned and linked in an intricate pattern reminiscent of Irish illuminations. The relief itself switches back and forth from bas to intaglio. Starting from the center, which shows Peter entering my and Zack's lives, the circles record all the major events in the life of our family, linked by the daily and annual events that define our days and our years: school, work, holidays, vacations. No one single event stands out from any other, though the traditional annual events seem to carry more weight overall, acting almost as a frame for the other things depicted. As part of his design, Ian had worked in every mark and scar the table held prior to his handiwork; each memory accidentally wrought was preserved in his deliberate creation of a memory record.

That first morning, when we had walked in on him and I dissolved into racking sobs at his cheery morning greeting, he had only gotten to the third ring of the seven, though the remaining ring designs had clearly been laid out. He and Peter had to work at soothing and reassuring me for quite a while before I was able to look clearly at what he had done and listen to his explanation of what was happening. Peter, who I believe had started yelling at the same moment I dissolved onto the floor in tears, had been distracted first by me and then by Ian's efforts to console me. We had both listened and ultimately marveled at Ian's depiction of family legends, stories he had not actually witnessed or had been too young to remember. Our appreciation grew as we realized that, unlike most of his works that disturbed the viewer, this work sent its message of calm love and family loyalties with only an undertone of morbidity.

We had agreed to let him finish, including the understanding that not only would everything be cleaned once the piece was artistically completed, but that it would be varnished and carefully sealed so that it could continue to be used as our kitchen table. Ian, who hadn't thought beyond sweeping up after himself, agreed, seeing these conditions as opportunities to learn more skills.

"These teeth marks, are they mine or Jen's?"

"They are Zack's. He was very mad at Jennie, this is when she was a small baby, she had been crying all night and day from an earache, and he tried to bite her, he was six years old. I caught him before he could chomp down on your sister and explained to him that people don't bite people. He turned right around in his chair and just bit the table.

"I wish we had had a bigger table, there is so much that isn't here, like today," I mused.

"And a lot yet to come. Maybe I'll start on the living room furniture while I'm home?"

"NO! You are old enough to build me a table to match this one to accommodate our growing history, and perhaps one day, a growing family. Take a class in table building when you go back to school."

He ducked his head. I knew I had hit something tender but perhaps he wasn't ready to talk about it yet.

"Ian, you are careful, aren't you? I mean you use condoms; you practice safe sex? I am sitting hospice with a man who is dying of AIDS right now. I can't bear the thought of you having to go through that… even if you were as old as he is, I couldn't bear it."

"How old is he?"

"Eighty-two. You didn't answer my question."

"Yeah, I'm careful. Don't use needles for my drugs, either."

"Ian, it isn't a joke!"

"Yeah. Tell me about this old guy. Why are you sitting with him? Don't you have people for that?"

I told Ian about Horace Cosgrove Drucker III, about his family, Horace the junior and Danielle Denise Drucker, about his house and staff, and his position in the business and social societies of San Francisco. We talked about his garden, and I told Ian about his folly, the pagoda, Cos's shrine, a seat you couldn't get to without wading. Ian was intrigued by the idea. I began to talk about the light in the bedroom and the garden, and how I felt when I sat with Cos. Finally, I told Ian about Aoife and the story Cos had told me of their life.

We sat alone though I heard Peter, and later, Todd, moving about upstairs. Ian put the kettle on again for more tea, and while standing at the stove, he began to tell me about school.

He had presented a piece of work in a class and during the discussion, the teacher had asked him what he was trying to do.

"That's what he said, 'What are you trying to do?' I mean, I'm never trying to do anything, I just do it, and then it is done.

"This guy got all over me because I told him I wasn't trying to do anything, and he said that wasn't good enough.

"Two weeks before I wrote to you, I got this offer from some other guy to buy three of my pieces from the show for thirty-thousand dollars. He's going to put them in some building in New York City, I think. There I was, I'm having this argument with a teacher who says my art will never be important if I don't know what I'm trying to do, and I got almost a year of that teacher's salary from some stranger who seems to think I've done something.

"Why should I stay in school if I can sell my art and do it the way I want to? I mean, doesn't this make me successful?

"You'd think I'd be all happy and stuff, but I got depressed. What am I trying to do? Make money? I never thought of it much. Is what I do meaningless or does someone thinking it is worth a lot of money make it have meaning?

"I guess it sounds real stereotypical, huh? But really, where is the meaning?"

"I think you did the right thing to come home. I'm sorry that you are going through this, but there is also a lot to celebrate in what you've just told me. I think your dad will be a big help for you to talk to about the practical aspects of your decision regarding school. I will tell you I think you should finish your education.

"The meaning of life, Ian, I don't know that anyone ever really knows more than what has meaning to them. This man, Mr. Drucker, I guess he and I have been exploring this same question in a way, except he maybe does know the answer, or maybe he just knows it doesn't matter."

I pulled a white bag of cookies from a hiding place in the spice cupboard. We ate the cookies while I told Ian about Cos's secret life as a spanker. As we talked, Ian pointed out how sad it was that even at the end of his life, Cos could not bring the disparate parts of his life together. The more we talked, the more interest and excitement Ian showed.

"Why don't we hold a wake for him!"

"What?"

"You know, a wake, only we do it while he is still alive. I can organize it. This guy should go out with people around him who know and get him. Todd and I can post online and hit the clubs with flyers and stuff. We'll find his playmates. It'll be like that wedding scene in The Godfather where there is this big party outside, but it is all quiet and reverential inside where people are meeting with the godfather. Come on Mom, this is a cool idea!"

Something about Ian's plan sounded correct, right. I didn't hesitate at all. I agreed to talk to Cos about the idea and about letting the boys help put it together, but I wondered about Hor and DeeDee.

X

<u>Parinibbana Sutta</u>

"All things in the world, whether moving or non-moving, are characterized by disappearance and instability."

I presented Ian's idea to Cos, and he had beamed. Subsequently, at Cos's request, I arranged for him to meet Ian. On that same day, Ian met DeeDee. Ian won her over by not mentioning anything about the spanking; it was only gay friends of her father's to be included as guests. DeeDee, excited to be planning a social event, wielded her influence and her brother Hor had agreed to the affair, with strong vocal reservations. I suspected he realized there was nothing he could do as long as his father was considered competent and in control of the family fortune. Ian masterfully concentrated his message to DeeDee, focusing on the idea of a chic party, and together they planned and executed the entire event. And an extraordinary affair it turned out to be. Todd and Ian posted on sites that Cos listed for them, using his private online moniker.

Cos surprised me by producing a private eye he had on retainer, who helped the boys track down past liaisons. I hadn't met him, but Ian and Todd spoke warmly of him.

The boys went to the trouble of meeting with each respondent and giving them engraved invitations if they exhibited genuine desire and caring to honor The Spankerman, as Cos was known in the online and alternative sexual lifestyle community. It was now mid-March, and planning the event was at its height of activity.

As I arrived one late morning, I saw someone pulling away from the Drucker house. His tanned arm resting in an old Volvo's open driver's side window gave me an odd déjà vu moment as I approached the door of the house.

When Lei opened the door, I felt out of sync, as if I should be able to recall why I recognized the man in the Volvo. Then I remembered: I was being followed. Shaking my head, I entered the house and refocused on my client who had become a friend and confidant.

My only role during this period of planning and organization was to sit with Cos. We listened to the trees outside his window, the leaves gossiping, repeating the rumor told to them by the westerly wind, a message sent in a whisper of regret. This change of season would bring an end. We talked but our conversations were those of memories.

"I began taking Hor to business meetings when he was ten years old. There were times I pulled him out of school to fly with me to Sacramento or Los Angeles. I believed he would learn more watching and listening in on these high-level meetings than he would that day in school. On our way home after a meeting, I would explain my strategy and the outcomes I wanted. He would give me his take on what had occurred.

"When he was a teenager, I gave him a small independent division within one of my holdings and some seed money. Within the year, he had reinvented the division and tripled its profits. Constantly, we would discuss why I was taking a particular stance or moving in a particular direction. I taught him all I know about business. He has simply become more ruthless and driven with experience.

"When he was twenty-five, twenty-six years old, after he got his JD, we did a joint venture. When it was established, I pulled back from the management of the operation and let him have free rein. The next thing I knew, he had changed direction with the firm and hired some questionable people in top-level positions. I came back into the company to regain control and he turned on me, filing a lawsuit. In order to stay out of court and avoid supporting the attorneys for several years, I agreed to let him buy me out of the venture. I never should have done that; I should have fought, but…

"Our relationship has been publicly polite but privately strained ever since. To pull something like that on me! In private, we have had almost no association at all, except for what DeeDee demands of us both. This just eats at me, he should apologize. To disrespect me! If we were a mafia family, he would be dead."

"Why didn't you take DeeDee to meetings?"

"I did, but she would become bored, and this told me she would not grow to be a strong businesswoman. She learned to play tennis instead."

"When you asked for her take on a meeting, what would DeeDee say?"

"As I said, she would be bored in the meetings so in our conversations afterward, she would be sullen."

"Yes, but what would she say in answer to your questions?"

"When she would discuss it at all, she would understand what had happened and my strategy, she often saw points I did not or noticed something key about one of the other persons. Why?"

"DeeDee struck me as shrewd underneath her layers of trivial chitchat. She is the one I... well, never mind, it just struck me, is all. Where was she when all this corporate fighting between you and Hor was going on?"

"She was my constant companion, she comforted me and stood by me. She tried repeatedly to bring Hor and me together. She was, during this time, my confidant..."

"What did you groom Hor to do, if not what he did? He had to do what he did, don't you see that?"

"He had to betray me?"

"He didn't betray you—he proved himself. He will always be your son, your first child, that is just the way it is for both of you. You trained him to be who he is. You taught him to win against everyone but that would never be good enough for him because he would still be your boy, under your wing. You have such a strong personality, how could he ever establish himself separate from you? He had to do what he did to prove he was a man, I mean, a grown independent person and someone for you to respect. Don't you see that? Until he conquered the king—you—he would never be an adult psychologically. I don't know what DeeDee's motivation was for whatever she may have done in all of this, but it all seems like pretty straightforward Freudian fodder to me.

"You must complete this. It is unfinished business for all three of you. You must welcome him back into your heart. I am not saying forgive him, I am saying come to a place of understanding where forgiveness is not necessary."

"I might suggest the same to you," Cos commented.

The next day, I was thinking about my last conversation with Drucker as I left the salon near my office. I could almost smell the change of season, and everything seemed bright and reborn. I felt a bit lazy, strolling in the afternoon sun, and thought about stopping for a coffee or even a bite of lunch.

I had traveled about a block and a half when I heard a voice behind me.

"You are either a concert pianist or you've just had your nails done."

I turned around to see the man I only knew from fleeting sightings since January. He was taller than I had thought, and better looking. He was standing about six feet away from me, a distance that seemed calculated to be non-threatening. His Hawaiian shirt fit snugly over a powerful frame. His left arm was slightly more tanned than his right, likely from hanging out a Volvo window so frequently. Chinos and casual loafers completed his outfit. His dark hair fell in untidy waves.

"You've been following me," I remarked, then looking at my hands, "I've just come from the nail salon. I can't play piano; I wish I could. Why did you say that?"

"Only a pianist would carry their hands the way you do when you walk. It is a very distinct mannerism. That, or you were a bit concerned about ruining a fresh manicure. It is part of my job to notice trivial things and make deductions."

He smiled so charmingly that I gestured for him to walk with me as I turned to continue down the sidewalk toward my office. We walked side-by-side in a comfortable silence for a few moments. I noticed he shortened his stride to match mine. When I glanced at him, he noticed, and that charming smile appeared again.

"Why?" I asked.

"Why have I been following you? I was hired to get to know about you. I am a private investigator.

"Why did I speak to you just now? I've succeeded in getting to know about you, and you intrigue me.

"I'm guessing you're hungry, I know I am. Can I buy you a burger?"

We had just come alongside the restaurant, A Lampreia, known as one of the best hamburger joints in the entire San Francisco Bay Area. I was hungry, hadn't I only moments before been considering lunch? I needed to assess who this man was and what he might know about me—and why. We were standing still outside the restaurant; he was just waiting, no impatience or fidgeting, just quietly waiting while I thought the situation through. I looked up into his eyes and nodded my "Yes." He immediately reached for the door, opening it so I could pass through first.

Inside, he gestured to what appeared to be the host and held up two fingers. She nodded, leading us past an opulent long bar and through an arch into a room away from the front windows and door. The wall on one side was lined with plush red leather booths, the opposite wall was brick with the restaurant's logo, a large firefly inside a circle, painted in the center. Against that wall were two tops whose chairs were also leather, but a muted light brown. She dropped two menus on the table and told us our waiter would be right with us.

"Is a booth alright, Ms. Mae?"

I nodded again, holding my menu unopened in my hands.

"Who are you? Who do you work for? Why me?"

He looked down at the table for a moment and chuckled. Then looking directly at me, he began to explain.

"My name is Clarence. I'm a PI, like I explained, but I only have two clients, both of whom have me on retainer. One is an extremely prominent defense attorney who specializes in murder cases. My job is to solve the murder, showing that his client could not have committed it, and if I am lucky, finding the person who did commit the murder. My other client you already know quite well, Mr. Drucker. It is he who has me investigating and following you. You should probably know I am exceptionally good at my job."

The server showed up at that moment. Neither of us had looked at the menus but we both knew what we wanted, a double cheese bacon burger with half fries and half onion rings, and a chocolate shake. This was the standard order for almost everyone when at A Lampreia. Once the server had gone, we again sat in silence, he calmly waiting for me to process, me trying, and for the moment failing, to think rationally about what seemed an invasion of my privacy, a violation. After a while, I took a deep breath and let it out, relaxing my body. I was perplexed by my lack of outrage or fear. He took the breath as a sign to open the dialogue again.

"Ms. Mae, would you like me to tell you what I have shared with Mr. Drucker?"

I nodded, bracing myself, my ever-present headache began to poke around the corners of my anxiety.

"I am not following you constantly, Mr. Drucker gave me very strict guidelines. I was to discover your typical weekly routines—home, office, offsite meetings, grocery shopping, nails every two weeks," he smiled gently, looking me directly in the eyes, "that sort of thing. Since establishing how you move through your days, I've simply been watching, observing from afar, for any activities that deviate from that usual routine. Mr. Drucker said I was not to look into your online activities or intrude on your correspondence. I did a background check for him. Oddly, I found no childhood history or family for Letty Mae using your social security information, and you do not have a passport. I couldn't even find a birth certificate issued to a Letty Mae who could be sitting here with me."

He fell silent, waiting for me, watching to see if he should continue. Our server showed up with our food, relieving some of the tension that was closing in on me.

"But here I am, shall we enjoy our meal?"

"Absolutely. May I ask you to tell me a bit about yourself growing up? Any truth you are willing to share with me. Nothing of our conversation today will go into any report or file. You have my word."

He picked up his burger with both hands and took a bite, wiping the edge of his lip with his pinky finger. His eyes were gentle, kind even, and for reasons I did not understand, I trusted him, at least as much as I trusted Peter.

"I grew up in Oklahoma."

He chuckled as he shook his head. "No, you didn't. I can't hear any Oklahoma in your voice at all, and I would hear it if it were ever there. Try again—truth only, this time."

"OK, I grew up in Montana." I paused, waiting to see what he would do. All he did was nod to continue.

"My family is all dead, but when I was little, we lived in a small city in Montana and spent time on a family ranch during holidays. I had no siblings."

He made a buzzer sound and waved a french fry at me.

"Try again, you're the oldest kid."

"I had a younger sister. She died before she reached adulthood."

I stopped there; he didn't need to know about Kelly's suicide. I thought I had sacrificed myself to save her, but in the end, I saved no one.

"Why did you decide to talk with me today? What has changed that you would blow your cover? Is that the correct term? 'Blow your cover?' Why are we having lunch? What do you want?"

"Nothing nefarious, I'm not here to threaten or blackmail you. Promise! I know you figured out you were being followed, it seemed only fair of me to let you know that was happening. Like I said before, you intrigue me.

"Oh, the ranch in Montana, you grew up around working horses, that is why you carry your hands and arms the way you do!"

He snapped his fingers twice in a sort of celebration. His face was like a little kid's, one who had just solved a puzzle. He was way too smart and I was getting nervous. I needed to think of a way to throw him off my scent. I had secrets to keep.

"What is it you think you know about my current life? What have you learned by following me?"

"I know that you've been having more sexual encounters than your staff or husband might suspect. You are going to a lot of trouble hiding your dalliances. No judgment, just a fact.

"Mostly, you are alone, working long hours running that hospice of yours, and now with Drucker demanding your time, no other social life to speak of as far as I can tell. You don't seem to have any best gal friends, and your husband only leaves the house for work. He is dull, but seems like a good guy. Did you hear what happened to that guy in the wheelchair right after your date night with him?"

I was looking down at my food, listening to him. At his question, I looked up, shaking my head. Something had happened to Moe? Clarence didn't get everything right; Peter was distant right now, but not dull. It was our marriage that was dull—maybe.

"What about the other guy who is following me? Is he your partner? If I have so little in my life, why does it take two of you to follow me?"

Clarence stopped eating. His eyes grew a bit wider and he studied my face. He was looking for a tell, something that would let him know if I had just lied to him, or was pulling his leg, or whatever. I waited. I know how to sit in silence. I thought about random people I had noticed in the past few months, deciding on what details I could use to embellish my story.

"I don't have a partner, I work alone. I am the only one who has been following you. What are you talking about?"

I made a buzzer sound like the one he had made earlier.

"Try again, you do have a partner. I've seen him, just like I saw you. An older white guy, dressed like a hippie with a very large, hooked nose and longish gray hair."

I was looking directly at Clarence. I concentrated on the memory of that man I saw sitting on a curb watching the boy in the umbrella. He was real, I was telling the truth—I had to believe I was telling the truth. Clarence and I held each other's gaze for a bit longer than was comfortable. In the end, I allowed my expression to change to quizzical and took a sip of my milkshake.

"Are you saying he doesn't work with you? Who was he, then?"

Clarence's eyes narrowed. Did I have him? Did he believe there was a second person following me? He shrugged and ate another fry. Then he asked me what kind of music I liked and we continued our conversation the way new friends do when getting to know one another. The lunch wound down slowly and when we left the restaurant, we found ourselves walking naturally together, chatting, sharing inconsequential stories, even laughing. At some point, I called my office and told them I was taking a personal afternoon off. I mentioned my headache, which by now everyone at Haven knew was plaguing me.

I couldn't remember the last time I spent a day in pleasant company with no agenda. Our conversations ranged from politics to memories of family holidays. I shared stories of my kids, even of Peter from better times. He shared what it was like growing up in Iowa, coming out to California to attend UC Berkeley, and ultimately making a life in San Francisco.

We found a bench in a park and sat for a while, people-watching and making up stories about them while they took advantage of the sunshine and warmth of the day.

"Your stories are based on knowledgeable observation," I laughed. "Mine are pure fantasy."

He reached out, taking my hand that had been resting in my lap, into both of his.

"Occupational hazard, I guess. Fantasy doesn't have much of a role in investigation.

"I enjoyed our afternoon. I appreciate you trusting me enough… but I have to check in with my attorney in about twenty minutes."

"Will you and your partner continue following me?"

He didn't answer for a moment, again studying my face as I gazed directly at him until a dog barked and I looked toward the sound. I kept my expression as neutral as possible, but I noticed the doubt in his eyes. I was convinced that he believed I thought he had a partner.

The air was getting a bit cooler, as it often does in the late afternoon in the Bay Area. The park had emptied. The colors of the grass and trees had changed, dampening down, preparing for the fog to roll over the hills and hide the colors in the flower beds. Clarence continued to hold my hand in both of his, lightly, their warmth spreading to my entire body.

"I am giving Drucker a final report tomorrow, I won't be following you again. But I would like to see you again. I would like to spend time with you. I would like to…"

His voice trailed off and again we sat in silence. Then he leaned forward very carefully, calmly, lifting one hand to brush a wayward strand of hair from my cheek before cradling my head as he gave me a deep lingering kiss. His hand still held me as he slowly released me from the kiss, then he leaned forward again and kissed my forehead. Letting go of my hand and my head, he stood up, looking down at me.

"When?" I asked.

Two days later, I found myself traveling down Van Ness Avenue in San Francisco. I began looking for parking once I arrived near Aquatic Cove. I had to circle around multiple blocks before I found a spot opening up near the bus transfer station.

I affixed a red felt hat with a wide brim to my head as I got out of the car. The day before, I visited Saks Fifth Avenue and purchased a suit in red wool, a pencil skirt and fitted waist jacket with big buttons. I visited the shoe department and bought matching red pattern stilettos and a purse. On the way out, I found the hat and some cute crochet gloves. I wanted a change of pace—I never wear hats or red. The whole shopping trip had cost more than I am usually comfortable spending, but I paid in cash and threw away the receipts. There was no buyer's remorse return option.

When I finished adjusting the hat, I took a quick glance in the car's side mirror. The woman in the reflection looked great, but the entire outfit was far out of my style and comfort zone. Definitely not me, still, it was right for this moment.

I walked the few blocks to Clarence's building on Chestnut Street, allowing myself to feel hopeful anticipation. He lived in one of several modern towers that lined this portion of town. His apartment likely had five times the value of my suburban home. Whatever Drucker and that attorney paid him, it was substantial, or he was from a wealthy family.

I checked the address I had written on a scrap of paper to make sure I was going into the complex through the correct doors. As I approached the entrance, I carefully watched the pavement where I was walking to avoid stumbling in my heels. There was no door attendant on duty at the desk, so I went directly to the bank of elevators. When the elevator doors opened, I was startled to find that the interior walls were all mirrors. Thank goodness for my hat! Looking at myself repeated endlessly from every angle would be excruciating! I kept my head down and used my hand to lower the brim even more across my face as the elevator ascended to the fifteenth floor.

When the elevator again opened its doors, I found myself in a drab narrow hall lined with pale wooden doors on one side, each with a peephole just below its brass apartment number. On the opposite wall were mid-century graphic art prints creating a parade of muted pink, blue, and beige splashes and geometric forms. I found Clarence's apartment number easily and pushed the small white doorbell button I found just below the mezuzah affixed to the door frame. The chimes I heard in response reminded me of something from my childhood, something I couldn't quite place, but the hint of the memory made me shiver.

I heard his footfall as he approached the door.

Clarence opened the door and stood in his hallway, his extremely fit torso shown off by the spotless fitted white shirt he was wearing. When he saw me, that same charming smile spread across his face. He stepped to the side and waved me in. A mirrored wall lined the left side of the hallway and continued into the open living and dining area. To the right, there was a closet and then the small, but fully equipped kitchen, which was also part of the open concept. As we moved further into the apartment, I saw an archway on the left leading to what I presumed was a bedroom and bath. The external wall of the apartment boasted floor to ceiling windows and sliding doors that led to a balcony running the full length of the apartment. The wall on the far right was another mirrored wall. Looking in either direction, infinite reflections of the room and its occupants were repeated. For a moment, I felt a bit queasy because it seemed like everything was moving.

Light poured in through the windows looking out on the Aquatic Cove breakwater and the entire San Francisco Bay from the edge of Fort Mason, sweeping across to Ghirardelli Square, and ending at the boats of Fisherman's Wharf. The whole apartment was light and reflection that pushed you to look outward toward the sparkling water and Santa Rosa County in the distance. It was stunning!

Clarence must have been used to the reaction of people first entering his home. He simply stood back and let me adjust to the surroundings. When I was able to focus back on the interior, I saw that everything was decorated in a sleek uncluttered midcentury modern, staying with the theme of the building itself. The colors were all blue and white with lighter wood tones, again reflecting the outside world of sky and bay. I noticed that the small round dining table was set for lunch and there was an open bottle of Napa Zinfandel on the kitchen counter next to two balloon glasses. I could smell goulash bubbling in the kitchen.

"Wow," I said softly.

"Life has treated me pretty well overall. Would you like some wine, or I have sparkling water?"

I indicated the wine, and he poured us both a glass. We settled on his couch, looking out at the view. I was getting used to the mirrored walls and the endless possibilities they displayed, but felt more comfortable with the stability of the panoramic view. He explained that while he made a good living as a private investigator, his family in Iowa had owned several manufacturing businesses in the state, exporting everything from air conditioners to tractors down to Mexico. Eventually, the family sold the companies to the unions, who made them cooperatives. Clarence, being the only son, inherited the fortune. He was conservative with the inheritance, investing in relatively safe stocks and high-yield bonds. He tried to live on what he earned from his investigative work. While I encouraged him to talk about himself, he never once tried to dominate the conversation. I felt like he was offering information about himself to balance things between us, as an offering to apologize for following me and invading my privacy.

After we finished our first glass of wine, he poured us both a second glass and served lunch. The goulash was delicious, and we talked about recipes and current affairs. The conversation did not include the Drucker family or my work. It was relaxing, enjoyable, and, for the moment, I felt safe.

When we finished lunch, we left the dishes on the table and at my request moved with our wine to the balcony. I wanted to feel the sun on my face and escape from the mirrors. The balcony was narrow and unfurnished, so we stood at the railing. I glanced down and confirmed that, as I thought, the only thing below was the parking garage that was perhaps three levels—one underground, one at street level, and the rooftop. The rooftop was empty of vehicles, but I guessed that was because residents were still at work.

I was taking a sip of my almost empty glass when Clarence brought up the subject of my other meetings with men.

"You know," he said, "It is the oddest thing but that creep, Marty, the one you met here in the City? Did you read the news article?"

"Oh, let's not ruin our afternoon talking about him! Please, may I have a bit more wine? Here, I will hold your glass while you get me a refill."

I took his glass and handed him mine. I knew he would circle back to the subject but first, he would politely fetch me my wine. He put on some music while he was inside. Sister Rosetta Tharpe began insisting in the background that it was Nobody's Fault But Mine. I could feel my headache pushing its way into my brain. I no longer felt safe. As much as I liked and even respected Clarence, he had violated my privacy, he had broken trust with me before we even met.

I had my purse with me and quickly took a pill out of a small vial I had tucked inside, just in case it was needed. When he returned, we exchanged wine glasses.

"Oh, I think this is a bit more than I can manage. Let me even the score."

I poured some of the wine from my glass into his until we had an equal amount. Then I saluted him with a toast.

"To secrets and private eyes." I smiled. "Lunch was so nice, this entire afternoon has been nice. Thank you so much."

I chattered on about my kids and the upcoming event in honor of Cos. It was lovely to watch him listen so intently, with real interest, as he sipped his last glass of wine. After a while, I could see that he was getting tired from standing on the balcony. I had him sit down in a chair that I brought out to him. Then I cleaned up my dishes, washing them and my wine glass. I dried everything I washed and put things away. I pushed my chair at the dining table in and made sure that the coaster I had used when we were sitting on the couch earlier was placed back in the stack from where it came.

By the time I finished tidying up after myself, Clarence was genuinely drowsy, but easily managed. I quickly took the chair from the balcony, putting it back where I had found it and placing the legs exactly where they had been before. Then I quietly left the apartment, making sure the door was closed, and walked to the elevator.

I guess I was a little tipsy from the wine, so instead of heading home, I drove across the bridge to Sausalito. There is a historic bar along the main strip that I have always loved. I found a parking spot some distance away. It was so sunny and warm that I decided to leave my hat, gloves, and suit jacket behind. Luckily, I had some more practical shoes in the car, so I changed out of the red stilettos and walked the half mile to the bar. Once inside, I found the ladies' room and changed into a more comfortable pair of tan slacks I kept in my car trunk. I enjoyed a cocktail and watched the tourists come and go, chatted a bit with the bartender, paid with my credit card, and finally headed home to Peter. Coming back into the City I made sure to get a receipt for my toll.

I liked Clarence so much, but I wouldn't see him again. He kept prying. I forgave him, I thought it must just be in his nature. That was why he was such a good investigator. My time with Drucker had changed me though. I wanted to explore my relationship with Peter, find the healing that would bring us back to intimacy. I couldn't risk my family to any further nosiness from outsiders. Still, I found myself tearing up when I thought of how it ended with Clarence.

Before I completely left the City, I pulled to the curb below an overpass and rolled my driver's window down. I gave ten dollars to one of the homeless women near my car. I also gave her the entire outfit I had worn that day, including the shoes. I could never wear it again. She giggled like a schoolgirl as she crammed each item into her shopping cart, the hat balanced alarmingly on her head.

As I pulled away, watching her in my rearview mirror, my headache faded to nothing.

XI
<u>Parinibbana Sutta</u>
"As a potter's clay vessels,
large and small, fired and unfired,
all end up broken,
so too life heads to death. "

It was early morning on the day of the wake. Rain, which had threatened for days, had finally come in the night and like a honky-tonk lover, departed at first light of day. I sat in my office, sipping coffee and looking out the window behind my desk, waiting for the magic that always came. I could see people walking to their cars and the bus stops, hunched as if it were still raining, all headed to daily chores.

Only I saw, just there on the stump across the street in the empty lot, a red-tailed hawk. He was often there in the mornings. He had caught my eye with the flurry of his wings as he snagged his prey on the hillside of mustard behind the business complex. He fed, as unconscious of the urban action around him as it was of him. He had little natural competition in this setting, but he would be gone soon. The stump where he sat used to be a tree. In some future tomorrow, it too will disappear, and a strip mall will rise in its place. This was not a new song but for the hawk, it may have been the last time it would be sung.

When I arrived at the Drucker house later that morning, I found the florist had come and gone, infusing every room with large exotic yellow and white flowers. The arrangements were unusual, having the stamp of Ian's creative instincts. The caterers were setting up the brunch in the formal dining room. In another room, I could hear DeeDee's voice in full command, apparently outlining the timing of the lunch and tea service. It was to be a day of food. I stuck my head into the front parlor to find a quartet unpacking and tuning their instruments. They introduced themselves as members of the San Francisco

Opera's orchestra, the first of three such quartets playing throughout the day.

Ian explained that the wake was divided into shifts beginning with a breakfast for business associates of the Druckers' enterprises, some flying in from Europe and the Caymans for the occasion. A transition to church members, family friends, and the City's high society would occur for lunch. In the afternoon, high tea would be offered for extended family, and finally, in the evening, wine and hors d'oeuvres for those persons responding to Ian and Todd's outreach. DeeDee had provided engraved invitations for each group. In all, there were three catering companies and any number of liveried staff. The entire event was downstairs with strolling available in the springtime garden. Access to the upstairs was to be monitored by Todd. Visitors from each group would be limited to those that could be seen during Cos's higher energy points during the day. Visits would be with one or occasionally two people at a time. The nurses and

I would monitor Cos's well-being throughout the day.

I went down to the kitchen and snagged a Krispy Kreme from a box delivered to the household staff, while Lei—or was it Long—cleaned the hem of my blazer where I had spilt the last of my latte on my drive from the office.

Once he finished drying my jacket, I went upstairs to join Cos. When I entered his room, I was surprised to find Ian sitting with him instead of one of Haven's hospice workers. Ian was pale but smiling, and Cos seemed to have just finished chuckling. After greeting me with a kiss on the cheek and a hug, Ian said goodbye to Cos with a slight bow and left the room.

"Are you ready for this?"

"The greatest joy is in giving and the greatest gift is the manner in which one receives. I am days past ready and am glad today has finally arrived."

Hor had been stationed in the study during the first wave, after greeting the bulk of the arrivals. Only those guests having a long association with Cos were scheduled to have time with him. The business associates would briefly pay their respects before they were ushered from Cos's bedroom into the study. Many of the guests simply joined Hor in the study, meeting three and four at a time.

This was the formal passing of the family torch.

I was told that during lunch, DeeDee managed the family friends, making sure that everyone felt included and had a chance to express their thoughts. Hor had joined the party downstairs, circulating and falling into his new role as the head of the Drucker family. Weeks before, Cos designed his son's responsibilities for the day after the two of them had a long conversation behind closed doors, first alone and then with attorneys and DeeDee included. It would seem that the two Drucker siblings were flexible enough to deny the reality of certain members of the guest list as long as their economic concerns and standing in powerful social circles were secured. I wasn't privy to what went on during those conversations and meetings, but perhaps some healing and resolution occurred.

The nurse and I carefully monitored Cos and once or twice delayed visitors outside his door. It was an exhausting day for all of us and I watched Cos become increasingly frail as the day wore on, but his resolve and eagerness for the event uplifted him.

Then it was a time of rest for Cos; most of the friends and church members had left and the few family members were arriving and being served tea. Looking down on the garden, now that it was the end of March, was like looking down from heaven onto the clouds. All the trees were in blossom, their white or pale pink petals flying off, sometimes swirling in eddies then blown apart, as if exploded, to float capriciously to the ground. Everywhere you looked, there were islands of color: iris, snowdrop, tulip, and crocus. The elms seemed cloaked in diamonds. The entire circus of budding life was reproduced in the mirroring pond.

"Oh, I see Ian is in the garden."

"I suggested he take a turn when he had the opportunity today. Can you move me to the chair so we can watch him together? I would relish having a better view of my garden."

"I wasn't… I suppose I am watching him, aren't I? Let's see if we can get you to this chair without calling anyone else."

Cos had grown so frail and light that I could lift him myself. The distance being short, he was able to get to the chair with my help and I pushed it closer to the window, removed the comforter from his bed, and had him gather it around himself like a shawl. In silence, we watched Ian stand by the pond at its widest point. He seemed to be looking at the pagoda but after a while, his focus changed. I looked down at Cos, who had leaned forward, reminding me of a child about to be handed a birthday gift, his eagerness almost contagious.

I returned my gaze to Ian in the garden, he was removing his shoes. A moment later, he stepped into the pond, but no—it was some trick of the eye. He was standing on top of the water, his feet still visible above the surface! Next to me, Cos clapped his hands, grinning so wide his lips began to bleed slightly.

Ian was moving his head like a hound casting for a scent. He took another step and paused, four rapid steps paralleling the shoreline of the pond, and he stopped again. He continued in a meandering pattern, walking on the water, one or two steps and then four or five. At first, the objective wasn't clear but suddenly I realized that he was drawing ever closer to the pagoda.

"My god, Ian!"

"Your boy has found out my secret. I thought he would, he is the first to see the possibility. He is walking on water."

Cos was rocking in his seat now, his hands still raised for clapping, humor burbling from him like the stream from the waterfall below.

Ian reached the pagoda, standing on the water just off its shore. He did not move for a minute, and then he turned and deftly retraced his path back to the edge of the pond. I could see his smile even from my aerial perch.

"Your son is a discoverer, not a conqueror. Do you see he respected the pagoda, being satisfied with having solved the riddle? He is quite unique, but I am sure you know that about him.

"When he gets back to the house, call him up here. I want him to take me out to my pagoda."

"You want to go out? Are you sure? Perhaps tomorrow would be better once you've had a chance to rest from today."

"No, today. Tell DeeDee that I will come down to greet the family and say my goodbyes, and from there, your son will take me to the pagoda. Come, Letty, you will accompany me. Don't you want to see the view from there?"

Ian and Todd, between them, carried Cos down the curving staircase. Less than two dozen family members milled in the front parlor and entry. DeeDee and Hor stood beside their father as he spoke to each nephew and niece, and the few cousins that made up their family connections.

At his request, DeeDee and Hor joined the sojourn to the garden. The boys moved slowly, stopping frequently so Cos could feed his koi and savor each element of his garden. As we stepped into the pond, Ian led the way as Todd cradled Cos in his arms, the rest of us trailing after in an odd, barefooted game of follow the leader. Even standing in the water and feeling the hard cool surface on which we walked, the eye could not easily discern on what we were walking.

"Follow this young man carefully, the walkway is narrow. I brought in artisans from Iran to design and build this for me. It is a crystal ramp. They are irregular blocks a little over a foot in depth, some are larger but all rest less than one inch below the surface of the water. In a few spots, there are gaps in the path to allow the koi access to the entire pond. These blocks were carved to reflect light and water perfectly during all but the darkest night; they are virtually invisible below the water's surface. Only Lei knows of this path, he is charged with keeping the surface perfectly clean.

"Tell us how you found the way, Ian?"

"The rocks. They did not fit with the rest of the garden's design."

"Yes! This garden was deliberate—the design layout, I mean—each component having a connection to all the other components. So, you knew it must have some other meaning or purpose?"

"They dot the 'i,' " replied Ian.

We reached the pagoda; Todd carried Cos up to the low seat in the center. Cos said his thanks to the two boys and asked them to see to the guests in the house.

I had brought down a quilt with me; I finished wrapping and tucking it around Cos's shoulders and lap, checking the temperature of his skin in the process. Hor and DeeDee settled onto the ceramic seats at his feet, and I stepped to the edge of the pagoda to allow them some privacy. As I stepped back, I watched Ian and Todd retrace the path back to the shore.

"When I was able, I would come out here and just sit, talking to your mother. This is where she is, and it is where I want to be. I want you to keep the house and gardens in the family, even if it means converting it to a family archive open to the public. Or live in it, but keep it in the family's holdings so your mother and I can rest here undisturbed for as long as is possible."

"Mommy is here? The funeral, the crypt… we thought she was in the crypt!"

"When was the last time you were there to visit her? No, never mind, this isn't about guilt. It may not matter where our ashes lie, but they must be somewhere, and I would like mine here. Your mother is here, but I also took some of her ashes and spread them in Japan in the place she was a child.

"In this whole puzzle that people call life, the one thing I truly fear is not being there when one of you needs me. I know… I know you are well into middle age. You are there for each other and I am comforted. I hope you will remember the good feelings we had as well as you remember anything else.

"I have only a few more things to say. Please listen.

"Don't expect anyone to be perfect, not even yourself.

"DeeDee, I am proud of you. You have style. You use fashion, rather than follow fashion. You are truthful to yourself, and you live in that truth. You need to teach that to Hor.

"I only recently came to understand how quick a mind you have and how strong a will. It is shameful that I did not know this before now.

"Hor, I was wrong in the world I presented to you. Courage, real courage, is the ability to stand by your beliefs but not be a fanatic. It is having an open mind. Bravery is a fool's word. Courage is being able to walk away. If you can walk away without a fight, do it, but if you must fight to walk away, do so.

"Hor has courage enough for you both, this is what you can learn from him, DeeDee.

"Both of you should be proud. You have achieved a great deal in your lives, and you have done it on your own merits. Just don't be afraid to ask for help, especially from each other, when you find your limits.

"My children, we have had our moments and certainly there have been many times we haven't liked one another, but I have always loved you. I love you now, and if you look for it, you will find my love continues the rest of your lives."

The three continued to talk until I could tell from the timbre of his replies that Cos needed to return to his bed. I began to call for Ian and Todd, but Hor waved at me to stop. The temperature had dropped, so we left the comforter a cocoon around Cos as his son and daughter carried him along the hidden path and back to his upstairs sanctuary. As we returned to the garden path, I understood the key to finding our way to the pagoda, Cos's shrine.

"It is Aoife! The pagoda is your place of peace, and love is how you get there; it is Aoife. The boulders dot the 'i.' "

Reaching out from the quilted cocoon and his son's embrace, he affectionately patted my arm, his laugh sending him into a fit of painful coughing, though his smile remained.

The nurse waited outside the room while they said their goodbyes.

I wandered back downstairs to fix myself a plate of food. I found Ian setting up a votive stand, but I did not disturb him because my attention was drawn to the men who now populated the downstairs, most not speaking to one another. They ranged in age from the mid-twenties to a few my own age or a bit older. The majority of the men seemed to be professionals, a few looked like they might be professors. I thought I recognized the appointed head of one of the City's major departments and a member of a Bay Area Board of Regents whom I had met once when I was part of a presenting panel. I saw several of them shyly acknowledging one another. The music was being played by what I guessed must be the third and final quartet. I couldn't put my finger on what they were playing, but it was clearly Mozart. I nodded and smiled my appreciation to them as I passed through the room, receiving the same in return. A few waiters still circulated, assuring that each person had a drink and offering trays full of luscious delicacies.

Since I had missed the more substantive meals, I went to the kitchen to see what might be available. Most of the catering staff had left. Sying, or was it Long, was alone in the kitchen. He fixed me a plate of luncheon leftovers and explained that the rest of the house staff had also gone home. Their employer had said his farewells to all of them when they first arrived in the early morning. They all expected to see him again tomorrow, I was told, and several had been puzzled by today's events, finding the entire matter so foreign to their own cultural experiences. When my meal was done, I returned to my bedside post. Hor and DeeDee had left the house.

When it was time, the evening's guests were ushered upstairs, each entering the room with a burning votive candle. The candles and the fire provided a flickering relief to the darkness of the room. The curtains were open to the night, creating a reflected canvas of disembodied flames burning in the black emptiness of the Bay, each separate and alone. In the room, the tiny lights quavered uneasily, perhaps a reflection of each man's internal feelings.

From the far corner of the room, Todd's single pure voice began to sing Ave Maria, a benediction on us all, the last note resonating in the room like a Tibetan meditation bell. Near the fireplace, a less practiced voice began to sing hesitantly in the stillness.

"Yesterday, all my troubles seemed so far away, now it looks as if they're here to stay. Oh, I believe..."

One by one, the other voices joined in this song. As it wound down, a flat baritone began "What would you think if I sang out of tune..." By the time they began A Hard Day's Night, there was a palpable atmosphere of joy, and everyone had gathered closer to the bed. Leaving their candles behind here and there about the room, each man came forward and grasped Cos's hand in turn, then left the room until only Ian, Todd, and I remained with Cos. They said their goodnights, receiving words of gratitude from Cos. Ian promised he would see me at home and they too left, arm in arm.

XII
<u>Parinibbana Sutta</u>
"Stop now! Do not speak!
Time is passing.
I am about to cross over."

I sat on the edge of the bed, holding his hand. Psoriasis and warts battled each other for supremacy. His voice was the damp rustle of reeds on the stream's banks, full of frogs and their creature foods. The house was empty now; only a nurse and one of his retainers lingered downstairs in the kitchen. We were kept company by Ravel's Mother Goose Suite; Cos had it played at some point during every recent visit, at which time he would focus only on the music. This night, it was just a friend in the room with us, keeping watch. The candles placed on all the surfaces of the room had burned low and sputtered in the background, the lost and weeping children of the fire that still blazed in the corner.

"Lisa, open the drawer and pull out what you find there."

I let his use of Lisa go; what was the point of correcting him? Opening the drawer, I lifted out an odd satchel just bigger than a binder. It was a thin unstructured bag made of deep burgundy velvet, inside of which I could feel the distinct shape of a manila file folder. As I placed it on his lap he took my hand tightly in his.

"Open it but before you do, promise me…"

"What, Cos, shall I call the nurse?"

"Promise me that when you see the contents of this, you will not leave the room. Promise me you will stay until I have no more to say."

"Yes, of course, you have my attention. Do you think you can shock me after all we have talked about? I am going to stay the night with you."

"Lisa, I have your word?"

"Yes, yes."

He let go of my hand and I took the bag, first stroking the softness of the material, noting dots of a moth's work and gently worn spots. There was the scent of cedar and sandalwood in the material so faint it must have been from some long ago association. I lifted the flap and pulled out the contents, setting a manila folder and a vial and syringe on the comforter. I looked at him, wondering what he wanted me to do.

"Set the morphine aside for the moment, look at the folder."

I opened the folder to find three pieces of newspaper torn from recent editions. I placed them on the folder to give myself a firmer surface and angled it toward the fire so I could see well enough to read.

The room froze. No fire burned. The failing flames of any remaining candles ceased movement. I felt myself telescoping to fill the room, like Alice in the rabbit's house. I was looking at an obituary. I lifted it to reveal a short article reporting a death, under which I found one of those society page columns reporting on parties that have the names being dropped in bold. One paragraph was circled with a red pencil.

"You will read them?"

I nodded.

SAN FRANCISCO — Moe Potholder, JD, PhD, 61, of San Francisco, died

Dec 14, 1941 – Jan 14, 2002

Moe Potholder, 61, of San Francisco died Jan. 14 in his home.

Mr. Potholder, raised in Palo Alto and an alumnus of Stanford, practiced Law as a partner in the San Francisco offices of Haw, Learman and Korkosky for 15 years. He left Haw, Learman and Korkosky in 1988 due to illness and went into a limited private practice. Mr. Potholder is survived by his children, Michael Potholder of Napa, Rebecca Hoffman of Palo Alto, and Melissa Epstein of Walnut Creek; grandchild Martha Epstein; brother Jason Potholder and sister Rachel Appelbaum. No services are planned; donations may be made to the Multiple Sclerosis Society.

SAN JOSE PLANET – Body Found in Ravine Identified

Staff Reporter

SAN BRUNO — Marty Sinatri, CEO of HuRe Systems, and a resident of Sunnyvale, has been identified as the man found dead Feb. 28 in a ravine off the ridge trail on San Bruno Mountain. This is the first death of its kind recorded on San Bruno Mountain. Alfred Newman, one of several homeless squatters who live in the park woodlands, found the body.

The park has had a growing number of squatters despite ongoing park management efforts. When police first arrived on the scene, it was thought that Sinatri was the victim of a mugging, but further examination did not bear out this assumption.

As reported in this paper in February, HuRe Systems is in extreme financial trouble and has pending lawsuits.

Authorities suggested Sinatri may have been suffering from depression and on medication when he went hiking alone on San Bruno Mountain, and later confirmed that alcohol was found in his system.

The cause of death is reported to be a blow to his head caused during a fall into the ravine and has been ruled an accident.

Sinatri was 49 years old and was originally from Manhattan, New York. He is survived by his parents Martin and Marie Sinatri, residents of New York.

PALO ALTO CHAT

PALO ALTO — The annual dinner dance held by the Palo Alto Actors' Theater was hosted this year by Bonnie Cross (pictured here with her husband Alan Cross and their daughter Anna Michelle Cross). Mrs. Cross is newly active in the theater company joining her husband, a longtime member, as a vigorous advocate of community theater. The dinner dance was a gala affair in the tradition of Noël

Coward, whose plays provided the theme for the evening. Alan Cross will be debuting as a director this coming season and looks forward to working on the effort with his wife of 25 years.

"When we first met, I asked you to be my midwife. Do you remember?

"I am tired, and I keep trying to sleep but I cannot. I want to find Aoife. I want to leave this place and awaken in my garden. My life is over, but does not end. Thanks to you, I have come to a place where all the pieces in my personal puzzle are present, and fit. I am done but cannot conclude. Midwives sometimes expedite a delivery when required.

"Dying is dying, of course, and it is messy business. Birth is messy and beautiful, so is death. Everyone tries too hard—my family, the nurses and doctors, my household. You are so self-involved, you see only the beauty, and remind me that I am alive, but I am dead. I am both. You are my pool of tranquility, even as I help you find it for yourself. This is why you are here. You are going to become my hands, my will. You will be my last vestige of control.

"Lisa, will you be my midwife?

"You are safe. My private investigator only knew pieces of this, you would have been safe regardless, but then you stepped in… I was the one who pulled it together because I knew what I was looking for. You are safe."

I noticed that the velvet on my knees was becoming wet. I looked at the wetness in wonder and saw a drop fall onto the bag. The headache that had receded in the days since Ian had come home jumped directly to the front of my consciousness, slamming down lead-footed, fireworks searing my vision. Just as quickly, it was gone, as if it had never been. I searched inside myself, like I was scanning with a flashlight, but could not find the crater that the pain must have occupied. It was just gone, and instead—I had memory. Memory that jerked the way your muscles can jerk as you lay on the precipice of sleep. Did I hear Cos? I must have because I knew his words, but they didn't seem to contain meaning.

Dying is not primarily an event punctuated by the cessation of breath or brain. It is more an event defining relationships—our relationship with ourselves, to those we love and those who care for us, and to the truths we hold for ourselves. I recognize and understand the pain of disconnection. It is important to understand the pain, and to provide relief from the pain. It can be so clear to me sometimes, but I know that an individual is often so caught up in their suffering that they cannot find their way to end it. I give myself in service to those in pain.

I was Lisa.

I was visiting my uncle's farm, as I did each summer while my parents took an adult vacation. One day, my uncle received a blow to his back and then he fell into an irrigation ditch and drowned. I think I was eleven years old at the time.

My aunt and I waited dinner for him. Sometime after I was sent to bed, she called neighbors to try and find him.

That night, after the television was turned off, no large dark figure entered my room, smelling of dirt and Aqua Velva. No scratchy whisper of cigarettes and alcohol lingered in my ear with words I did not fully understand.

"Lisa, little Lisa, I'm alone—all alone. No one understands my pain. Lisa, you want to help me, don't you? You don't want me to feel sad, do you, Lisa? Little Lisa, pretty Lisa."

No hands pinching my nipples or poking at me, digging a hole of pain that I had come to eagerly anticipate. No one pried my cousin's baseball bat from my arms as I slept. No guilt disturbed my sleep that night, or ever again.

Then.

It was a Sunday not long after our divorce; I went to Zack's father's apartment in Cupertino to pick up Zack after a weekend visit. I knocked on the door repeatedly, and finding the door unlocked finally just walked in. Zack, a toddler, was asleep in the bedroom and his dad was smoking crack in the kitchen. He hardly knew I was there. That was the last time we saw him.

The police had taken one look at the drugs in the apartment and immediately ruled it a drug deal gone wrong.

I became Letty.

I lied to Zack when he was old enough to ask. I said his dad had just run off and disappeared. This is what I told everyone. This is what I told Peter. This is what I told myself.

Then.

I had returned with Moe, to his apartment, with sexual promises after our kiss. He had gone into the bathroom to undress, being more comfortable doing it in private. I removed my shoes and went in. He was startled and half out of his chair. It was so easy to tip him into his shower. When I clutched his head, he tried to reach me, and I, too, had slipped, avoiding his hands but ripping the knee of my pantyhose. I cracked his forehead on the tile lip of the shower entrance. As I was pushing his torso further into the shower, angling his head toward the drain, his colostomy bag burst and splattered my pretty dress. His cheek and lips covered the drain, blocking the flow. The hot water filled the shower's shallow basin and overflowed into the bathroom. The wheelchair turned on its side, the clothes he had removed, and a hamper knocked over now were all a soggy mess. I grabbed a small towel as I left and dried my hands, using it to open the door and pushing the button on the elevator with it, leaving my dress untouched. I removed the ruined pantyhose, stuffing them into my purse. When I returned to the car, I threw the used towel in the back seat.

Then.

Marty was so easy, so pure in the action, for I had learned from Cosi-san the concept of magic. As he rested with his head in my lap, he rolled to kiss my denim-clad crotch as he might have kissed the top of his dog's head, except he had no dog. It was in that moment I used the rock I had laid by, first crushing the back of his neck before opening his skull with a second forceful blow, using his polo shirt to catch the blood. When I was very sure he was gone, I rolled him and then the rock down into the ravine. As I held him by his wrists, in his last moments, his fingers curled and pressed into the dirt, scraping as if for a hold as his body slid, and with a twist, rolled down to the brush below. I knew the rain coming that night would finish my work for me.

Then.

Clarence, he had been so deliberate, so sure of himself. I had liked him so much, but he was a threat to me, to my family. Flunitrazepam is easy for someone in my position to squirrel away. A fall from the fifteenth floor onto concrete has no chance of survival. It was sad, but necessary.

Truth is life affirming. It is the best ascetic, embracing our own higher nature. When we know the truth, we know death is not separate from life, suffering not separate from joy. Truth brings us to ourselves.

I knew what I had done. I knew what was in me. I knew who I was.

"All the pieces…"

"Lisa, would you give me the morphine now? I am in pain."

"The nurse? It couldn't be time?"

"Lisa, I want you to do it. It is just a little extra so I will sleep, not enough to be noticeable, really. And then you can use the pillow.

"Lisa, you are my midwife, you can help me."

I gave his hand a squeeze and nodded. Retrieving the vial of morphine, I found his IV's injection site and administered the drug.

"The bag and its remaining contents are part of my gift to you. I have shared what I know only with you. You are safe.

"Lisa, you have been my last best friend. Thank you."

I made him comfortable, adjusting his kimono as I moved him into a more reclined position for sleeping, smoothing the bedclothes, and adjusting his pillows. I held the extra pillow, which I had removed from behind his head.

"Are you comfortable? Is there anything else?"

He smiled at me and raised his hand, resting one finger on my cheek, lifting away a tear and placing it on his bottom lip as if it were an ice chip. I arranged the velvet bag over his face and over that, I set the pillow. I used both hands to hold it in place, watching as the last of the candles died, one by one, until I was sitting alone in the dark with the glow of the fire's coals my only companion. The music no longer played; I was alone.

I put the pillow where it normally rested and took the velvet from his face, slid the used vial, syringe, and the folder with its contents into the bag. I put the entire package into my briefcase and called the nurse and Sying on the intercom.

While the nurse confirmed that Cos was dead and went back downstairs to call the doctor and family, I began the last task as his hospice worker and friend. I could hear Sying sobbing at the top of the stairs. In the bathroom, I found the copper basin, oils, a large sea sponge, and plush purple towels Cos had chosen just days ago. I filled the basin with warm water, adding a few drops of the oil, and carried everything out to his bedside.

I stripped the bed down to the plastic sheeting. I removed his kimono and diaper. Taking great care and moving with reverence, I washed him. Looking at him as I sponged his face and patted it dry, he became the most beautiful man I have ever known.

"Cosi-san, you have died. Whatever ultimate kindness there is, you have now found it. Your relationships here are ending.

"Rest now. Rest in Aoife. Rest in memory. Rest in love, Cosi-san."

When all was clean and dry, I remade the bed with red satin sheets. I dressed Cosi-san in his solid black kimono with gold thread woven at the hems. Taking the oil, I dipped my fingers in the bottle and anointed his forehead, his lips, and his chest. I pulled the drapes aside and opened the windows, letting the evening air further cleanse both of us.

I sat with him, our final time together, resting.

XIII
<u>Parinibbana Sutta</u>
"This is my final teaching."

It's been frosty for days and now, snow has fallen. They have snowplows, borrowed from Sacramento, on the highways that cross the coastal range. The roads are being salted but it doesn't seem to help.

This morning, we had something different here in our yard. This morning, even now at 10:30 a.m., every bit of the yard and the neighborhood looks as if fairy wands have touched it. Every leaf and needle, every blade of grass sparkles in the cold, cold sunlight. This isn't the frost that kills the grape or orange crops. This is weightier and infinitely more beautiful. Celtic tunes of elfin frost slip in and out of my mind. The neighboring roof is a layer of crystals glinting with such brightness I can barely look at it from the upstairs window. The sky is clear and sunny, but oh so cold. I can look out over the neighborhood and see far distances not usually available to me. The world looks foreign and almost a mirror of light. It is an out of the ordinary May here in the Bay Area, where snow never occurs and frost is rare.

Huddled on the back porch are dozens of birds of all diverse kinds. Poor small creatures, they look like refugees massed there beneath the potted roses. I am trying to find a portable heater to set outside for them; we must have one somewhere. What brought me out into this Narnia of frost was a cracking sound. I found two deer in the very back, one of them breaking the ice over a deep puddle.

This day's beauty brings the death of so much that I find beautiful in my yard. I wouldn't miss it for the world. I think I have begun a love affair with the cold this morning. I thought I knew what the promise of spring meant, but now I know it differently. Now it is a promise in which my part is faith.

The doorbell rings while I am on the telephone with Nancy; the younger Druckers have finally dropped their lawsuit. I walk to the front of the house to find the FedEx carrier at the door. I make signs with one hand and gather a box into the curve of my arm. I wave her off after signing for the package. It is addressed to me, marked personal. I hug the package closer and turn it so I can read the label. The return addressee is Horace Cosgrove Drucker III.

I hold the unexpected delivery like a newborn as I finish my conversation and hang up. I put it on the table, just staring at the package, while I have a cup of tea and a cry. I had been given a friend and had him taken away all in the same moment.

The boys have left, Ian deciding to go back to school the day after the wake. Peter comes home while I am sitting at the table and says a brief hello from the hall, scooping Cain from his perch where he was monitoring the freezing birds; they go directly upstairs to his office. I can hear the click of the latch as he closes me, our world, out. I am tired of crying, and tired of being lonely. I wipe my face with the back of my sleeve and pick up this last gift from Cos, holding it tight in both hands as I go to our bedroom.

I run a bath while I sit on the edge of the bed with the box on my lap, and open it. Inside I find his tarot deck, an old teak brush with sable bristles, and a piece of paper with a short, handwritten note and typing:

What the Pastor said – Cosi-san

"Prayer is the joyous acknowledgment of perfect God, perfect man, and a perfect universe, wherein there is nothing left undone, unfinished, unsupported, or unsupplied. Since every idea was created as part of God's all-inclusive plan, there is not an idle, useless, or superfluous idea in existence. As God's spiritual reflection, man has boundless opportunities, infinite capabilities, ceaseless occupation. His capital is Mind's resources, unlimited and ever available. His business, being the reflection of God's business, must be active, progressive, productive, prosperous, and successful now."

I soak in the tub until the water is cold. I stand, damp-dry, looking at my more than fifty-years-old body. Finally, I walk over to the door and open it, calling down the hall.

"Peter, come to the bedroom. Right away, please!"

Stepping back into the room, I wait, holding the brush in my left hand. Slap, slapping it, soft on the palm of my right hand. Peter comes in, Cain at his heels.

"Peter, things are going to change."

I pick Cain up, placing him back in the hall and closing the door. I face my husband. Slap, slapping.

The End

Albert Einstein (1950)

"A human being is part of a whole, called by us the 'Universe,' a part limited in time and space. He experiences himself, his thoughts and feelings, as something separated from the rest—a kind of optical delusion of his consciousness. This delusion is a kind of prison for us, restricting us to our personal desires and to affection for a few persons nearest us. Our task must be to free ourselves from this prison by widening our circles of compassion to embrace all living creatures and the whole of nature in its beauty."

Writer's Notes for Readers

<u>Overture</u>

- Aoife (EE-fa) - Irish, means "beauty"
- Slingbag - Shibari and Kinbaku styles of Japanese rope bondage
- Farrah - Arabic, means "joy"
- Cosi-san - *san* is used as an honorific in Japan to mean *dear* or *honorable one*

<u>Chapter 1</u>

- *Glengarry Glen Ross* - Play by David Mamet (Fair Use)

<u>Chapter 2</u>

- Zhifu Li - Zhifu = getting rich, Li = strength or sharp
- Messiaen experienced music as colors offering a confused but brilliant sensory complexity.
- *Saint Francois D'Assise* - This opera has no plot, but rather a series of scenes linked together similar to the concept of this novel. It is a reflection of inner struggle, confrontation of the fear of death and suffering. (Fair Use)

  The person with leprosy - Francis overcomes his own fear and revulsion to embrace and kiss the diseased man, and in doing so, cures him. The allegory is that once we overcome our fear of the different or unknown it is no longer something to be shunned or judged.

Chapter 3

- Sakura tree - In the story of the origin of the cherry tree, a goddess, Princess Konohanasakuya, is said to have sprinkled from the heavens the first cherry seeds from atop Mt. Fuji. The cherry tree is, therefore, a tree of the mountains, and associated with Sakami. The next part of the word is *kura*. A kura in old Japanese was a seat that gods would rest on—a holy seat and resting place for gods.

  It is the symbol for new beginnings and for forgetting the past.

- Operation Meetinghouse - Allies Bombing of Tokyo (10 March 1945)

Chapter 4

- *Liszt's Liebestraum No 3* - this is one of three piano solos that create Liebstraum, which means "Love Dreams." It is based on the following poem by Ferdinand Freiligrath (public domain):

  O love, as long as love you can,

  O love, as long as love you may,

  The time will come, the time will come,

  When you will stand at the grave and mourn!

  Be sure that your heart burns,

And holds and keeps love

As long as another heart beats warmly

With its love for you

And if someone bears his soul to you

Love him back as best you can

Give his every hour joy,

Let him pass none in sorrow!

And guard your words with care,

Lest harm flow from your lips!

Dear God, I meant no harm,

But the loved one recoils and mourns.

O love, love as long as you can!

O love, love as long as you may!

The time will come, the time will come,

When you will stand at the grave and mourn.

You will kneel alongside the grave

And your eyes will be sorrowful and moist,

Never will you see the beloved again –

Only the churchyard's tall, wet grass.

You will say: Look at me from below,

I who mourn here alongside your grave!

Forgive my slights!

Dear God, I meant no harm!

Yet the beloved does not see or hear you,

He lies beyond your comfort;

The lips you kissed so often speak

Not again: I forgave you long ago!

Indeed, he did forgive you,

But tears he would freely shed,

Over you and on your unthinking word –

Quiet now! – he rests, he has passed.

O love, love as long as you can!

O love, love as long as you may!

The time will come, the time will come,

When you will stand at the grave and
mourn.

- Rainer Maria Rilke - "Love and Death are
  the two greatest gifts that are passed on to
  us, and usually they are passed on
  unopened." I believe from one of his

letters but I can't find which one. (Fair Use)

- Sweet - A British glam rock band. *Love is Like Oxygen* "Love is like oxygen, too much you get high; not enough and you die." (Fair Use)
- Beatles - Lyric from *The End* composed by John Lennon / Paul McCartney. "The love you take is equal to the love you make." (Fair Use)

Chapter 5

- Minerva and Neptune - MINERVA (Athena), the goddess of wisdom, was the daughter of Jupiter (Zeus). She was said to have leaped forth from his brain, mature, and in complete armour. She presided over the useful and ornamental arts, both those of men—such as agriculture and navigation—and those of women: spinning, weaving, and needlework. She was also a warlike divinity, but it was defensive war only that she patronized, and she had no sympathy with Mars's (Ares) savage love of violence and bloodshed. Athens was her chosen seat, her own city, awarded to her as the prize of a contest with Neptune (Poseidon), who also aspired to it.

  As the first king, Cecrope unified the populations of the Attic villages of the Acropolis, the tale ran that in the reign of Cecrope, who was half man and half snake, the two deities contended for the possession of the city. The gods decreed that it should be awarded to the one who produced the gift most useful to mortals. Neptune gave the horse; Minerva produced the olive. The gods gave judgment that the olive was the more useful of the two and awarded the city to the goddess; it was named after her, Athens, her name in Greek being Athene.

The Parthenon was built in her honor. Built near the very first olive tree, the Parthenon became a symbol of Greek culture, freedom, and peace.

- Guardians of principle or prophets of doom -

Christian Bible

Revelation 11:3-13

"And I will give power to my two witnesses, and they will prophesy one thousand two hundred and sixty days, clothed in sackcloth."

4 These are the two olive trees and the two lampstands standing before the [b]God of the earth. 5 And if anyone wants to harm them, fire proceeds from their mouth and devours their enemies. And if anyone wants to harm them, he must be killed in this manner. 6 These have power to shut

heaven, so that no rain falls in the days of their prophecy; and they have power over waters to turn them to blood, and to strike the earth with all plagues, as often as they desire.

The Witnesses Killed

7 When they finish their testimony, the beast that ascends out of the bottomless pit will make war against them, overcome them, and kill them. 8 And their dead bodies will lie in the street of the great city which spiritually is called Sodom and Egypt, where also [c]our Lord was crucified. 9 Then those from the peoples, tribes, tongues, and nations [d]will see their dead bodies three-and-a-half days, and not allow their dead bodies to be put into graves. 10 And those who dwell on the earth will rejoice over them, make merry, and send gifts to one another, because these two prophets tormented those who dwell on the earth.

The Witnesses Resurrected

11 Now after the three-and-a-half days the breath of life from God entered them, and they stood on their feet, and great fear fell on those who saw them. 12 And [e]they heard a loud voice from heaven saying to them, "Come up here." And they ascended to heaven in a cloud, and their enemies saw them. 13 In the same hour there was a great earthquake, and a tenth of the city

fell. In the earthquake seven thousand people were killed, and the rest were afraid and gave glory to the God of heaven.

- I named his tree Peace, Jennifer's Witness, and Ian's tree was Light. -

Homer wrote that olive branches ensured that the souls of the dead successfully crossed the river Acheron to the underworld on Charon's boat. For the same reasons, the Spartans buried their dead on a bed of olive twigs; those who attended the funeral wore crowns of olive branches to protect themselves from evil.

"The dove came back to him in the evening, and lo, in her mouth a freshly plucked olive leaf; so Noah knew that the waters had subsided from the earth..."

The foliage of the olive tree has been used for centuries to honor victory, wisdom and peace.

Chapter 6

- Sying or Lei or Long - Star, Thunder, Dragon
- Hor - Pharoh Hor, from the early 13th dynasty, was an insignificant ruler. He had seven months of rule around 1760 BC. Didn't have time to build his own tome

and was buried in a small one belonging to someone else.

- Zen - a Japanese sect of Mahayana Buddhism that aims at enlightenment by direct intuition through meditation.
- Virginia Wolfe, *Jacob's Room* (1922) "Nobody sees any one as he is… They see a whole, they see all sorts of things, they see themselves.. One must follow hints, not exactly what is said, nor yet entirely what is done." (Fair Use)

Chapter 7

- Kinbaku-bi - translates to "the beauty of tight binding," a Japanese art of rope bondage.
- *Tom Sawyer* - Tom is whipped in several chapters by his Aunt Polly and several teachers.

Chapter 8

- Chihuly - Dale Chihuly is a famous American glass artist
- Vargas - Alberto Vargas is a Peruvian–American painter who specialized in pin-up girls
- Janis Joplin - *Work Me* "Though I've looked everywhere, and I can't find me anybody to love, to feel my care." (Fair Use)
- Entrecote vom Grill mit Zweibel, Bratkartoffeln un Tomaten Salat - German (Deutsch) - Grilled rib eye steak with

onion gravy, fried potatoes and tomato salad

Chapter 9

- uno a uno - Spanish "one on one"

Chapter 10

- Sister Rosetta Tharpe - *Nobody's Fault But Mine* (Fair Use)

Chapter 11

- *Ava Maria* - by Franz Schubert, "Ellens dritter Gesang" ("Ellens Gesang III", D. 839, Op. 52, No. 6, 1825), in English: "Ellen's Third Song", was composed in 1825 as part of his Op. 52, a setting of seven songs from Walter Scott's 1810 popular narrative poem *The Lady of the Lake*, loosely translated into German. (Fair Use)
- *Yesterday*, composed by Paul McCartney of the Beatles "Yesterday all my troubles seemed so far away, now it looks as if they're here to stay. Oh, I believe…" (Fair Use)
- *Help From My Friends*, composed by John Lennon and Paul McCartney of the Beatles "With a little help from my friends…" (Fair Use)
- *A Hard Day's Night*, composed by John Lennon and Paul McCartney of the Beatles (Fair Use)

<u>Chapter 12</u>

- Ravel's *Mother Goose Suite* - Ma mère l'Oye is a suite of five pieces depicting fairytales (Fair Use)
    1. Pavane de la Belle au bois dormant: Lent (Pavane of Sleeping Beauty)
    2. Petit Poucet: Très modéré (Little Tom Thumb / Hop-o'-My-Thumb)
    3. Laideronnette, impératrice des pagodes: Mouvt de marche (Little Ugly Girl, Empress of the Pagodas)
    4. Les entretiens de la belle et de la bête: Mouvt de valse très modéré (Conversation of Beauty and the Beast)
    5. Le jardin féerique: Lent et grave (The Fairy Garden)

<u>Chapter 13</u>

- Note from Drucker - *Seeking First the Kingdom* by Louise Wheatley Cook Hovnanian, CSB, *The Christian Science Journal,* November 1916 (Public Domain)

<u>Endnote</u>

The quote is attributed to a letter written by Albert Einstein in 1950. There is an entire article about it with images of the possibly original letter and a handwritten draft in German attributed to him. The article transcribes the quote in the original German and gives an alternative translation. It appears that the version used here—and which was at the back of *The Tibetan Book of Living and Dying* by Sogyal Rinpoche—was a 1972 *New York Times* translation of the original Einstein letter.

Einstein willed all of his materials and copyright permissions to the Hebrew University in Jerusalem, however, Princeton University manages permissions for any works published after 1971. Permissions for anything before 1971 are handled by Hebrew University. Sogyal Rinpoche does not cite Einstein as the author. Given that we reached dead ends in all our efforts to discover the genuine copyright, and that we reached out to every possible source we have come to the conclusion that this falls under Public Domain.

www.ingramcontent.com/pod-product-compliance
Lightning Source LLC
Chambersburg PA
CBHW031436160726
47994CB00005B/1745